# SHORTY IS IN *Love* WITH A REAL *One*

A NOVEL BY

## SHVONNE LATRICE

*© 2020*

*Published by First Class*

*Publishing Group*

*www.TheShvonneLatrice.com*

## ALL RIGHTS RESERVED



**Contains explicit language & adult themes suitable for ages 16+**

$19.99

ISBN 978-1-966375-17-3

51999>

# CHAPTER ONE

## Khyle Luke

$\mathcal{I}$ sat at my vanity, brushing down my hair, as my mother fussed about how dirty my room was. She always did this shit, even if it was just one or two pairs of jeans lying around. I was going out with my boyfriend tonight, so I did get a bit carried away with the outfit changes, but so fucking what; I was gonna clean it.

This was the exact reason why I applied to go to college out of state, and in just three weeks my ass would be gone. I loved my mother but damn, was she a buzz kill. She needed to just come right out and say she didn't like me because it was obvious that, that was the case.

Soon I would be attending college in Las Vegas, Nevada where my sister Shayne currently lived. She moved out there because she wants to become a Vegas showgirl, but I'm not too sure how well that's working out for her since I haven't heard anything. Her boyfriend Pierce was another reason she skipped town, because he was gonna be this big football star. He was supposed to play for UNLV and then get drafted soon after. He got on an NFL team, but something must've gotten in the way because I never saw him play in the games. I asked

Shayne about it, but she just danced around the question, obviously not wanting to tell me. Anyway, I miss my sister and I want to be away from home, where I can do me how I want and how late I want. My parents weren't strict, but they kept a close eye on me and expected a lot of me, especially my father.

Once my fresh press was brushed down the way I liked, I stood to my feet and went to slip on my sneakers. My mom was still running her damn mouth, and with every word that came from her I was rolling my fucking eyes. I didn't know why she treated Shayne like some princess but acted as if my mere existence annoyed her ass. Sometimes when I got in my feelings I would wish we could be close, but then again I really ain't give a fuck. As long as she wasn't trying to kill my ass or backstab me in anyway, we were good. I knew she loved me but she just didn't *like* me. Hey, I was a daddy's girl anyway.

"Mama, I'm about to go," I sighed, finally happy she'd shut up long enough for me to speak.

"Get that damn starch out of your voice when you talk to me, Khyle."

"What is starch, mother?" I cocked my head, letting my long hair fall to the side. It was recently done so it was soft just the way I liked it.

"I hate when you get condescending. You're not the only one who went to college in this family so stop acting like it," she barked back as she roughly placed my new Guess sweater on a hanger. "Are you going out with that boy?"

"Brian, yes. You know I'm gonna be gone soon, mama, so he wants to get as much of my time as he can."

"You're only gonna be in Vegas. He'll live… with his clingy ass. I think it's good to be away from him."

My mom liked Brian when we first got together because he was going to be a doctor soon. But over time she for some reason became annoyed by him. Yes he was a bit clingy at times, but I'd rather him wanna be up under *me* versus wanting to be up under another bitch or two.

"Is that my college bound daughter?" my father peeked his head in wearing the biggest grin on his handsome face.

"Yes, Daddy," I smiled shyly, using the small voice I always used for him.

"Better tell that little nigga to keep his hands to himself, Khyle. Tell him whatever he does to you, I will do to him."

"James, that's kind of nasty if you think about it," my mother turned her nose up, before both she and I began laughing.

"Just tell him that for me, and I bet he will act right."

"Daddy, he knows I'm waiting until marriage to give myself to a man," I nodded as I pushed my stud earrings into my earlobe while looking into the mirror.

My smooth, cinnamon complexion was very vibrant and not faded at all. My long dark hair hung down my back, sweeping the top of my tailbone. My frame was small, but not skinny if that's what you're thinking. I liked the way I looked, and that was the only person's opinion I gave a fuck about. I'll be damned if I'm out here changing my features to impress these bum ass niggas in Los Angeles, shit, Las Vegas too. All of them can kiss my small, round ass.

"Good, have fun, baby." My father interrupted the tongue-lashing I was giving in my head with a forehead kiss. I gave him a faint smile as I reached for my brown leather watch and the matching bracelet.

I was a cool, laidback dresser. I mainly wore sneakers, jeans, jean shorts, or crop tops. I had some dresses and shit too, but I saved those for dates or parties. I admit I bought some more little sexy dresses for my new college life in Las Vegas, just in case. I'd been corresponding with my roommate, and she told me that there was always a party at my school, and I wanted to be prepared. I wasn't sure how she knew that since she wasn't from Nevada, but she didn't seem like the type to make shit up.

My phone buzzed, so I picked it up to see it was Brian. I chuckled as I thought about how I'd lied to my daddy and told him I was a virgin. I wasn't a hoe by any means, but I was fucking Brian. He was my first, and he would be my last since he was the man I planned to marry. In all honesty, sex wasn't really about shit and I never even found a reason why bitches would be moaning and screaming about how they were about to cum. Brian was lucky if I didn't dry up in the middle of him breaking a sweat over me. However, I enjoyed the emotional part of the sex, whilst he enjoyed the physical. Could I go without the shit though? Hell fucking yeah.

Grabbing my Louis bag that I got for my birthday earlier this month, I rushed out of the house and closed the door behind me. The cool air of Los Angeles hit me in the face, and I relished in the moment. I would miss the little things about my hometown, but it wasn't enough to make me go to college out here. And it's not like I was gonna live in

Las Vegas for good, it would just be for four short years.

"Hey, baby girl," Brian leaned over and pecked my lips once I got into his car.

He looked good in his white polo, with matching white jeans, and all white Adidas. Brian was perfect in the sense that he was smart with a little tiny bit of hood to him. I mean he didn't know how to move weight or cook up drugs, but he could handle himself when it came down to it. He was my baby, and a part of me hated to leave him behind. But like my mother said, it would only be four hours away.

"Hey," I finally replied and pulled my phone from my back pocket.

"Why are you always on that shit?"

"Because it's always ringing and shit, what do you mean?" I sucked my teeth and rolled my eyes. I hated when he complained about me being on my damn phone. I'm 18, the fuck did he expect?

"Whatever, Khyle. My mom is at work now, so let's go to the house first and then we can go out."

Go to the house in Brian's language meant 'let's fuck'.

"That's cool."

He sped off in his Mustang, and turned up the Problem CD he had playing in his car. I bobbed my head to a couple of tracks, and finally we were pulling up to his mother's home in Carson. It was a quiet street, far away from commercial businesses, which I guess was cool if you were old and didn't like to do shit. The only upside for Brian and I was that none of these old folks told on us when they'd spot us leaving his home.

After swooping into his driveway, Brian hopped out and made his way to my side. I gave him a seductive smile as he opened the door for me and helped me out. Brian was tall as fuck, 6'8, and I loved that shit. He was hella skinny, but I'd grown to love that part about him too. It was true that skinny nigga's had a big dick, but like I said before, that big dick didn't do shit for me.

"Thank you, baby," I said as I slipped my hand into his.

As soon as we got inside of his house and hit the doorway of his bedroom, this nigga was gnawing on me. I could barely walk backwards as he kissed and groped me with his big ass hands. Before I could even mutter a word, he had my shirt off, and my jeans and panties at my knees. Falling back onto the bed, I allowed him to remove my sneakers, and then take my panties and jeans all the way off.

"You wet already," he groaned. *You's a got damn lie, nigga,* I thought but just chuckled sweetly instead.

As I laid back, he latched his warm wet mouth onto my clit and began sucking. I let my thighs rest on his shoulders, and closed my eyes to imagine the new life I was about to live. Not to mention, I would be closer to my older sister whom I adored.

Shayne was so dope, and I'd looked up to her since I was a young child. I loved that she always went for what she wanted and didn't care what people thought. My lawyer parents hated that she moved away to be some sports player's wife and a showgirl, but she didn't care. She left with her boyfriend Pierce, and never looked back. My dad still felt some type of way about it, but my mom forgave her with the quickness because that was her favorite child. I didn't—

"Khyle!" Brian barked as he stood over me shirtless.

"What?" I frowned, pissed that he'd interrupted my fantasy. "Why'd you stop?"

"Because you ain't even moaning you're just lying there like I ain't putting my fucking jaws to work!"

I was irritated, but just sat up to unbuckle his jeans. I wanted to get this sex session over with because I needed to get home and handle some shit for my move. Once his jeans and boxers were off, I unhooked my bra, and then laid on my back, making sure to go easy on my freshly straightened hair.

"Condom!" I pointed to his drawer with my long ass acrylic nail.

"Baby come on, think of it as a going away gift," he gave me that sexy smile of his.

"Get me some diamonds or some new sneakers, but not a baby, nigga. And hurry up before your mama gets here."

He sucked his teeth but got that condom and rolled it down. Once it was in place on that monster of his, he got on top of me, but I pushed him back. He never let me get on top, and I wanted to try it. I pushed myself down onto him, and sucked on my bottom lip as I moved up and down. No matter how hard I tried, this shit was not working... for me at least. His mouth was all open as he groaned and growled like a grizzly bear. Placing his fingers on my clit, he began to massage it, and finally I was feeling it. I began grinding against his fingers, and when that wasn't enough, I placed my hand on top of his and began guiding his hand myself. But typical Brian saw I was in control, so he flipped me onto my back and slammed into me until he came.

We tongued it up for a bit, before I nudged him off of me so I could go to the bathroom and fix myself. He followed, and once we cleaned up and washed our hands, we returned to the bedroom.

"Victoria said she can still get you into USC, even this late, babe."

"Brian, I am going to Nevada. I have my dorm, classes, and everything. My parents have paid for a full year, which is a lot of money considering I'm an out-of-state student, so I can't back out now."

"I'm sure they have some sort of refund policy."

"Brian, stop. You're gonna see me on every major holiday, what is the damn problem? And I won't be too far so it will be even more frequent maybe."

"I just don't want you forgetting about a nigga. College is not high school, you'll be on your own and in Vegas, you can get caught up in that shit." Brian wore a worried expression as he spoke. Little did he know the shit he was saying only excited me more.

"I'm only 18, I can't do that much."

"I know, but niggas gon' have a heart attack when yo' fine ass touch down."

"So silly," I giggled and kissed him. "Let's go before your mom comes."

"Aight, wanna get food?"

"That's cool. I'm in the mood for some tacos from Diana's."

"Right around the corner from me," he said as he slipped his boxers and jeans up his skinny frame.

"I know."

We left the house in time, since his mom texted that she was on her way home literally as soon as we got to Diana's, which was only about 10 minutes from him. We ate there, and then headed back to my parents' home in Torrance.

"I will text you later." I pulled on the lever to get out of his car.

"Can I see you tomorrow? I wanna go to an arcade or some shit, since you love those." He was talking to me but looking down at his phone, texting. I swore I saw a girl's name, but Brian wouldn't cheat on me.

"You're so sweet, baby, but no. Emery is coming over tomorrow and we're gonna go to dinner, the movies, and all that. You know she's gonna spend the night."

"I don't like you hanging out with her hoe ass." He placed his phone faced down in his lap, which was a red flag, but I brushed it off.

"Stop being disrespectful, Brian."

"And ain't her ass gonna come visit you a few weeks after you move?" he frowned.

"Yes, but she still needs to see me. I will see you soon, damn," I scoffed and tried to get out of the car, but he grabbed me back and shoved his tongue into my mouth.

"I love you, Khyle."

"I love you too, baby." I half smiled and then got out.

As soon as I was out of the car, I rushed inside of my house and into my bedroom. I undressed, and then took a nice bath before brushing my teeth and getting some fruit to eat. I then pulled out my college's pamphlet to look it over, and answered a few emails from my roommate before calling my sister on the phone. I was more excited to leave home than I let on, but Brian had nothing to worry about. This shit wouldn't change me one bit.

# CHAPTER ONE

# Shayne Luke

*Las Vegas…*

$\mathcal{I}$ swayed my hips to "No Limit" by Usher, as I sipped my glass of Patrón and pineapple juice. I was waiting for tonight's main event, Oden Bishop. Oden was every girl's dream, the ones who resided in Las Vegas and even the ones who didn't. He was tall, handsome, hood, and rich. I loved everything about that nigga; well, as much as I could love since I'd never met him really. I'd been in the same clubs as him like right now, but as far as me holding conversation… nah, I wish.

Tonight was the grand opening of his and his best friends, Anton and Truman's new club, Palace Nights. And on top of that they were debuting their liquor line Brown Sugar Bourbon. The club was lavish as fuck, costing a minimum of $50 to get in. Under the club floor was a whole fucking strip club, and not them funky cheap ones, some upscale shit. It was so sexy how Oden was about his business and his bread. There was nothing like a hood nigga who still knew how to conduct business like a professional. Just thinking about it made my panties wet.

I moved to Las Vegas with my boo Pierce, and at first I was the happiest bitch on Earth. We felt it was a good idea to move here because I wanted to be in Vegas shows, and the football coach of UNLV promised him that if he played two years he'd get drafted to the NFL. I just knew Pierce was gonna make it, and I would be a rich ass football wife, living in the lap of luxury. I planned to shop at the priciest stores, and dine at the fanciest restaurants too. Life was gonna be lit, because life before the NFL was even great. Being the girlfriend of soon to be football star Pierce Warden got me so many perks at that time. Just the thought of it *used* to make me smile.

I was so in love with Pierce, but that was before he got picked up by the San Francisco 49ers, and then dropped before the first damn game. I wasn't sure what happened exactly because the nigga was crying like a bitch as he explained it to me, but I just knew that I wasn't gonna be rocking those Yves Saint Laurent stilettos I'd had my eye on. So now, I was planning to leave Pierce in the dust for something bigger, finer, richer, sexier, and overall better… Oden.

"What time do you think they're coming? It's already 11pm," my friend Alanna shouted over the loud music.

I met her when I moved out here, and the only reason she even associated with me was because she'd lost her nigga, Earl Jr. Unlike Pierce, he'd made the team and stayed on, but once he got a taste of that NFL superstar life, he dropped Alanna like a whore's panties. It was shady as fuck, and I felt for her a little bit, but I'm sure it was her fault. Alanna wasn't meant to be with a boss nigga, which is why I didn't understand her need to constantly check up on when Oden, Truman, and Anton would arrive. She was way too meek, and let Earl Jr. dog her whenever he got the chance. And then one day he just told her to kick rocks. You have to be strong when dealing with these niggas who have the world in the palm of their hand.

"He'll be here. Keep Oden off of your mind though because he's mine, Lana."

"I know that, damn. I'm asking for you, you know I'm still waiting on Earl." See, listen at her. The nigga left her a year ago and she was still sitting by the phone for him.

"That's your damn problem, and the reason you lost that nigga. These men don't want no weak ass bitch who sits at home crying for them. They want someone strong who can ride alongside them."

"Like you," she sucked her teeth.

"Be sarcastic if you want to, bitch, but my man is at home still sniffing this pussy. Yours on the other hand, is out doing him."

"Whatever. Oden's drink is free at the bar until 11:30pm, don't you think you should try it?" she cocked her head, trying to change the subject. She could ignore my advice if she wanted to, but she would forever be that bitch who couldn't keep a man, unless he was a fuck nigga who liked weak hoes.

"I will get some when he comes so I can have a fresh drink," I winked at her and she shook her head with a smile.

Like I said, Oden was the owner of a liquor line named Brown Sugar Bourbon, and he owned a luxury car dealership too. He had money coming in from multiple fucking sources, making him just my type. He and his homeboys Anton and Truman ran everything together, and they made plenty of money doing so. I mean there were rumors that the boys did other things, but that just made Oden sexier because he had some mystery to him. He was feared by many niggas and loved by all of us women. I smiled widely just thinking about his sexy ass and that beautiful head of wild curly hair.

"Ladies and gentlemen, are you ready to find out who we have in the house?" the deejay yelled, causing my breathing to become shallow. The club roared with screaming women, and you're damn right I was one of them. The deejay told us to shut the fuck up, but nicely, and once it was quiet he continued. "We have Oden, Tru, and Tony in the building!!" he shouted with a raspy tone, and the club went wild as the three men approached the balcony of the VIP.

"What's good everybody? It's your boy Oden, and I apologize for being late but—"

"We love you Oden!!" some stupid thirsty ass females shouted since it was quiet. I admit it was smart since the club was somewhat silent. Everyone paid attention when niggas like Oden, Truman, and Anton stepped into the building.

Upon hearing the girls express their love for him, Oden's beautiful smile appeared. He had the whitest teeth I'd ever seen. He switched the mic to his other hand, and blinded the whole damn venue with his diamond watch, as his fine ass homie Anton stood next to him.

Anton was fine as fuck too, with his smooth chocolate skin and perfectly lined goatee. But, he had too much female drama in his life, and I didn't need that shit. Yeah, bitches went dumb for Oden, but

Anton had hoes claiming he was their baby's father. I wasn't dealing with that shit, plus, I just overall preferred Oden's personality. As for Truman, he was not my type at all. He was tall, skinny, caramel, and had gold slugs in his mouth. He was sexy but he had a girlfriend that *everyone* knew he did dirty but her stupid ass.

"We love y'all too, but make sure you enjoy the liquor, and everybody just have a good time tonight. There are some newbies here who ain't from Vegas, so we need to show them how we do it, aight?" Oden finished with a cocky, sexy smile as everyone cheered and screamed like he was Michael Jackson. Lustful thoughts filled my mind as I watched his full lips move.

The beat to "2AM" by Adrian Marcel dropped, and everybody started to get wild. I made my way to the bar with Alanna trailing me, and got my free glass of Oden's liquor brand. I took a sip and was surprised by how smooth and tasty it was. I didn't fuck with dark liquor because it was known to grow some hair on your chest, but I could rock with this, especially if it got my pussy closer to Oden Bishop's dick.

"Come on," I smiled at Alanna, and she let out a nervous sigh before following me to the VIP stairs.

Oh shit, I almost forgot to tell y'all how fine my ass was. I had a smooth light complexion, long hair down to my ass, full lips, pretty brown eyes, and long eyelashes. I had a big round ass, but small titties, which I was gonna fix soon. Niggas didn't care though, they still damn near broke their necks when I walked past them. My red dress rose up my toned thighs as I made my way up the stairs, and instead of fixing it, I let it do its thing. When I got up to the bouncer, he licked his crusty lips as he eyed Alanna and I.

"What's up with Oden?" I threw my hair behind me and batted my long ass eyelashes.

"What you gon' do for me?"

"Nigga, bye! Get me in here or I will do it myself!"

"Shayne!" Alanna shouted but in a whisper. I sucked my teeth at her and she shut the fuck up. I hoped she stayed quiet too.

The bouncer rolled his eyes with his trash ass, and then turned around to go speak with Oden. I watched my future baby daddy closely while dancing sexily to "24 Hours" by Teeflii. He listened to the bouncer speak, and then looked in my direction once the bouncer pointed. I waved and flashed my perfect smile that years of braces had given me, and he licked his lips. *Got em!* I yelled in my head. He turned his attention back to the bouncer, and advised him of something, before the bouncer wobbled back over to me, almost knocking Alanna and me down the stairs with his belly.

"Gon' head," he slurred in his somewhat southern accent. He sounded like he was fresh off the plane from New Orleans. Louisiana people had a different accent than other southerners in my opinion.

"Thanks." I grabbed Alanna's hand and sashayed inside, right up to my boo. I let her hand go, and then shooed her ass off so she could mack on some dick of her own, if she even knew how.

"Hey," I cocked my head, letting my long locks sway perfectly.

"What's good?" he smiled and moved down a little bit from Anton so I could sit. Anton was already all over some hoe that he was clearly finger fucking. Truman was nowhere to be found, so he must have been fucking something too.

"You asked to be up in here with me, and I know it wasn't just to talk, right?" he raised his brow, while nibbling on his bottom lip. I was a bit caught off guard at how forward he was, but I was a bitch that could roll with the punches. Moving his wild curly hair from his face, he waited for my response.

Inhaling his Clive Christian cologne, I said, "No, it wasn't just to talk." I crossed my legs slowly and he caught all of that.

"Red panties," he grumbled in a low raspy tone, which made him even sexier.

"Yep," I nodded and smirked.

"Come show me something." He stood his tall ass up, and I admired his wheat colored thermal, black Balmain jeans, and his black Jordan retro 12's.

"Umm." I didn't get to finish because he walked off. I followed behind him like an obedient puppy, and we made it to this little room in the back of the VIP. The lights were purple, and so were the plush ass couches. "Here?" I asked as he placed his hand on top of my head and guided me to my knees. He licked his lips sexily, and nodded after tucking them in. Thank God the carpet was plush and fluffy because my knees were comfortable. "Aren't you scared we're gonna mess up the carpet in here?"

"Nope."

"Oh," I whispered softly as my trembling hands unbuckled his expensive jeans.

He smelled so good, and I was happy to be here. However, even though I'd like to think of myself as a champion dick sucker, I prayed that I sucked the life out of this nigga so that he'd keep me around. Oden was known to tire of bitches quickly, and throw their asses to the side. I lost count on how many hoes had cried in the hair salon about how he'd gotten tired of their dick sucking skills and whack ass pussy. I refused to be a part of that crew.

"Mmm," he mumbled lowly once my full lips wrapped around his tip.

I moved my mouth up and down his shaft, while holding the rest of it. He had a nice big dick, and I couldn't wait to feel that shit inside of me. Pierce was packing too, but he wasn't Oden. I continued sucking him up sloppily, giving that shit my all as if I were a high paid porn star. He gripped my hair, and although I wanted to smack his hand a bitch knew better. Sucking, licking, moaning, slurping, I was doing it all and once I felt his grip on my hair tighten, I knew he was about to explode. I let his tip hit the back of my throat, and he called out loudly before spilling his seeds into my mouth.

"Shit, I fuck with you," he chuckled and bit down on his lip as he buckled himself back up. He then stroked his chin hairs as he stared down into my face. This man was way too fine Lord, way too fine. Running his big hand down his face he said, "Go have fun at the party *downstairs*, and I will hit you with an address to come through later." *Nigga what?* I wanted to say.

"Wait, so we're not gonna chill?"

"We just did, and I will get at you later." He grabbed on the door handle and opened it for me to walk out first.

"I don't wanna go downstairs, Oden. I wanna be up here, baby," I whined, and his face went from soft to irritated with the quickness. I just sucked his dick and he was sending me to mingle while he macked on other bitches? I'd never ran across a nigga like this ever in life, but it made me want him even more.

"Kill that whining shit. I told you the deal and in a minute that shit is gonna be dead. What's your number?" He pulled out two iPhones before slipping one back into his pocket. I read it off to him and he frowned. "You ain't from 'round here?"

"Nah, I'm from Los Angeles."

"Dope. What's your name?"

"Shayne." Damn this nigga had me sucking him up before he even knew my damn name.

"Aight, I'll get at you." He nodded and briskly walked past me, allowing me to take in his sexy cologne. I watched as he dapped people up and talked to hoes as he made his way downstairs to see the strippers. I felt a tingle between my legs just thinking about riding him.

I slipped into the bathroom to rinse my mouth with some Listerine and check my appearance, then came back out. As I was walking to save Alanna from some fuck nigga who was trying to get at her, my phone rang. I looked down to see it was Pierce, so I made a U-turn and went back into the room I'd just given head in.

"Fuck you at? You said y'all were just going to dinner!" he shouted, barely allowing me to say hello.

"We're just out getting a damn drink!"

"Why couldn't you text me that? I've been texting your ass for the longest with no damn response."

"Fuck you, aight." I wanted to start a fight so that I'd have a reason not to come home to him. Niggas did the shit all the time, so why couldn't I?

"Fuck me? Fuck me? I'm the one busting my ass to take care of yo' ungrateful ass, and you can't even provide me the courtesy of texting back, Shayne?"

"Bye nigga, see you later." I hung up on that ass and then continued on to get Alanna so we could go downstairs to the dance floor.

I didn't have time for these low budget ass niggas. The only dude I was trying to rock with was Oden Bishop. I got one more glance at him laughing with some hoe who was kissing all over his face downstairs, before taking Alanna with me. This nigga was a hoe but I was with it.

# CHAPTER ONE

## Oden Bishop

*The next morning…*

I woke up to my blaring alarm, and wiped my eyes before glancing to my right to see old girl from last night. I wish I could tell you her name but a nigga forgot. All I remember was that she gave me some bomb ass head at the club last night, and I had no choice but to take her home. She was a bit thirsty and had the stench of a gold digger, but I was interested to find out what her pussy was about since her mouth was so phenomenal. After letting my eyes dance all over her naked body for a few, I sat up, cut my alarm off, and gathered my things for a shower.

It was already 8am, and I usually liked to get my day started around 7am so I was behind. Being a business owner, especially of multiple businesses, it was pivotal that I used every damn hour in the day to do what I had to do. I wasn't gonna complain though, because there was a time where I really didn't have shit, and only dreamed of being where I am in life right now.

Despite my rough exterior and brash demeanor, I liked to think of myself as a good guy in a sense. I mean, I've had my fair share of women and all that jazz, but it wasn't because I was some little boy who was scared to commit, it was because I'd only come across garbage for lack of a better word. Best believe if I ran into a girl that I felt was about something, I would wife her ass in a muthafucking jiffy. Contrary to popular belief, it was just as hard for a man to find a good woman as it was for a woman to find a good man, especially if we had money, a little fame, and good looks like myself.

For as long as I can remember, I've always had women on my dick. I wasn't sure if I was just that damn good looking, or if it was my hair. Bitches loved to touch on a nigga's hair like I was a puppy or some shit, but I hated it. My hair was sacred, to me at least, and touching that shit was a privilege that only a girl I was wifing would have, and I had yet to run across her. I was a stand up dude, but what I wasn't gonna do was waste my time on a bitch that I knew was only good for one thing. Only women do shit like that, try to make a husband out of a nigga that can only give them an orgasm and nothing else. So although everywhere I turned there was a bitch ready and willing, if she wasn't up to par, she was getting fucked and nothing else.

Like old girl lying in my bed right now; I would never wife her. There were plenty of reasons why, but it was mainly because I knew what type of chick she was. She was the type that you fucked and gave nothing else to. This wasn't even where I laid my head, this was what my homeboys and I called the Hoe Crib. I would never take a bitch like her to my actual home… ever. She was only interested in riding the dick of someone who had fat pockets, and I was only interested in smashing, no need for her to know my home address. And I didn't give a fuck where she lived either.

Once I finished brushing my teeth, flossing, and rinsing with mouthwash, I hopped into the shower to scrub off last night's festivities. I partied hard and drank a lot of fucking liquor to celebrate. I'd busted my ass all of my life, and there was nothing like partying after accomplishing something, especially something as big as opening a damn club and a new liquor line. That was some major shit, and it made me smile from just thinking about how much more bread me and my boys were about to make.

I wouldn't say I had it too easy, because my mom died of a drug overdose, but lucky for me, my grandpa stepped in and raised my ass right. Every time I tried to get out of bounds and do shit that would potentially get me locked up, he got my ass right back in line. He did the same with my boy Anton since his mom and mine were needle buddies. That's why I never told him that Anton and I were running a luxury car theft ring, because I was sure my grandpa would have gone into cardiac arrest. He passed last year though, unfortunately, and that made me want to get into more legit shit, hence the club and liquor.

It's not like I woke up one day and decided I was gonna be into some illegal shit, I just gradually maneuvered into it. It all started when I got a job in the summer before my senior year of high school at a Range Rover dealer. It was just a way for me to get some money, and I probably wouldn't have even gotten the job if my grandfather hadn't known the manager. One day while I was bringing donuts to the whole office, some African cat named Akachi, dressed sharper than a knitting needle, pulled me to the side and asked me if I wanted to make some real money. I was apprehensive at first, but when he invited Anton and I to his humungous crib, and began explaining what all we could obtain, I was down.

At the beginning, Anton and I would steal the cars, and because we were so good Akachi moved us up, and that kept happening until we were damn near eating at the table with him. A couple years ago Akachi decided to retire, and it was a no brainer that he'd pass it down to Anton and I, and he did.

I moved a little smarter though, since technology had changed, making it harder to steal cars. That's why I obtained a luxury pre-owned car dealership, so that I'd be in cahoots with other dealers. By saying that, it was nothing for these dealers to cut keys for me, matching the VIN of the car that was to be stolen. Anton, Truman, and I were making so much damn money that it felt unreal when I checked my safe or my account. And now, we were adding Palace nightclub, and Brown Sugar Bourbon to the mix. My funds weren't planning to dry up any time soon.

I cut the shower off and stepped out to wrap a towel around my waist, before spraying cologne all over my body. As soon as I opened the bathroom door, the girl from last night was standing right there looking up in my face. She was beautiful as fuck for sure.

"Aye, what's your fucking name again?" I frowned because it was bugging me.

"For real, Oden?" she grinned as if I was joking. When I continued to stare at her with a blank expression, her smile faded. "Shayne, Shayne

Luke."

"Oh yeah, you did say that," I chuckled lightly as I slipped past her and headed to the bedroom I used when I slept here. She followed behind me too. "Get dressed, Shayne, I have to be somewhere."

"Where?"

"A bunch of different places to handle some business." I put my boxers on, right along with some black jeans that weren't too baggy, a black thermal, black low top chucks, and black diamond studs. She watched me the whole time as I secured my watch and chain, and as I rubbed some unscented lotion on my hands. "You ready?" I snatched my keys off of the dresser.

"Yeah. I like your place." She tilted her head back to take everything in as we made our way out.

Don't get me wrong, Shayne was bad as hell, but she was hoe. Granted, she was the bourgeois type, meaning she only let niggas hit who had money, but a hoe was a hoe. And I knew I'd seen her before but I wasn't quite sure where.

I let her step outside of my apartment door, and then closed it for a second to grab my gun and secure it in my waist under my thermal.

"So how old are you, Oden?" she questioned once I stepped outside, locked the door, and started off towards my car.

"I'm 24. Ain't your car that way?"

"Oh yeah, so you'll call me?"

"When I need you," I grinned, biting down on my lip, and she blushed before looking off for a few moments.

"Well I hope that's soon."

I just shrugged and continued to my car without another word. I wasn't lying to her; I would text if and when I needed her. Who knows when that would be, but one thing I knew for sure, was that it would only be for one thing and nothing else.

***

Walking into Bishop's Luxury Car Dealer, I spotted my homeboy Truman on his way to his office. Truman, better known as Tru, was a childhood friend of Anton's and mine. He was the manager of my dealership, and he also kept an eye on the chop shop Anton and I had built underground. The dealership was some extra money that we didn't need, but it's sole purpose was to help me build relationships with luxury car dealers who were looking to sell their old leased vehicles to me since my dealership was for pre-owned cars. Most of them niggas were crooked, and always willing to help me out when I needed something regarding stealing a whip. It was a quid pro quo situation. It was dangerous having so many people in your shit, but if you wanted to make the proper amount of coins, you couldn't be a small time nigga.

"The two Maseratis and one Bentley were brought to the chop shop last night," he said as he followed me to my office. Usually I would be in a suit, Banana Republic namely, but since I wasn't planning to be here all day, I dressed down.

"What's the status of them now?"

"They've been taken apart already, VINs have been switched out and everything. They're gonna be shipped out tonight." He closed my office door once I sat down.

"Good, good. Everybody informed about the meeting tonight, right?"

"Yeah, I told them to be at the parking lot with the Del Taco by 9pm. A van will come by to pick them up and bring them to the warehouse."

I had a solid team of muthafuckas who burglarized luxury cars all around Las Vegas. The majority of the time they were instructed to get at cars that had the keys in them already, or to rob the valet booths of expensive restaurants or private upscale parties. I even had a relationship with valet companies. If neither of those situations presented themselves though, then we'd take the car at night using one of our many tow trucks.

We had a couple of occasions where the owner ran outside, not knowing why they were getting towed, but these rich muthafuckas put so much of their responsibility on other people that when you told them their car payments were behind, they believed it. And by the time they figured out that it was all a scam, their car's VINs would already be switched, and the vehicle itself would be shipped out already.

That's why I kept a nice little staff at the chop shop to make sure that cars were processed as quickly as possible. If a whip was sitting in there for more than 24 hours, somebody was getting a bullet to the dome. I was a cool nigga, but I ran my business with an iron first so niggas knew not to fuck with my money. And now that we had Brown Sugar Bourbon and Palace, I really didn't have time for the games. My car theft ring was the biggest on the West Coast, and although that was the case, we weren't even close to getting caught.

"Well, after I make a couple calls, I'm gonna be meeting Anton at the club. Tru, make sure those cars get out tonight. If they don't, get rid of them niggas… for good."

"I got you," he nodded before leaving.

It was tough being me at times, but I wouldn't have this shit any other way.

# CHAPTER ONE

*Freshman year... Three weeks later...*

The Uber driver pulled up to the school, and threw the car in park. I smiled at the sight and quickly hopped out, forgetting to thank him. That was the least of my worries; I was finally a college girl. I adjusted my duffle bag on my shoulder, and started towards the dorm hall that I was assigned to. My parents, Brian, and I came over a week ago to bring my stuff, so my room was already set up for me. I was excited just thinking about being so far away from home, free to do whatever the fuck I wanted. I was gonna miss Brian, but honestly, I was happy to be away from his ass too. He smothered me a bit, and hated for me to do anything with Emery, my best friend.

I finally made it to Dayton Complex, my dorm hall, and entered, gaping at my surroundings. It was a huge building with a washer room, a wall of mailboxes, and even a big lounge area with a television. I loved this place already. I was eighteen and feeling grown as fuck.

I double checked my room assignment, and then got onto the elevator to get to the right floor. I made my way down the hall until I reached the right door, and then used my school ID to enter. The other bed already had a pretty comforter on it, so I knew my roommate, Tasmine, was here. I came a week earlier though, just so I could choose which bed I wanted first, which was the one by the window. I was happy she wasn't a petty bitch, and just accepted what was left.

I placed my bag onto the floor, and then plopped back on my bed while smiling. This was just the beginning, and I knew I was gonna have the time of my life here in Nevada. I couldn't see myself missing California at all.

"Finally you're here! Girl, I was looking through all of your clothes earlier, and you have some cute ass dresses!" Tasmine beamed, prompting me to sit up abruptly. She'd left the door open purposely for some reason.

Tasmine was really pretty. She had a caramel complexion, long brown hair, which was pressed and sweeping her shoulders, and a slim thick frame. She had big boobs though, but it went well with her shape, and her eyes were a light brown. Her perfume was hella strong, but at least it smelled good.

"Thanks, I got them just for school. I remembered you told me about all the parties they had here. If you don't mind me asking, how do you know that?"

"I came to visit earlier in the summer."

"Dope. Is this complex really only for freshman?"

"It is, but sometimes shit gets mixed up so we may run into an upper class boy here. Are you ready to party tonight?" she sat at the desk on my side of the room.

"Tonight? Damn, already?" I frowned. "I kind of wanted to settle in."

"I mean you can if you want, but these guys named Oden, Tru, and Anton are having a barbecue, and you don't wanna miss that shit."

"Yeah chica, you don't." Some Spanish girl switched in, wearing the littlest shorts I'd ever seen, and a bandeau top that was barely covering her breasts. "Bella," she smiled and stuck her hand out to me. "I live right across from you guys." I guess she and Tasmine had become cool already.

"I'm Khyle," I half smiled. "And who the fuck are Oden, Tru, and Anton?"

"Baby, you can't be in Vegas and not know who they are, so let me put you up on game. They're some rich ass cats and they're all fine as fuck. They own Bishop's, the car dealership, this new club Palace, and have you heard of Brown Sugar Bourbon?"

"I don't really fuck with dark liquor," I replied.

"Well you will tonight," Bella smiled at Tasmine, before sitting on my bed with me like she knew me well enough to do so.

"Y'all can have Oden and Tru, just don't touch or look at Anton."

"I'm sure I won't want either one of their asses, I have a man back home in Cali." I was serious. I wasn't trying to have no nigga that all these bitches wanted anyway. I needed someone I could have to myself with no problems, and that was Brian.

"Your boyfriend was cool with you being away in Vegas, chica?" Bella raised a brow at me. She was much prettier up close, like for real pretty with her full lips, brown eyes, and a mole above her lip. She had super long golden brown hair that was more wavy than curly. Her frame was small, but she had nice legs and a super flat stomach. She smelled like some kind of sweet Bath and Body Works lotion. I was all for hanging with her and Tasmine because I didn't hang with ugly bitches.

"Yeah, he's cool because he knows I'm gonna behave. It's only niggas who can't control themselves, women have no problem."

"I feel the same. My boyfriend, Dean, trusted me to leave the state too," Bella nodded. I noticed a bruise on her inner forearm as I scanned her.

"That's until you need some dick and don't feel like driving for hours to get it," Tasmine sucked her teeth before picking up her iPhone.

"Sex ain't even all that for me to be jonesing and shit." I got up and checked myself out in the mirror. Right now I had on some terry cloth shorts in gray, with the matching terry cloth crop top that had a hood attached. I wanted to show off my belly piercing and tattoo on the side of my stomach now that I was away from my parents. They didn't know shit about my body modification.

"You just ain't had the right dick," Tasmine retorted, and the three of us laughed.

"Girl, your body is sexy. I hope you're gonna wear that to the night barbecue," Bella complimented me, and I smiled at her before speaking.

My body was sexy in its own way. I wasn't skinny at all, nor was I Amber Rose, but I had nice legs, an ass that could be grabbed, and matching titties. They weren't on Tasmine's level, but they were enough for me to have some cleavage.

"I ain't going." I brushed my long hair down, and then turned to make sure nothing was on the back of my shorts since my period decided to show up today. I was loving this big ass mirror by the sink. I just hated that the sink was out here in the room, instead of in the little bathroom with the toilet and shower.

"She's going," Tasmine cut in, and I playfully rolled my eyes as I walked back to my bed to sit down.

"So who has a car?" Bella questioned, darting her eyes from me to Tasmine.

We both stayed quiet because I guess we both didn't. My father was gonna get me one, but when I chose to go to UNLV, he, for some reason, felt I didn't need one anymore. But he said if my first semester grades were B's and above, he'd buy me a Jeep. I was bummed about not being able to have a car to whip while out in Vegas, but then again, it was all the more reason I wouldn't be able to drive home, which was oddly a plus.

"Looks like we can't get to the partyyyy," I chuckled.

"No, my roommate told me she has a car. She's kind of shy and nerdy, so I'm sure she won't mind taking us and picking us back up. Her name is Perry, I think she said."

"We can just take an Uber," Tasmine suggested.

"You gonna pay for that shit? My mom is only giving me $200 weekly, and I ain't trying to blow it on Ubers. We're gonna be partying off campus a lot, ladies, so it's best we secure Perry as our designated driver now. Hey, you never know, we may turn her out," Bella popped her ass making Tasmine and I laugh loudly. I was happy as fuck I had Tasmine for a roommate and not Perry's ass.

"Well, let's get some food from the dining hall," I stood up.

I was gonna try to eat there as much as I could because in a way it was like eating for free. Before coming down here you had to purchase a dining plan, so all we had to do was swipe our ID to get food. It was better than using the credit card that my dad gave me. It was attached to his credit card, so it wasn't like I could go hog wild anyway. I had my own debit card too now, but like Bella, I was only getting a certain amount—$500 to be exact, every two weeks—and I wasn't about to throw it away on food.

We grabbed our purses and then went across the hall to get Perry. Bella said we needed to butter her up so that when it came time to ask for a ride, she'd be more than willing. I didn't like using people, but Bella had a point, and maybe Perry needed friends.

"Perry, these are my new friends, Khyle and Tasmine."

"Nice to meet you," Perry rose to her feet. She was an okay looking girl. All I could tell was that she was half Asian or something. She was about 4'8, skinny, had freckles, and reddish brown hair.

"I don't like asking people this because I hate when people ask me, but what are you mixed with?" Tasmine frowned at her.

"My mother is Irish, and my father is Black and Asian," she replied nervously.

"Right, umm, wanna go get some food with us?" Bella questioned, before swinging her long gold hair behind her back.

"Uh, sure, yes." Perry grabbed her purse and we all left out, heading towards the elevator.

A couple of guys whistled and yelled out irrelevant ass comments as the four of us walked by them through the lobby. All of us ignored their asses and kept it pushing towards the dining hall. After using our ID to get inside, we immediately went our separate ways, arriving at our food station of choice. As I was looking over the food, I saw Perry come up next to me and smile.

"You from Vegas?" I asked her and she nodded. "Why don't you live at home?"

"My parents thought it'd be good if I had the whole college experience."

"Smart choice. I think the four of us are gonna have a lot of fun this year. Are you coming out tonight? To the barbecue?"

"I have some studying to do."

"Already? Class doesn't start until Monday, well for me."

"Mine are Tuesdays and Thursdays, but I like to go over some of the curriculum before I get to the class. It's my nature to be ahead of things."

"Suit yourself," I raised a brow before going to get myself something to drink. Once I had everything I wanted, I walked out to where the tables were, and spotted Tasmine and Bella sitting already, so I joined them. Perry came over a few moments after. "She said she's not coming tonight."

"Perry, you should come. I know you said you wanted to study or whatever, but don't you think it's a good idea to make some friends at least?" Bella turned her lip up in disgust.

Perry glanced back and forth between the three of us, before sighing and saying, "Fine, I will come. But I don't drink at parties, I know they roofie people."

"Don't trip, we're gonna get twisted before we go in," Tasmine grinned, and so did I at the thought. I wasn't sure how we were gonna get liquor, but I was sure Bella had a way. I'd learned already that she was the type to figure out how to make shit work by any means necessary. I had to admit I liked that about her.

If my first day was already this interesting, I couldn't wait to see what else was in store. But my first stop was gonna be this night barbecue.

# CHAPTER TWO

# Shayne

*Khyle: There is a party tonight, you should come.*

*Me: Already going to something boo, and I'm sure where I'm going is better.*

*Khyle: Where?*

*Me: We can just have breakfast together since you didn't come see me once you got here.*

I didn't want her coming to this particular shindig.

*Khyle: Because someone was too busy to get me from the airport so I had to take an Uber.*

*Khyle: Have you heard of some niggas named Oden, Tru, and Anton/Tony?*

My heart dropped as I read her text.

*Me: Yes, that's the party I'm going to.*

*Khyle: Oh my gosh! Me too! What time are you heading over?*

I sucked my teeth and set my phone down on the dresser,

deciding not to respond. I really didn't want my sister at this party because I hadn't quite bagged Oden yet. Yeah, we fucked a couple more times since that first night, but we didn't really talk outside of that. He would just randomly hit me up, even late as fuck at night sometimes, and I would hop my happy ass up and go see him. I was tired of lying to Pierce about how Alanna was having a hard time over Earl and needed me. I was ready for Oden to make that move and claim me as his girl, ask me on a date, shit, something. The nigga had to be half blind because if I even gave a nigga eye contact, he was on my shit and tough.

But see, if Khyle goes to this party, I'm sure Oden will be salivating like a dog. My little sister was pretty as fuck, and for some reason, niggas were always on her tip. We looked a lot alike, except I had a bigger booty and hips. She wasn't flat in either areas, but I was obviously winning in those departments. However, despite the fact that she was lacking and I wasn't, dudes gravitated towards her and I swear it never failed. I didn't know if it was her boisterous personality or the way she dressed, I just wasn't fucking sure, but if we went out, it was a sure thing that the nigga would look her way first before me. Even Pierce tried to fuck with her before he found out she was only 16 at the time. Only then did he try to come my way. I usually didn't fuck with a nigga who tried to get at me as a second choice, but because I thought Pierce was gonna be the next Reggie White, I swept that itty bitty negative under the rug.

I felt bad that I was envious of my baby sister because I knew she loved me and meant no harm. I mean, it wasn't her fault that dudes gaped upon seeing her, but it was just so damn annoying. That was why I didn't like hanging with her sometimes though, because some days I wanted to be the prettiest bitch niggas saw.

Like, Alanna was beautiful as hell too, but I looked better and niggas recognized that when we were out. That was how I liked shit. Hopefully, tonight would be the one night I won over Khyle. Oden wasn't your typical nigga, so I kind of doubted that he would be smitten with Khyle like these other simpletons. At least I hoped he wouldn't be smitten.

Plus, Khyle had Skeletor aka Brian back home, who she swore she loved. I knew that nigga was cheating, but little Miss Khyle thought she was the crème de la crème and that a nigga would be stupid to fuck around on her. As true as that was, niggas were dumb and she'd realize it one day.

After spreading my Kat Von D lipstick on, I slipped it into my clutch and snapped it. Tonight I was rocking a tight fitting black dress that was long sleeved. The dress code for tonight was supposed to be casual, but I liked to go above and beyond just a tad bit. I would much rather be overdressed than underdressed any damn day. You wouldn't catch Shayne Luke slipping no fucking where.

As I was running my brush through my long ponytail, I saw Pierce walk into the bedroom through the mirror. He was dressed to the nines and smelling like a million fucking bucks, which made me wonder where he was going. Yes, I was over him, but that didn't take away from his looks. The nigga was fine, he just didn't have the bread or demeanor to match.

"Where are you going?" I frowned, dropping my brush onto the dresser.

"Barbecue party on Buffalo." *What the fuck? No! Shit!*

"Oh, for real? Well, I guess I will see you there."

"We can ride together, Shayne. No point in using gas for two damn cars, especially since you don't fill up either damn one."

"Look, don't be snapping at me because you ain't clocking million dollar contracts, bro. I'm just as fucking mad about it."

"I ain't snapping at you about that, but I do think that you could contribute a little more, not only to the household but to the damn relationship," he frowned his sexy face.

Pierce had blemish free brown skin, was about 6'2, had a perfectly lined goatee, and a nice amount of muscles but wasn't too buff. What I loved about him was his kindness, and how he treated me. He never once cheated or disrespected me like most niggas who were on their way to NFL greatness. Our shit was perfect, and sometimes I just wanted to slap his ass for fucking our future up by getting cut. I hate to leave him, but it is what it is.

"I don't want my mood ruined before the party, so can we go? I told Alanna I would pick her up so we have to stop at her crib."

"Where she stay?"

"South Grand Canyon, remember?" He just nodded, so I walked by him but he grabbed me by the wrist.

"Stop acting so cold," he spoke in a low tone with a sad expression. I just leaned up to press my lips against his, and then wiped my lipstick off before taking his hand into mine so we could leave. Boy, bye.

***

*Coogi down to the socks like I'm Biggie poppa, keep your girl head in my Tommy boxers. But really though, she's a silly ho, cause you know the Fergenstein gettin' plenty dough.*

A$AP Ferg's "Work" played loudly as fuck as Alanna, Pierce, and I entered the back area of The Wyatt where Oden, Truman, and Anton lived. I wasn't sure why three niggas who made so much bread lived together, but then again, a bitch didn't care. It was bittersweet being here because I wouldn't be able to do my dirt with Oden, but at least I got to be around him.

The party was in full effect, and there were plenty of bitches surrounding the pool in little ass thong bathing suits. I hadn't gotten the memo that this was a pool party, but I wish I had so I could've shown Oden what he would be missing tonight, thanks to Pierce.

People were also dancing, some in the grass, some girls were giving lap dances in the little beach chairs around the pool, and some people were just straight up kissing. The weed smoke in the air was potent, and the drinks were already being passed around. All in all, this party was already flying high.

I scanned the party for Oden, and when I spotted his homeboy, Truman, on the grill while talking to his girlfriend, Pilar, I knew Oden couldn't be too far away. As I kept looking, Alanna nudged me subtly and pointed to Oden and Anton coming out of the sliding doors and dapping people up. They both looked sexy as fuck, and were dressed to fucking impress. When they sat down, I purposely made the three of us go in their direction so we could pass them.

"Oden, Tony, what's up?" Pierce smiled down at them with his thirsty ass. I hated that he tried to act like he knew them.

"What's good, P, this you?" Oden question with a grin. *Wait, he knows Pierce?* I glanced at Anton who was smiling just as widely, so he must've known Oden fucked me. Shit.

"Yeah, this is my girl, Shayne. And this is her home girl, Alanna."

"Nice to meet you two," Oden replied in his raspy voice, while eyeing me lustfully with a smirk. Great, now he thought I was a hoe. I got lost in his stare for a bit though, because he was just so damn sexy that it made no damn sense. I just wanted to touch his pretty ass hair. "Aye Pierce, can you do me a favor?"

"Sure, what's up?"

"I need you to go pick up some more weed. It's just around the corner. My boy Lyle is gonna be in front of the Chipotle in the shopping center on Arroyo Crossing Parkway. Give him this, and take the box."

"Umm, okay, fasho. I'll be back, babe." Pierce kissed my lips but I didn't kiss him back. It was quick anyway so he didn't notice.

"Come with me." Oden stood up and I followed him inside the building and up to his apartment.

He took me right to the bathroom, bent me over the sink, and yanked my panties down my legs without saying a word. He didn't even wanna talk. I listened as he rolled a condom down, and then entered me slowly, causing me to whimper. We made eye contact in the mirror as he rammed into me from behind, and I could barely muffle my moans. I bit down on my lip to keep from screaming out, as he hit my spot time and time again, pulling my orgasm out of me.

"Odeeeen, fuck," I cried out. His long thick dick was filling me up, and it felt so damn good. I had to be with this nigga, and if he had to send my nigga away to fuck me, then I was sure I had him. Khyle wouldn't have a chance.

"Shit," he grumbled in his sexy voice before delivering a few more pumps and exploding. After we caught our breaths, he pulled out of me, so I turned around to kiss him but he blocked me. He never let me kiss him. "You just kissed that nigga in the mouth, back up."

"Jealous?" I raised a brow as I grabbed a wet wipe from my clutch.

"Why would I be jealous when all he got was a kiss? Shit, at least I got some pussy." He used a wet, warm towel to clean his dick before tossing it into the hamper and washing his hands.

"When are we gonna go on a date? I'm tired of just fucking and saying goodbye."

"I'll let you know." He dried his hands and then left out of the bathroom.

This nigga was working my nerves with his fine ass, but I was a determined woman.

# CHAPTER TWO

"I'm ready to fuckin' party! Remember we still have to go across the street to Von's for the liquor," Bella smacked her lips as she checked herself out in the mirror in Tasmine's and my room. She was wearing some white shorts and a red bandeau top. I was starting to see that, that was her outfit combination of choice.

"I'm ready," Tasmine replied after running her flat iron over her hair. She was wearing some tight ass skinny jeans, a goldish-yellow halter-top, and some gold gladiator sandals. Her brown hair was sweeping her back, with a headband holding it back.

"Khyle?" Bella quizzed as I slipped on my tennis shoe. I had on my same terry cloth fit, along with some Huaraches, so I was good. I wasn't about to get dressed up for this shit, because for one, it was last minute, and two, Bella said it was casual. There was nothing wrong with what I had on.

"I'm ready," I sprang up with a smile as the girls laughed. Perry had on some skinny jeans, an orange t-shirt, some kind of beige sweater that swallowed her skinny body, and these pointy toed flats. She looked like the mother of the group, especially because Bella, Tasmine, and I were showing either our stomachs or back.

"Alright, ladies, and remember, we can't stay long." Perry stood up and headed to the door. None of us responded because we all planned to stay as long as we wanted. I'd told the ladies that my sister was gonna be there, so if anything, she could give us a ride home.

We left the building and the Las Vegas air was so humid and hot, even at night. I smiled as we made our way across the parking lot to get into Perry's car because I was so happy to be here and free from restrictions.

My phone buzzing interrupted my thoughts, and I saw it was Brian's ass blowing me up with text messages. I'd spent the whole day with these ladies, and I'd gotten so caught up in our conversation and the shit we were doing, that forgot to reply to him. I knew he missed me, but I just wished he would back off a little bit. I mean, damn, this was my first fucking day, dude.

We finally got to Perry's fresh ass BMW, and I laughed at Bella when she high fived her.

"Perry, why didn't you tell me we'd be riding in style?" Bella quizzed as soon as we slid into Perry's plush ass leather seats. Tasmine and I shared a smile of approval before reaching for our seat belts.

"I guess because I've had it since eleventh grade, it's not really a big deal to me," Perry chuckled softly as she cranked the car. The shit was smooth as fuck.

"You got a car in eleventh grade? Damn, bitch, you're lucky," I shook my head at my thoughts.

"I know that's right. If I even mumbled the word car to my mom in eleventh grade she probably would have slapped my ass," Bella touched up her mascara in the visor mirror.

"Where are you from?" I asked Bella, astonished that we'd been talking all day and I didn't know. I knew Tasmine was from Kentucky, because in our emails back and forth, she told me she couldn't wait to get away from home. We bonded over that.

"Hot ass Arizona, mami."

"Why'd you come here?" I questioned her further.

"Because I wanted to go somewhere that I knew was on that turn up tip, but I wanted to be close enough to be able to drive home if I wanted. Not that I would, but I like that I can. And the fact that they offered me a scholarship didn't hurt either."

I nodded at her response, remembering that she said she had a boyfriend back home, and that they were engaged. She had a ring on, but it was little as hell. She also said she was Spanish, black, and Italian, a mix I'd never seen before. She was gorgeous though.

Perry pulled into a parking space at Von's Grocery Store across the way, and the four of us got out to get some liquor. Tasmine had taken her older sister's ID so she'd be able to get the alcohol for us. We'd already given her some money on it before we left the school. After picking out some cheap ass Smirnoff, juice, cups, and gum, we checked out and went back to the car. We immediately began filling our cups with the pineapple juice and vodka; well, all of us except Perry.

"Cheers to our first night in Vegas, and many more to come." Bella turned around in her seat to face Tasmine and I, wearing her pretty smile.

"Cheers!" Tasmine and I said in unison, before the three of us chugged it down.

We refilled once more, before Perry typed the address of the party into her GPS and sped out. Tasmine had her phone hooked up to the radio through Bluetooth, and my roomy had all the fucking ratchet shit on her phone. If I didn't know before, I knew now that we would get along great. I loved sensible music too, but there was nothing like the shit that made me want to pop my ass with my tongue out. As we rapped along with "Mobbin' On Em" by Smoovie Baby, Perry had finally pulled up to our destination and shut her engine off.

"Perry, you need a fucking drink," Tasmine giggled along with Bella and I.

"No, I don't like the way it tastes," she turned her nose up and laughed.

"She has to drive us home anyway, so she shouldn't drink," Bella chimed in and I nodded. "You think they have weed? These niggas better have weed."

"I hope so, but if not I'm sure my sister Shayne has some."

"Whose idea was it to give y'all boy's names?" Tasmine questioned.

"My dad. He wanted two boys, and since we were girls, he just kept the same names he was gonna give his sons," I explained. I could hear loud music from behind the apartment building, so I knew the party was cracking all ready.

"Well come on, y'all. And remember, Khyle, we have to behave because we're in relationships," Bella and I chuckled in unison. I had no problem with that, I knew I was gonna behave. Brian was my boo.

The four of us exited the car and made our way around the back to see the party in full effect like I'd expected. People were swimming, dancing, eating, smoking, drinking, laughing, just having a fucking ball in this bitch, and I was so ready.

I spotted my sister sitting down at one of the tables with some light-skinned girl who I assumed was Alanna. I'd never met her, but she was always in my sister's stories. Shayne was sitting on Pierce's lap as they both sipped from their red cups and swayed.

"There goes my sister," I pointed.

"There is Anton," Tasmine shrieked, but low enough so that only the four of us heard as we headed towards my sister.

Anton was sexier than a muthafucka! He had sexy chocolate skin, a tapered fade, muscular build, and he was tall as fuck. He wasn't 6'8 like Brian, but he was definitely about 6'4. I saw why Tasmine was on his tip, that nigga was the truth. I was a bit jealous that she'd called dibs first, and mad that I had Brian back home.

"Aye, Tony, take this," some light-skinned guy with big curly hair walked out holding a box.

"Pick your jaw up, baby girl," Bella chuckled as she lifted my chin. "That's Oden."

Oden was fine as fuck. I know I said Anton was, and he was, but Oden was just gorgeous. His skin was like a toasted vanilla, he was about the same height as Anton, and had scruffy chin hairs which I would love to play with. He was wearing a Chicago Bulls jersey, which exposed his muscular arms covered in tattoos, and on his bottom half he wore dark jeans, and red low top chucks. I didn't like dudes with hair, but that shit had changed in a matter of seconds. Also, his wild hair was more afro-like but filled with beautiful coils. His demeanor, even from afar, spoke volumes. I knew he was exactly what these girls claimed he was: a fucking boss. He had my pussy wet just from watching him talk, with that blunt in his hands.

"Khyle!" Tasmine barked, and when I looked her way, I saw she, Bella, and Perry were already sitting down with Shayne, Pierce, and Alanna.

I glanced back just for one more look at this fine ass specimen, and my heart stopped when he looked over at me while still talking. His full lips made my mouth water, and I felt a tingle between my legs when he shot me a cocky smile after letting his eyes run amuck all over my body.

Pulling my eyes away, I went over to my friends, and gave my sister and Pierce a hug. I was about to sit down but "Wavy" by Ty Dolla $ign came on and that was my song. I began dancing, and so did Bella. I decided to give Perry a lap dance since she was so shy, making everyone at the table chuckle. When I looked in Oden's direction, he was on his way over. Shit!

# CHAPTER TWO

# Oden

$\mathcal{I}$ was just minding my own damn business, taking this blunt to the head, when my eyes landed on this pretty little bitch at my party. She was staring a fucking hole through me, and I didn't mind at all. I usually didn't go after women unless they were just bad as fuck, so right now I was making my way over. If anything, I just wanted to smash one time. As long as I knew what the pussy was like I'd be good.

"Oden." I walked up on her, and she stopped popping her ass on some shy girl who was 'bout red as a damn tomato by now.

"Khyle." She pushed her hair behind her ears and then shook my hand with her small dainty one. I was about to speak again, but she turned her back to me and rounded the table to sit next to some pretty Spanish girl. I chuckled lightly because I could already tell what type she was.

"Khyle, come talk to me for a second," I squinted my eyes, shoving my hands down into my pockets. The side of my face began to burn, so when I looked over I saw Shayne grimacing. Right then it hit me that she was related to Khyle because they favored. Khyle was more attractive though.

"I'm good, but thanks for inviting us to the party. Y'all got any more weed?" Khyle shut my ass down, which was a muthafucking *first.*

"Yeah, come with me and get it," I grinned, making her shy away before gaining eye contact with me again. Rising from her seat, she grabbed the Spanish chick's hand so that she could come with her.

"Fuck you think, I'm gonna rape you? Let yo' friend chill while we get the weed." She paused for a bit, but when the Spanish girl flashed her a smile, she rolled her eyes and made her way over to me.

"Come on," she snapped. I gestured for her to walk in front of me so I could get a good look at her ass. She was slim thick; that perfect in the middle shit. And with every step she took towards the apartment building, I was imagining putting her in all kinds of positions. *I wonder if she's flexible.*

"How old are you, baby girl?" I asked once we got inside, away from the loud music, conversation, and just all around ruckus.

"I'm 18, you?" We got onto the elevator. Damn, I didn't like them that young at all. However, despite the makeup she had on, I knew she was young before I even asked.

"I'm 24. You look young as fuck, but you're sexy as hell."

"Thanks."

"Why are you so mean? You don't even fucking know me and you're low-key coming at me foul up in my fucking crib. I don't take too kindly to disrespect."

"I ain't mean to be disrespectful, I'm sorry. I have a boyfriend and it just seemed like you were trying to get at me." Her tone calmed all the way down, and I could sense that she was a bit afraid of me.

"So what if I am?" I cornered her in the elevator, and she inhaled sharply, gripping the handlebars.

"Then I have every right to be rude to you so that you'll back off."

"You smell good, what's that?"

"Very Sexy Now by Victoria's Secret."

"Name fits, baby girl." I licked my lips as she slipped past me and sauntered off the elevator. I hated when girls fucked their bodies up with big ass tattoos, but the one on the side of her stomach was sexy. Everything about this little mean ass girl was sexy. If I was lucky, I'd be able to hit by tonight.

She waited until I got off, and then followed me to my door. I stood there for a second, just admiring her, before chuckling at the fact that she'd rolled her eyes for like the hundredth time tonight.

We entered the apartment and she immediately began aimlessly walking around, running her pretty hands across shit. I didn't really trip because this was the hoe crib and we only somewhat fixed the shit up to make it look like something. Aesthetics were everything, and a room being decorated nicely did impact your mood. A nice painting or two always assisted me and the homies in scoring some pussy.

"You want something to drink?" I quizzed her.

"No. We're not staying up here, we're just getting the weed and bouncing." She plopped down onto the couch and pulled her iPhone from her pocket. She had some long ass nails, which I hated, but it was fly on her. She kept herself up which was a turn on.

Chuckling, I nodded and went towards the bedrooms as if the weed was really back there. Pierce went to get it a little earlier when I was banging his girl, and we left it down there for everyone to enjoy.

It was thirsty for me to lie to get Khyle up here, but I was a very ambitious ass nigga. So when I saw something I wanted, I went after it and did what I needed to, to get it.

"Shit, I forgot I left the shit downstairs." I returned to the living room, smiling hard, even though I'd tried to hide the shit.

"You didn't forget," she chuckled softly. Finally, a smile. Damn!

"Nope." I sat down next to her and she tried to scoot away, but I tugged her so that she'd stay in place.

"Don't be grabbing me up like that," she spat before smirking. Her smile was so damn pretty. I wanted to ask her how she knew Shayne because they favored, but I decided against it because I really didn't care.

"I'm sorry, I can't help but touch you," I spoke honestly.

"Well, let's go back downstairs and join the party then since ain't shit up here." She attempted to stand, but I sat her little ass back down. Her long dark hair slapped me in the face, but I didn't mind. "Is this a weave?" she had the nerve to ask me as she touched my hair. Now usually I would have snapped her fucking wrist for feeling on my shit, but I didn't mind, oddly.

"Nah, this ain't no muthafucking weave, fuck kind of niggas you run into back in California?" I frowned as she chuckled. Her laugh…

her fucking laugh.

"How did you know I was from California?" she frowned. I wanted to tell her it was because I knew she was related to Shayne, but I was sure she would ask me how I knew her and I didn't want to go there. Something told me that if she knew I smashed her kinfolk, she wouldn't even let me breathe her same air.

"You got that look that girls from California have."

"What look is that?"

"Fine than a muthafucka," I replied and we both laughed together. "What you doing out here in Vegas, baby girl? You're too young to really have fun."

"I'm gonna be attending UNLV for the fall semester."

"Dope. I go there too. I'm getting a certificate in business."

"Why a certificate and not a degree?" her perfect eyebrow raised up.

"Certificate is quicker and easier to obtain."

"But a degree would be more beneficial." I was liking her mind already. She wasn't one of them pretty bitches who had pebbles for brains.

"True." I moved her hair behind her shoulder, prompting her to look into my eyes innocently. I wanted to game her up so bad in order to fuck, but I couldn't. She was feisty but she was a good girl, meaning she wasn't the type that you fed dick to and kicked out afterwards. "You got me staring at you and shit like some thirsty nigga," I scoffed with a smile.

"It's not thirsty. If I felt you were thirsty I would have gotten up and left. You're too fine to ever be considered thirsty."

"Take your shoes off," I instructed.

"What? Why?"

"Take them off, please."

She stared into my face for a bit, and then leaned down to pull her shoes off. Her pretty hair fell downward into her face as she did so, and she flung it when she sat back up. I grabbed her legs and placed them in my lap so that I could get a good look at her feet. I hated ugly feet, and I was happy to see she had some sexy ass ones. Her toe polish was white, which I'd never seen before. Her shit just looked so soft like the rest of her.

"You got a foot fetish or some shit?" she turned her full lip up. I wanted to suck on them muthafuckas, and a couple of other things too. It was rare that I ate pussy, so the fact that she had me wanting her to sit on my face was new.

"Nah, I just don't like girls with ugly ass feet."

"It shouldn't matter what my feet look like because I have a man, remember?" She removed her legs from my lap and put her socks and shoes back on.

"Not for long, but enjoy him while it lasts."

She stared at me for a few, and then began laughing hysterically. She was clapping her hands and everything, making her bracelets clink together loudly.

She rose to her feet, and adjusted her shorts while standing in front of me, showing me how sexy her stomach was. Sinking my teeth into my bottom lip, I attempted to keep myself from salivating at the thought of eating her pussy. I knew it was pretty, and that shit probably tasted like strawberry Starbursts. Reaching my hand up, I ran my fingers down her stomach, toying with her belly ring, before making my way over to the tattoo of the dream catcher on her side.

She stayed silent as I gripped her waist, so I pulled her down into my lap, inhaling her coconut and vanilla scented perfume. I brushed my lips across hers as she let out a stuttered breath. As soon as I pressed her body down so that she could feel how hard she had my monster, someone started beating on the door.

"Khyle!" Shayne shouted. I wanted to draw my heat and kill her ass from behind the door.

Khyle shot up from my lap, and rushed to the door to open it for Shayne. Shayne stared me down before making eye contact with Khyle again.

"Your friends are looking for you. The party is getting wild anyway, so y'all need to leave, boo," she explained to Khyle as I chuckled lightly at her hating ass. "I will meet you down there."

Khyle looked over her shoulder at me before walking past her sister to leave. I stood up and sucked my teeth when I saw Shayne close the door behind her and glare at me.

"Don't you have somewhere to be?" I furrowed my brows.

"So you fuck me and then try to get at my little sister, nigga? Really?"

"I ain't know that was your sister. Not that I care though."

"Leave her alone, she has a boyfriend."

"So did you, but that didn't stop me from fucking right?"

"It's supposed to be me and you, Oden."

"Girl, get yo' ass up out of here and tend to yo' nigga. I already got what I wanted from you so you can step."

I opened the door, and she rushed out with an attitude. I followed behind her, and when I got down to the party, I immediately began scanning it for Khyle. I saw her talking with the Spanish chick and the shy one, just before she pushed her other friend into Anton purposely. Baby girl was a handful, and I planned to fill my hands all the way up.

# CHAPTER TWO

# Tasmine Randall

"Damn, girl," Anton turned to me frowning after Khyle's ass pushed me into him. She'd been telling me to talk to him, but every time I looked up, he was in some bitch's face. And for the last 30 minutes, it'd been the same bitch who was now frowning at me for interrupting her time with him.

"Sorry, I tripped," I lied before glancing at a laughing Khyle.

"You good. What's your name?" His brows dipped in confusion as if he'd seen me before. I was so mesmerized by his beautiful chocolate skin, brown eyes, and full lips. He came straight from heaven, I was sure of it.

"Tony!" the girl screeched when he asked for my name.

"Aye, chill the fuck out. Go to the Jacuzzi, I will be over there in a minute."

She looked from him to me while moving her tongue around the inside of her mouth, and then finally turned on her heels and switched her flat booty ass away. He watched her for a bit, as I admired the tattoo on his neck. Finally, he turned back to look at me, giving me a whiff of his cologne that smelled expensive as fuck.

"Name?" he inquired again.

"Tasmine."

"Tasmine, that reminds me of Tasmanian devil," he chuckled, flashing his pretty white smile. His eyes were low from getting high, making him even sexier.

"Thank you, I guess."

"I ain't mean to clown on your name, baby, it just reminded me of that shit. You got some pretty ass eyes, what color is that?"

"Hazel, and thank you." I couldn't help but giggle because a bitch was ecstatic that I was actually talking to Anton Nickerson.

I'm sure you're wondering how the hell I even knew him, because of the simple fact that I was from Louisville, Kentucky. Well, in order to come to this university, my parents wanted to visit first so the three of us plus my older sister flew out to look at the school. When night hit, my sister and I ditched my parents to go to some party that was being thrown a street over from the strip, and the hosts were none other than Anton, Truman, and Oden. From the moment he spoke his name into the mic, I was drawn to his fine ass. That night my sister and I found his Instagram and I made sure to follow him. He followed me back, but I guess he didn't remember me.

Don't be fooled, I wasn't the type of girl who went crazy for a nigga who hadn't even talked to me once. I usually had to swat niggas off of me with a fly swatter, but there was something different about Anton. His swag was different from the dudes that I turned down on the daily, and I was immediately attracted to that. He was exactly the type of dude that a girl like myself was supposed to be with.

The only downside to him was all the rumors about him fathering kids all over Las Vegas. I wasn't down for fucking with a deadbeat ass nigga, nor was I trying to play step mommy to six kids, or fight with eight baby mamas. I was young, and looking to have fun while finding love. I hated drama.

"I feel like I've seen you before, baby." The way he said 'baby' in that deep ass voice had my legs weak as fuck.

"We follow each other on Instagram." I immediately burst into laughter because he jerked his neck back in amazement when I said that.

"We do? Damn, baby, I'm gonna be honest. I just follow back whoever follows me, especially if she's pretty as fuck like you." *He thinks I'm pretty.*

"That's cool… I guess."

"Yeah." He looked over his shoulder at the girl he'd sent away. She was shooting daggers at me with her eyes as she soaked in the Jacuzzi. "Well, it was nice meeting you, little mama. I hope you come to some more of our parties." He licked his lips and then walked away, tipping his red cup up to finish off the contents.

"What happened?" Bella asked me as she, Perry, and Khyle rushed to me.

"Nothing. He just told me I had pretty eyes and that was it. He didn't even ask for my fucking number."

"It's a process, baby. At the next event, he will go further, and so on and so on," Bella smirked. "Well, Perry is sleepy, so we'd better go get food now so we can get back to the dorms."

I nodded and the four of us headed out of the big ass apartment's backyard. I got one more look at Anton, as he felt up on that bitch in the Jacuzzi.

Perry drove us to this place named Blueberry Hill on Flamingo. It was a 24-hour diner that sold everything from breakfast to dinner food. No one was there, so we were seated immediately and had our drink orders taken. As far as the inside, this place really needed to upgrade their systems because it was way too old fashioned for me.

"So what happened with Oden, Khyle?" I asked, and noticed her face light up a little bit.

"Nada. We were just talking and shit since he *forgot* that the weed was downstairs with the party." She used air quotes when she said forgot.

"You like him?" Bella asked.

"I have a boyfriend, and plus, I think he has something going on with my sister. She came beating on the door like the police, and she was glaring at him when I answered the door. Something wasn't right, and he seems like a dirt ass nigga who would try to fuck two sisters."

"I noticed she didn't speak to you when you said bye," Perry finally made a peep. She'd been fairly quiet all damn night.

"Yeah, exactly. She acts like that when she's mad. She loves for people to try and figure out why she's angry instead of just telling them, but I ain't got time for that bullshit. I came here to get an education and experience, not to be chasing behind her ass," Khyle spat.

"Wasn't that guy her man anyway?" Bella frowned as the waitress set our juices down.

"Yeah, Pierce. She moved here for him in a sense. But I know my sister, and the way she looked at Oden said a lot."

"Well, you have a boyfriend, Khyle, so no need to worry," Perry smiled.

"You're exactly right." Khyle nodded her head in agreement, but something told me that she had just that quickly found interest in another man. I couldn't blame her though because Oden was sexy and aggressive as fuck. I knew if he wanted her he would have her, and that was all there was to it.

We continued conversing for a little bit, and once our food came, we went the fuck in on it. As we were scarfing down our pancakes, a group of niggas walked in talking loudly. They had on UNLV branded attire, so it was obvious they played something for the school. When they got closer, I saw a football sewn into the side of the windbreaker jacket.

"Bella, what's good?" this sexy caramel-skinned guy approached our table, as his group sat at the booth next to ours. He was tall, built as fuck, and he smelled like Irish Spring body wash. All in all, the nigga was fine as hell.

"Hey, Santino," Bella replied dryly, avoiding eye contact. Khyle, Perry, and I all looked at her suspiciously because her usually boisterous ass was acting like a church mouse to this nigga.

"I'm happy to see you came to Vegas too." He leaned down to

look into her face since her head was lowered.

"Yep, me too."

"Ladies, I'm Santino. Since Bella is too rude to introduce me, I will do it myself," he smiled, and his deep ass dimples appeared.

"Tasmine."

"Khyle."

"Perry."

"Nice to meet you, ladies. See you around, Bella."

"Who the fuck—"

"I will tell you bitches later," Bella cut Khyle off, making us chuckle.

For the rest of the meal, Bella and Santino kept stealing glances. When it was time to pay the check, Bella handed us her cash, and went to wait outside as the waitress processed us at the register. I couldn't wait to find out who Santino was if he had crazy ass Bella shook.

# CHAPTER THREE

*Official First Day...*

Chris Brown's soulful voice blasted from my phone, letting me know it was time to wake up. Throwing the covers off of myself, I laid there staring up at the ceiling for a few before sitting up.

I was excited for my first day, but that didn't make me any less sleepy. Not to mention the fact that I hadn't been able to get Oden's sexy ass off of my mind since that party over the weekend. No guy had ever made such an impression on me in that short of amount of time. Matter fact, niggas didn't impress me at all. I never sweated them one bit. As Jay Z said, I had ninety-nine problems but a nigga was never one. However, Oden had me smiling for no reason as I pictured him licking his lips, or running his tattooed hand down his wild curly mane.

"Get it together, Khyle," I said as I got down from my bed and grabbed my phone. When I did, I saw I had about five texts from Brian's ass. I decided I would text him back after my first two classes since I had a big break then.

I made my way to the sink to brush my teeth, and giggled when I saw Tasmine toss and turn in her bed. She was really knocked the fuck out. It made me a bit jealous that her first class was at 11:15am, and mine was at 8am. After flossing and rinsing, I went ahead and showered before slipping into a summery yellow dress. It was still hot as hell in Vegas right now, and I was not about to wear any form of pants, not even to bed. After slipping on my sandals, necklace, and bangles, I sprayed on some of my Victoria's Secret mist and bounced.

My class wasn't too far away, but the heat had me pissed at the fact that I decided to wear my hair down. I hated that Las Vegas was just sitting heat, with no type of wind anywhere. I felt like I was in some pizza oven or a brisket boiler.

I finally made it to the building my class was in, and then double-checked the room number before going up the stairs. When I got to the right room number with no problems and at 7:55am, I was happy as fuck. I just knew I was gonna have a hard time finding this class, *and* all of my other classes, but I was wrong, thankfully.

I scoped the room as I found a seat in the middle because I didn't want to be in the back, and I damn sure didn't want to be right up front. Although this would be a fairly easy class since it was Women's Studies, I liked to text a little here and there, and sitting up front would force me to give up that luxury. I was glad that I'd listened to my father who told me to put the easy and/or interesting classes in the morning, and the boring or hard shit in the afternoon, so that I'd be more willing to wake up, and if I did miss it, it wouldn't kill me in the long run.

As I was scrolling on Instagram, I decided to check and see if Oden had one. Tasmine followed Anton, and since Oden was his best friend, maybe he had a profile too. I typed his name in, and then realized I didn't even know how to spell the shit so I just gave up. I needed to calm my hot ass down anyway. I'm finding time to look for this nigga on social media, but not finding the time to text my boyfriend back.

"Damn, I'm glad I chose this class." Some guy walked up and sat right next to me. I think I remembered seeing him last night with that Santino guy at Blueberry Hill. I declined to say anything, so he stared at me for a little while before continuing. "You know I only picked this class because I knew it would be some bad ass females up in here."

"Well, I hope you find what you're looking for."

"Oh, I have. I saw you last night with some friends. What's your name?"

"It's Khyle, yours?" I decided to not be so mean to him because I did in fact want to make friends in this place, and a sports player was a good place to start.

"Huelo." He stuck his hand out to me and I shook it.

"That's a pretty name, what are you?" He looked to be Tongan or something. He was tall, buff as fuck, and pretty cute.

"I'm Tongan. I like your name too, even though it's a male's name."

"Thanks," I smiled just as the professor walked in. She was wearing a pantsuit and tennis shoes, which clashed horribly in my opinion.

"Good morning, class, how is everyone?" She dropped her bag down and smoothed her curly brown hair back.

"Good," everyone said simultaneously almost.

"Who here is majoring in Women's Studies?" She stuffed her hands into her pockets and paced the room. People raised their hands, and I just prayed she wasn't kicking people out who weren't majoring in Women's Studies, because I was majoring in Political Science and Criminal Justice. She was about to speak again, but this guy entered the room.

"Is there a…" he pulled out a piece of paper, "Khyle Luke in here?" The professor looked at us, so I raised my hand slowly. The boy nodded and then waved someone into the room. Another guy walked in holding a big ass bouquet of red roses, and a big bag from Marciano. He walked it over to me, set the flowers on my desk, and then the shopping bag on the floor next to me.

"Sorry about that," I said once the two guys left. I had no idea who would bring me all of this shit, but I had never been so embarrassed in my life.

I waited impatiently for class to be over, and once it was, I ripped open the white card that was sitting in between the roses. It read, *You forgot to give me your number. - Oden.*

*Hmm, he spells it with an E.*

I half smiled before placing it into my purse. I then picked up the Marciano bag, and pulled out a box. When I opened it, I saw it was a pair of stiletto sandal heels. Another note was inside that read, *I want you to wear these for me, you got some pretty ass feet. I swear I don't have a foot fetish. - Oden.*

I placed the shoes back into the bag, and had to unfortunately lug all this shit to my history class. Once that was over, I stopped to grab some food in the student union, before strategically carrying everything back to my dorm complex. Upon entering, I saw Oden's sexy ass chilling in the lobby, typing on his phone. He was wearing a black Nike t-shirt, gray basketball shorts, socks, and Nike slide ins. He was also sporting an Apple Watch, and a small gold chain hung around his neck. He wasn't dressed up at all, but damn did he look good. When he spotted me, he ran his hand over his shoulder length untamed curly hair, like always, and then walked towards me. His cologne permeated the air, and I almost closed my eyes to enjoy it.

"Really?" I lifted the shit up, along with my food.

"Yeah, really. Do the shoes fit?"

"I don't know, but somehow you got the right size, so most likely, yeah. Look, Oden, this is sweet, but I have a boyfriend, I told you that."

"And I told you that I didn't care. I don't give a fuck about you having a nigga," he frowned his handsome face, and placed his hand under his shirt, exposing the top part of his boxers and a little of his abs. Damn. I was used to skinny ass Brian, not a nigga with all this muscle.

"Why would you even want a girl that would leave her man for another?"

"You wouldn't leave me… ever." He got more in my personal space, and smiled down at me when he saw how nervous I became. My pussy was ready to snap off and go with him on its own if I didn't.

"Oden, thank you, but I have to go."

"Come back down after you put your stuff up so we can go get something to eat."

"I have food, but thank you." This nigga was not gonna give up, and the more he asked the more willing I was becoming.

He snatched my food from my hand and tossed it into the trashcan, causing me and two other bystanders to gasp in surprise.

"Now you don't, and hurry up because I don't wanna have to come get you. Matter fact, I'm coming along." He started towards the elevator. I paused for a few, and then just followed after him.

"Hey, Oden," some pretty brown-skinned chick flirted as she walked off of the elevator.

"What's good?" he nodded his head up, and although she stared at him for a little bit, he was watching me as I joined him on the elevator. Seeing that he wasn't so thirsty to the point that he had to size her up turned me on. I loved a nigga who wasn't aching for pussy all the time from every female.

As we rode the elevator to my floor, he grabbed the Marciano bag from me so he could carry it, and then took my free hand into his. I wanted to pull away, believe me I did, but I couldn't. His strong hand felt so good wrapped around mine. As we walked down the hall and past a few people, the girls were staring hard, looking like the Scream mask. That shit was funny to me, and since I was petty I intertwined our fingers.

"Oden, what are you doing in here?" this girl named Raquel asked.

She was caramel with long curly hair, and big ass eyes. She was pretty though. She reminded me of Tracee Ellis Ross, except her hair wasn't wild. I only knew her because she lived next door to Tasmine and I, so we shared a bathroom with her and her roommate, Siena.

Oden just gestured towards me as a response to her question once we neared my room. She stared at me in confusion and a little bit of disgust as I entered my room, making sure Tasmine was presentable. Raquel then opened her own door, and I could hear her talking in an annoyed tone to Siena as the door slowly closed.

"Tasmine, you remember Oden," I said when we walked into the room.

"What's good, baby girl?" he said in his sexy voice, before walking to my bed to sit on it.

"Yeah… hey." She was caught off guard, I could tell, but when his back was turned, she smiled widely at me. I just shook my head 'no' at her, as she grabbed her purse and left the room.

"How did you know that was my bed?" I asked.

"Because you got this big ass K over the headboard." He checked his phone but pointed to the K without looking.

"Whatever. Would you like something to drink while you wait?"

"While I wait? You're just putting your shit down and that's it," he turned his lip up. He was so damn fine; I couldn't deal.

"No, I have to make a phone call first."

"Okay, what you got?"

I bent down to my miniature fridge, and opened the door to check as if I didn't already know what I had in there.

"I have Kerns strawberry banana juice, water, sp—"

"Fuck all that shit. I thought you had something a real nigga would like." He kicked off his slides and laid back on my bed like he lived here.

"I was gonna sit there while I made the call."

"Come sit." He ran his tongue across his full bottom lip while patting the bulge in his basketball shorts. My clit throbbed, but I rolled my eyes as if his gesture had dried me up like the Grand Canyon.

"Never mind." I plopped down in the chair at my desk, and then pulled out my iPhone to dial Brian before he got angry and drove over here.

"Damn, baby. In a minute, I was gonna drive out there to you," Brian answered.

"It hasn't been that long, Brian. I was just trying to get settled." It irritated me that he wanted to talk to me all fucking day. I wanted to hang out with my roommate, and have fun, not sit up in my room conversing with him 24/7.

"Still, you shouldn't go days without hitting me up."

"We talk every day, just not *all day* like you want to."

"We're both in college. Shit, I'm in a pre-med program so if I have the time, you should have the damn time too, Khyle."

"I have another class in 10 minutes," I lied. My next class wasn't until 3pm, so I had a nice, healthy break. "Meaning, I have to go."

"Wait, baby, have you met anybody? Like, tell me something? I wanna know how everything is going up there for you," he questioned, making me smile at the fact that he was interested. I glanced over my shoulder at Oden, and he was texting on his phone while cheesing which made me a little jealous.

"Uh, I, it's great. My roommate is really nice, but that's expected since we talked the whole summer. I met two other girls, Bella and Perry. I love Bella, she's so dope. Perry is okay. She doesn't really say much but she has a nice ass car. We went to a party over the weekend."

"Damn, already? You should've stayed in Cali for the weekend if you could go and party."

"Really, Brian? What the fuck?" Suddenly, the phone was snatched from me, but I knew who it was because his cologne invaded my nostrils.

"Aye homie, let me bust first and then you can finish talking to her." Oden hung up as my jaw hit the floor.

"Did you really just say that?" I attempted to grab my phone but he kept moving it around. When I got up close and personal with him, he wrapped his free hand around my waist, grinning.

"You'll get your phone back when I'm done with you."

# CHAPTER THREE

# Oden

"No, I want my phone right now or I'm not going anywhere with you," Khyle stood there looking prettier than a muthafucka.

I just laughed at her and continued out of her dorm room. A few moments later, she came out after me with her face all contorted, but I didn't mind because her mad face was cute as hell. Stopping in my tracks, I waited for her to catch up to me, and then draped my arm over her shoulder before kissing her face. I saw some bitches that felt like they knew me, watching us, but they were the least of my fucking worries. The only thing I was focused on was making baby girl mine, and I was gonna succeed.

"Where are we going anyway?" she finally said something once we got outside of her dorm.

"To eat."

"I know, Oden. I mean where to eat in particular? I don't just eat any damn where," she switched, and I had to adjust myself because I was getting hard as a rock.

No matter how a nigga came at a female, our goal at the end was to fuck. Some niggas wanted to smash and never talk to the girl again, and sometimes niggas wanted to spend the rest of their lives with her. Whatever the case was, we all wanted to hit. I don't care what type of nigga he is, he wants to fuck at some point.

After walking towards the back lot where the visitors parked, she stopped and turned around to face me. She held her hand above her eyes to block the sun, and pushed her hair behind her shoulder as she waited.

"Right there." I hit the alarm on my Lexus truck with red leather interior and espresso colored wood. I had way nicer cars, but my daily driver was this. I got to my car before her, so I opened the passenger side, prompting a smile to appear on her face. "You're welcome, rude ass," I joked, making her giggle, while handing her phone back to her.

"This is a nice ass car, Oden," she said as she rubbed her fingers over the wood portions of the car. "I love the red leather; that's so extravagant, just how I like."

"See, we already have shit in common."

"I guess, and that's probably where it ends."

"You're funny." I started the engine.

We made it to the Encore hotel, and after getting a ticket from the valet guy, I took her hand into mine. I led her to this restaurant named Andrea's, where they had the best fucking sushi in the world. I didn't know if she liked sushi, but she looked like she did. And if not, there were other things that she could order.

"This place is so pretty," she spoke lowly as we approached the entrance of it. I enjoyed the scenery as well, and I felt like it would be a good ass place to get to know her.

"I know; I come here a lot," I nodded. "Reservation for Oden Bishop," I told the lady at the front.

She scanned her list, and said, "Okay, I've found you. Follow me." We trailed her to a table, and once we got there, I pulled Khyle's chair out. I may have been a hood nigga, but I was a chivalrous one. My grandfather taught me a lot about how to treat a woman, when she deserved that shit. "A waiter will be with you in a moment. Would you like some waters?"

"Please, thanks," I replied before turning my attention back to Khyle.

"Reservation? So you not only knew my class schedule, but you knew I'd agree to coming on this little date with you?" She sounded bothered, but she was smiling.

"I told you that I was gonna have you. Your boyfriend don't mean shit to me, and he won't mean shit to you in a little bit."

"I love Brian."

"That's good for him, but you gon' love me too." She just laughed since the waitress approached our table. We put in our orders, and she got sushi like I knew she would. After the waiter left, I asked, "So what's wrong with dude?"

"Brian? Nothing."

"Has to be, or you wouldn't be here with me."

"I'm being nice and you threw my damn lunch away, so of course

I came. I'm hungry, nigga."

"That doesn't explain why you were straddling my lap at the party, or how I was close as hell to kissing you before your *friend* came to the door with her hating ass."

Khyle could front all she wanted, but if that Brian nigga was everything she claimed he was, she wouldn't have even fed into my advances. But the fact that she did showed that, that nigga wasn't doing a lot of things right. Khyle was complex as fuck, and it took a certain type of nigga to keep her satisfied; a complex nigga like myself. She couldn't be with a weenie, and I knew Brian was one because if a nigga got on my girl's phone talking that bullshit, he would have been dead before he hung up. I don't care how far away I am.

"I'm just being nice to you, Oden, stop trying to make it seem like Brian is lacking."

"Whatever you say, baby." I licked my lips slowly before tucking them, and her little ass didn't miss a beat. I had her, and I couldn't wait to make her heart and body mine. I was tired of waking up to a new bitch every morning.

"Speaking of my sister, what do y'all have going on?"

She asked that burning question, and I wish she hadn't but I knew it was coming. She caught on to how her sister was mugging me that night, and only a fool would believe it was for no reason. But damn, I was hoping Shayne was her cousin, not her fucking sister. I called her, her *friend* earlier, hoping she would confirm my theory that Shayne was lying about them being siblings.

"Nothing. I smashed a couple times and that was it."

"Wait, you fucked my sister and then sent me flowers, shoes, and now we're out on what I guess is a date?" she frowned. I loved her full lips. Her light cinnamon complexion had some type of glitter on it, so I knew she had on makeup. I didn't like that shit, but I liked Khyle so if that was how she got down, then so be it.

"I fucked your sister before I knew you, Khyle. How was I supposed to know that she had a little sister that I would like better? You can't fault me for that."

"I think she really likes you though," she looked off for a second.

"Do you like me?" I quizzed and she nodded. "And I like you, so why can't we work on something just because I smashed her? She has a man anyway."

There was no way in hell I was gonna allow Shayne to come between Khyle and I. Yes, I fucked, but had I known Khyle first, the shit wouldn't have happened. I hadn't planned on hitting again either, now that Khyle had my full and undivided attention. Shayne had better go be with her man and be happy.

"So you don't wanna be with her?"

"Hell no! I don't mean to talk about your sister, baby girl, but she's not exactly the same breed as you outside of genetics."

"I know, but I like that she does what she wants to do, and doesn't care what people think."

"You're the same way, you just have boundaries, which I like. But answer my question, why are you seeking love elsewhere?" I clasped my hands and leaned onto the table.

She pushed her long hair behind her ears, sipped her water, and then looked deep into my eyes.

"There are different things. I feel like he doesn't take my goals in life seriously, because he's gonna be a doctor and anything outside of that is bullshit to him. And sometimes I get the feeling that he's being unfaithful, but I don't have any proof. It's just a feeling in my stomach. I honestly feel like no one is as loyal as I am to them, and I think that's just the way the world is."

"I'm a very loyal person." I reached across to grab her hands into mine.

"Yeah right. I know how you are, Oden."

"I promise I am. But just out of curiosity, what kind of guy am I?"

"You know."

"No, I don't." I knew exactly what she was gonna say, but I wanted to hear it actually come out of her mouth before I jumped to conclusions.

"The type that only chases women for the thrill of it, and once you get them, you're over it. Or you treat women how you treated my sister. Those types of niggas are not loyal."

Yep, I was right. I knew exactly what she was gonna say.

"Yeah, I can be like that, but not to a woman that I'm actually interested in, which has never happened to be honest. And your sister presented herself to me in a certain way, so that was how I treated her. I'm not gonna treat a woman like a queen when she doesn't even see herself as one."

"So because a woman likes sex, or has had more than a few partners, she deserves be to be treated badly?" Her brows furrowed as the lady set our plates down. She asked us if we were okay, and then pranced off.

"No, a woman's past doesn't matter to me, because if she approaches me on some different shit, I'm not gonna care. However, any woman that sucks my dick within five minutes of meeting me is not gonna get top notch treatment, I'm sorry. I know prostitutes that make you work harder. And all women love sex, by the way, not just certain ones."

"Not me." She ate one of her sushi rolls.

"You doing it with the wrong person then."

"No, I just think I'm not the type to like it. I've never came or whatever, and when I looked it up, it said some women just can't."

I stared into her big brown eyes for a second before laughing a little loudly.

"I can make you cum for sure," I nodded as I stared down at my plate. I was talking to myself more so than her, because I couldn't believe she'd never had an orgasm.

"No, no one can."

"Right." I ate some of my food. I couldn't wait to make that pussy cum for the first time. "But I'm serious, Khyle, let me show you. I have a bad reputation in your eyes, I know, but I can be loyal, just like you want."

She just sipped her water, keeping her eyes on me the whole time.

We finished off our meal while keeping up with the conversation. To be only 18, she had great conversation skills and didn't bore me with bullshit. I liked that she had more depth to her than what it seemed. She was feisty as fuck, but she had her calm moments where she could really get deep with you.

By the time we were leaving the hotel, it was 2:30pm.

"You should come see me after your class," I said once I got in on the driver's side.

"You don't have class?"

"Not today I don't. I like talking to you and I want you to come back tonight."

"Oden, I can't. I have a boyfriend. Regardless of how much I like you, I need to be faithful to him."

Her loyalty to him was turning me on, and only made me want her more. I knew if I made her mine she would be down for the long haul. Especially if she was willing to stick it out with a nigga who wasn't about shit and couldn't even make her nut. I could only imagine how down she'd be for me.

"I'll text you my address, and if you ever wanna come through just do so. If I'm not there, text me and I promise I will make it to you."

"I know your address, I went to the party." She unlocked her iPhone and handed it to me so that I could text myself. Once I got the text I sent, I replied with my address, handing her phone back in the process.

"That's not my address that I sleep at. Don't give my shit out either, baby."

"I wouldn't do that," she smiled.

I swooped into a park in the lot behind her dorm complex. We both got out, and I walked her up to her dorm because she said she needed to get her math book. When we got inside of her room, I decided to make my exit right then because I could sense that neither of us wanted to part just yet, and I would not be the nigga that caused her to miss class and shit. Grabbing her small arm, I pulled her into me and crushed my lips against hers. She was tense at first, but then her body relaxed as our tongues came in contact.

"Oden," she finally pulled away from me, avoiding eye contact. "I'm gonna be late."

I declined to respond, turning the doorknob and exiting. Khyle was gonna be mine, and there was no one who was gonna get in the way. Not her boyfriend, and especially not her hating ass sister.

***

*9:30pm that night...*

I was chilling on the couch, looking over this contract sent to me by this new steakhouse that was opening up on Tropicana Avenue. They wanted to have my liquor listed, and I was ecstatic about the shit. Going to school to get this certificate in business had really helped me out in scoring business deals, because truthfully, there was a science to this shit. When my grandfather first told me to go to school for it, I waved him off because I was a natural born hustler. Granted, I did achieve a lot prior to enrolling, but I have to admit that the knowledge I've gained has really helped a nigga out.

*KNOCK! KNOCK!*

I got up from the couch to get the door, assuming it was Anton or Truman since they lived over here as well. When I looked through the peephole, my natural reflex was a grin upon seeing Khyle's pretty ass standing there in tights and an oversized long-sleeved t-shirt. She checked her phone before pushing her long hair behind her ears, and when she brought her face back up, I saw she had no makeup on, or at least what seemed like no makeup. She looked the same pretty much, which was a plus.

"No warning text?" I answered the door. She stared at my bare chest, and then her eyes dropped to my crotch. "My bad. Come in and I will get a shirt." I walked away from the door so that she could come in.

"You said just to come through. Hope I'm not intruding on anyone."

"Never. I told you I don't bring women here. I take them to the Wyatt, where the party was." I grabbed a t-shirt from my laundry room and pulled it over my head. When I came out, she was sitting on the couch, all in my shit. "Damn, nosey."

"Sorry, what is this contract for?"

"To get Brown Sugar Bourbon in Quarter Steakhouse."

"Wow, really? I heard they're building a new one out here. I love their food, especially the lamb. That's so dope, Oden," she beamed as if it were an opportunity for her.

"Thanks. Thirsty? Hungry?"

"No, I don't know why I came here. I just… came." She looked off before turning her attention back to me. "Why the name Brown Sugar?"

"Part of my great-grandmother's secret recipe. She used to mix up bourbon for people and sell that shit. She got arrested so many times." I sat down next to her.

"Why?"

"In her time, you couldn't sell alcohol from your damn porch. I still don't think you can now, but she was doing that shit and making a killing. The story is on the back of the bottle." I pulled one from the cabinet portion of the coffee table.

"Can I have this one?"

"I guess."

"Thank you," she chuckled.

"Do you have makeup on?" Her skin was for real flawless.

"No, I washed it off in the shower. I was planning to go to bed, but I couldn't sleep. I was restless, so I decided to take you up on your offer," she spoke, as she scanned the living room with her eyes. "Your place is nice."

"Yeah, it's cool. Wanna come to my bedroom? I've been up all day and I wanna lie down. I swear I ain't trying nothing."

After looking into my eyes for a few, she finally nodded. I grabbed her hand as we both stood up, and led her to my big ass bedroom. I took my shirt off, pushed down my sweats, and then got into the bed. She took off her tights, and I wished her shirt wasn't so big because I wanted to see something, anything.

"Do you put anything in this hair?" she toyed with my curls.

"I just wash it every two weeks and put this cream in it that… umm, I found."

"Some girl must have told you about the cream," she chuckled. It was true, but I wasn't gonna say that. We didn't need to be thinking about anybody but one another right now. "It's soft and so big. I thought I would hate a guy with big ass curly hair, but it's cool."

"I've thought about cutting it a few times, but I can't. And I don't fuck with braids, that shit is weak as hell, not to mention ugly as fuck."

Propping her head up with one hand, she let her other trail my many tattoos on my chest and arms.

"Lorena?"

"My grandmother."

"Can we be friends, Oden?" she questioned after a few moments of silence.

"No, because we're gonna try and fail."

"Why would we fail?"

"Because we don't wanna just be friends. But because you want to waste your time with old boy back in L.A., we're gonna try the shit out and eventually give up."

"Don't be so negative."

"It's negative to you, but positive to me. I told you I want you, and I'm gonna have you. What I don't know is how long it's gonna take for me to get you."

She straddled my lap, and my dick immediately started hardening under her. She had on some thin ass lace panties, which seemed to be telling my dick to come out. Gripping her hips, I pressed her body down into me, while staring into her eyes. A soft moan escaped her lips as she subtly grinded against my hard dick.

"I've never been turned on before," she whispered. "This is the last time I'm coming over here." She leaned down to kiss me, and our tongues immediately came in contact.

We laid there kissing, groping, and talking until the both of us dozed off.

# CHAPTER THREE

# Shayne

*Two days later...*

I hadn't talked to Khyle in almost a week, and her ass made no attempts to call me or anything. I wanted to wait it out and see how long she would go before hitting me up, but it never happened. Then my home girl who goes to UNLV told me she saw her and Oden coming and going a couple times. That shit had me hot as fish grease, because he knew I liked him and that she was my sibling. I thought he and I were working, yet he was chasing after my little sister. I knew this shit would happen if he saw her, and now I wish that I had just taken her to dinner that night or something.

I walked into her dorm complex and took a seat on one of the couches before dialing her number. I needed to convince her to stop fucking with Oden, because I knew he wouldn't listen to me. Matter fact, he'd blocked my damn number. Yeah, I'd called and texted him a little more than I should have, but what did he expect? Nobody just fucks me and keeps it pushing, I don't care how fine they are.

"Hello?" Khyle answered.

"Hey, where are you?"

"Coming from my last class, why?"

"I wanna talk to you. I'm at your dorm, you'll see me as soon as you walk into the lobby."

"Fine," she hung up.

About 10 minutes later, she entered the building looking as pretty as ever. I wondered if she'd fucked Oden as she made her way over to me wearing a small scowl. Was she really mad? She had her nerve!

"Can we go up to your room and talk?"

She nodded and turned on her heels to walk off. I followed her to the elevator, and we rode it up to her floor. This dorm was nice as hell, and almost like an apartment building. As we walked down the hallway, those same girls that she came to the party with spoke to us, just before we went into her room.

"One of those your roommate?"

"Yeah, the one with the pretty eyes," she replied dryly as she set her books on the desk. She then plopped down onto her bed, and I sat at her desk.

"Khyle, I wanna talk to you. I did something bad, and you're the only person I trust and want to tell," I sighed dejectedly.

"Okay."

"I cheated on Pierce, but the worst part is that I think I'm in love with the guy I cheated with. He's so sweet to me, and we have such a good time together that I'm thinking about leaving Pierce for him."

"You're not talking about Oden, are you?"

"Yeah, I am. How did you know?" I played dumb.

"Because it's obvious y'all have done some shit with the way you were looking at him the night of the backyard barbecue."

"Well, yes, it's him. We've been messing around for some time now, and he's asked me to leave Pierce, but I kept refusing. But now I think I'm going to." I needed her to purchase this wolf ticket I was selling.

"Shayne, Oden did not ask you to leave Pierce. Look, he told me the deal with you two and it's not that deep at all. You need to stick with Pierce. He loves you."

My heart dropped to the pit of my stomach once I processed what she'd just said to me. The fact that she knew the actual situation between Oden and I was embarrassing to say the least. My little sister looked up to me, so for her to know that I was pining for a nigga who didn't see me as anything more than a quick fuck, had me ready to pull a brown paper bag down over my head.

"He lied, Khyle. Duh."

"He didn't lie, Shayne." She got off of her bed to go into her mini fridge for some juice.

"So you're gonna believe him over me? Really, Khyle? He likes you so he's gonna tell you whatever to convince you to fuck with him."

"I have a boyfriend, and he knows that. He didn't tell me anything to convince me of shit, Shayne. I asked him what the deal was between you two and he told me the truth."

"What happened to sister code? If you knew I liked him, why did you hang out with the nigga? That's shady as fuck!" I hollered louder than I wanted to.

"He and I are just cool. You're telling me I can't be his friend because you like him? Shayne, grow up."

"Wow. You haven't even been here a damn month and you're already acting like an Oden groupie," I scoffed, getting up from her desk.

This conversation was pointless. Somehow, in less than a week, Oden had gotten into her head. Brian had better enjoy what was left of he and Khyle's relationship because I knew it would be ending soon.

"I'm a groupie?" She placed her hand against her chest before gulping down some of her juice. I loved her but hated her at the same time. I didn't get why Oden liked her instead of me, when I was more of his type. "You're the one who has slept with him already. I haven't and I don't plan to."

"Whatever, Khyle. You know what type of guy he is, and sooner or later you're going to be in his bed, cheating on Brian. If you really love your boyfriend, you know what to do." With that said, I grabbed my bag and headed out.

On my way down, my phone chimed, and I pulled it out to see I had a text from Alanna.

*Alanna: He's here.*

*Me: Thanks, on my way now.*

I had her sitting outside of Oden's apartment building on Buffalo Drive every day this week, because when I'd dropped by a few times, he wasn't there. I had other shit to do, like chill with Pierce and audition for a couple of shows, so I thought it was a better idea to have Alanna do the work for me. I mean, she didn't have shit else to do. She'd gotten a job working for a call center at home, so she had more free time than me.

As soon as I got into my car, I tossed my purse into the passenger seat and peeled out. Oden was a hard man to catch, especially now that he'd blocked my fucking number, so I didn't want to miss him. He and I had to talk because if he thought he was gonna be smashing my sister, he had shit fucked up and twisted.

I pulled into the townhouse like community, and just admired how beautiful it was. His shit was so much nicer than the place Pierce and I stayed in over on Tropicana.

I rolled my eyes up in my head as I thought about Pierce. He was becoming less and less attractive to me every day. I missed when he was a ball player, on top of the world, with sponsors and scouts blowing his phone up. Now he wasn't anything but a regular ass nigga from California who wasn't about shit. I was a boss ass bitch, and niggas of his current caliber didn't stand a chance with me. I was almost embarrassed to be out with his ass because I had a reputation to uphold. He was lucky he was finer than a muthafucka with some bomb dick, because otherwise, I would be single until I got Oden.

I saw Oden so I swooped into a space, and tried to shut off the engine before I even put the car in park. I needed to slow the hell down. After changing the gears, I turned the car off and hopped out, almost tripping along the way. I guess Oden heard all of my ruckus, because he stopped sifting through the mail to look over his shoulder at me. Once he saw who it was, he sucked his teeth and ran his hand over his big curly mane.

"Aye, you're crazy as fuck," he chuckled lightly, avoiding eye contact as he kept his attention on the mail he was looking through.

He looked so fucking fine in his wife beater, which displayed his muscular arms, covered in tattoos. Gray sweats were on his bottom half, and the waistband of his Ralph Lauren boxers was exposed. After enjoying the smell of his cologne, I finally decided to speak.

"What the fuck are you doing with Khyle?"

"Why is that your business?" he raised his brow, slightly turning his full lip up. His toasted vanilla complexion was so vibrant and smooth.

"Because she's my little sister, Oden! You know what you're doing is wrong! And don't try to tell me that you guys are just friends like she did."

"I don't wanna be her friend and I won't be. And don't be rolling up on me, questioning who the fuck I talk to, Shayne. You doing way too much to be a girl I only smashed a few times." He looked so irritated by me, and although it hurt my feelings, I couldn't deny how sexy his screw face was.

"So that's all I am, Oden? A girl you smashed a few times?" I shifted my weight from one hip to the other, and smiled when I saw his brown eyes scan my frame lustfully.

He finally brought his attention back to my face, and chuckled before saying, "Umm, yeah." He started off to his car with his mail in hand, and I was right on his damn heels.

"If you think that you're about to be sleeping with two sisters, nigga, you have shit confused! I can have any nigga I want, and I refuse to be one of your bitches, along with my sister."

He stopped in his tracks, and turned to face me since I was fussing into his back.

"That's the thing though, I don't want you. So looks like the problem is solved," he shrugged, looking down at me. He was so fucking tall; I loved it. But… I hated his mean ass attitude.

"I'm not gonna let you play my baby sister."

"I won't." He got into his car before I could reply. If I weren't a little bit scared of him, I would've bashed his fucking window in.

The fact that he said he wasn't gonna play her bothered me a bit. Not that I wanted Khyle to get played, but why was it okay to do me dirty and not her? Usually, when niggas went for Khyle over me, I just left it alone, but this time I couldn't. I'd had my eyes on Oden Bishop for the longest, and there was no way I could just lose out on him to Khyle. Nope, no way, no how. For once, I was gonna get a nigga that Khyle liked, whether Oden wanted me or not. And with the way he was checking my body out, I'm sure it wouldn't be too hard to get him to fuck me again, hopefully with no cap.

# CHAPTER THREE

$\mathscr{I}$ had time to think about the things that Shayne had said to me, and part of it was right. I couldn't continue to be friends with Oden. I made this decision not because Shayne likes him and is obviously upset about the way she chose to come at him, but because I had a boyfriend and I could recognize my attraction to Oden. He even said it himself that we would try to be friends but it would eventually develop into more. I've had friends that were guys before, and I was able to leave it that, but I knew I liked Oden, which had never happened with any of my other male friends, so I knew better.

I stared at my phone for a few before finally pressing Oden's name. My body became hot, and my palms started to sweat as I listened to the line ring. I kind of hoped he didn't answer, and just as the thought crossed my mind, he picked up.

"Baby girl, I miss you." His voice was soooo damn sexy it made me close my eyes and shiver a bit, even though it was hot as hades right now.

"Oden, I was just calling to let you know that we can't really hang out and stuff anymore."

"Your sister."

"Not really, more so my boyfriend that I have no intention of cheating on." I paced the room just as Tasmine walked in with Bella.

"What do you think kissing me in my bed with your pussy pressed against my dick was? Just because I didn't fuck doesn't mean you didn't cheat. But, whatever. I have shit to do and it doesn't involve playing games with you."

My hands began to tremble lightly because I didn't like him being mean to me. This was a side of him I didn't know yet, and I loathed it already. It just made me want to tell him I'd changed my mind and to come pick me up so we could hang out. Why couldn't he understand that I didn't wanna break our friendship off just as much as he didn't, but I had to. I was being responsible. My parents told me I had to be when I went off to college, and I was trying but he was making it hard.

"Oden—"

"See you around, aight?" Before I could answer, he'd hung up.

"Oden? What were y'all talking about?" Bella sucked her teeth as she switched to my side of the room, with Tasmine trailing her.

"Just told him to back the fuck up off of me," I attempted to sound hard. That was my personality, so I had to make sure I stayed stoned face.

"Why?" Tasmine frowned as she sat next to me on my bed.

It was around 6pm in the evening, so the sun was going down. I loved how Vegas looked when it started to become night. Despite the large areas of just dirt and sand, it was beautiful, especially Las Vegas Boulevard, which was literally right down the street from my dorm complex.

"Because I have a boyfriend and shit got too intense between us. I told y'all I almost had sex with him the night I went over there."

"I could've told you that you might have had sex with him. I feel you though, girl. If you love your man, then you need to let Oden go. There is no such thing as being friends with a guy like Oden Bishop." Bella put some mascara on using her compact mirror.

"I agree," I said in a low tone as Tasmine looked to me with a worried expression. I knew she was thinking exactly what I was thinking… this shit was gonna be hard.

***

*Three weeks later…*

"I'm so happy you're here, and just in time!" I beamed, as my best friend, Emery, and I rode back to my dorm in an Uber.

It was Friday and she'd just flown in to stay with me. I was happy because there were so many parties this weekend, as usual, and because since I wouldn't be in class until Monday, I had all the time in the world to hang out with her.

"Girl, me too. I wanna meet some fine niggas to mess with just for the weekend," she smiled, as the Uber pulled up to the front of my dorm and turned on his hazard lights.

The two of us hopped out, and got her rolling suitcase from the trunk before entering the lobby of my dorm. Some guys from the football team were sitting in the lounge area as we passed it, and Emery was focused on each and every one. Some of them were eyeing her as well.

"Damn, do all the niggas look this good in Vegas?"

"Nope, but we do have a lot of handsome dudes here as students. Calm your little ass down, you can only do so much in one weekend. Or should I say so many."

"I know, relax. I ain't about to be a hoe in front of your peoples. So where are your other friends?" she asked once we stepped off the elevator, headed to my room.

"Well, Tasmine is in the room chilling, and Bella is probably in there too," I responded, just as we walked up to our rooms.

Bella opened the door of her room, and I saw Tasmine and Perry were in there with her.

"Bella," she stuck her hand out to Emery.

"Emery."

"Why don't you guys come in here? We're just chilling before we get ready for the party tonight," Bella suggested as Tasmine came up behind her to introduce herself to Emery.

"We will, she just needs to put her stuff down," I answered and Bella nodded.

Emery and I went into my room, and I showed her around a little bit before placing her suitcase by my desk. She looked around with a big smile on her face, and I watched her with one on mine.

Emery was beautiful with her brown skin, slim thick frame, and short curly hair. She was a bit on the wild side, but so was I, so we immediately clicked upon meeting. The only difference was that I liked to party, get high, and tease niggas, where as she liked to party, get high, and actually fuck.

"I don't like your two friends," she sighed. That shit caught me off guard.

"Really? Why?"

"I feel like Bella thinks she's better than me, and Tasmine was sizing me up for sure."

"Emery, Bella is really nice; I think you'll like her a lot. And Tasmine is super sweet. She would never size anyone up."

Emery was a bit possessive, but that's how all best friends were. I didn't care too much for people she introduced me too and vice versa. So by saying that, I wasn't gonna trip off the fact that she wasn't really feeling Bella and Tasmine. She wasn't gonna be out here like that anyway, so it wouldn't change me hanging out with them. I really fucked with them.

"Well, I don't like her. Are we going to the same party they are?"

"Yes. It's a party thrown by one of the fraternities so a lot of people who go here will be there. Don't be mean. Emery, Bella and Tasmine are nice." I started out and she followed after as she rolled her eyes.

We walked right across to Bella and Perry's room, and I knocked, waiting for them to answer.

"Somebody said they saw Brian hanging out with Jacqueline." Emery sprung that shit on me just as Perry opened the door for us. "So,

I guess you should be friends with Oden again." My mouth opened and closed because I was speechless for a moment, wondering if I should respond to her with everyone in earshot, or just wait.

Jacqueline was this bitch that I told Brian to stay away from after she told me she wanted to fuck him and was going to. I warned her ass, but she didn't care about that; she was still on his dick. He agreed to keep away from her, but I guess now that I was gone, he decided to disobey the rules. And here I was cutting Oden off to make sure I stayed faithful to this nigga, and he was painting the town red with a hoe I deliberately forbade him from seeing.

Speaking of Oden, I hadn't talked to him in almost a month, and every day it got harder. I would see him at parties in passing, looking so fucking bomb, and I just had to look the other way. He wouldn't even look at me, though; he would always walk right by me like he didn't even know me. I thought about hitting him up, but I had too much pride and was scared that he wouldn't respond. I never chased niggas, ever, and I wasn't about to start now. I would get over that shit soon, and never look back.

I decided to ignore what Emery had just told me because I wanted to have fun this weekend and show my best friend a good time.

"So, are you in college as well, Emery?" Tasmine questioned as Bella showed me something funny on Instagram.

"No, boo. Not everyone can afford a higher education," Emery low-key snapped.

"Okay," Tasmine looked to me and I just shook my head.

"Would anybody like some water or something?" Perry offered, and everyone shook their head 'yes' in response.

Tonight was gonna be interesting.

# CHAPTER FOUR

# Tasmine

*K*hyle and I had the Problem and Iamsu! mixtape blasting in our room, as me, her, and Emery got dressed for tonight. There was this party at this house on Hollymead. It was a cool ways away, about 20 minutes, but this party would be worth the drive… so they say. Niggas had been talking this shit up for the longest, so nobody was gonna miss it, not even Perry; we were making her ass go.

I ran my little flat iron down my hair, and stared into the mirror for a little bit, making sure nothing on me was out of place. I had on tight, red high-waist pants, and a red bandeau top with thin ass straps attached to it. On my feet were some all red pumps, and my shoulder-length hair was hanging down, sweeping my shoulders. I chuckled as I thought about when Khyle said I wouldn't be able to wear this fit in California unless I wanted to be dodging bullets.

As I took in my appearance, I smiled. I knew Anton would be there, and this time I was determined to make him not only see me, but be interested to hang out. It wasn't enough to be cute; I needed to draw his ass in. If I couldn't pull it off tonight, then I don't think I'd be able to pull the shit off at all.

"Sexy!" Khyle grinned.

She was wearing a white skirt, with a white crop top that looked like a bikini top in the breast area. Her sandal stilettos were white, the same ones Oden bought her. I wondered if she was wearing them because they matched, or because she knew he would be there tonight. I wasn't sure, but I just prayed we had a good time because her best friend Emery had been a little salty all day. I wasn't one for confrontation, so I'd been ignoring her little smart comments all day; but if she kept that shit up, I had no problem decking her ass between the eyes. We got down in Kentucky too.

*KNOCK! KNOCK!*

I went to get the door, and in walked Bella and Perry. Bella was wearing blue skinny jeans, a blue halter-top, and some sexy gold and blue heels. Her blond curly hair was straightened, and like Khyle, her makeup was flawless. I laughed inside as I took in Perry's look. We'd taken her to the mall earlier, so she had on a black dress that was supposed to be tight, but it was slightly baggy on her frail frame. It was so difficult to find something small enough for her. I'd never met anyone that skinny in my life.

"Y'all ready?" Bella danced slightly as she walked further into the room.

"Yep!" Khyle and I said in unison.

Emery rolled her eyes as she picked her purse up. She was wearing some short jumper with heels, and you could see the bottom of her ass cheeks hanging out. I wasn't one to judge, so if that's how she liked to dress then so be it.

The five of us left out of the dorm, ignoring the niggas and their catcalls to us. We piled into Perry's car, and I made sure Khyle sat in between Emery and I. I hadn't written her off yet, but I damn sure didn't wanna sit next to her ass right now.

As usual, we drove to Von's and bought some alcohol using my older sister, Tasia's ID, and then pregamed in the car. If you don't know, pregaming is getting drunk or high before you get to the party. So anyway, we poured up the Hennessy and apple juice and started drinking up, as Bella and Khyle rolled some blunts. Once they were done, we opened the car doors and started smoking. Perry didn't want us hot boxing in her car, and since none of us wanted to smell like weed, we agreed to keeping her doors open.

After getting high *and* tipsy, Perry's sober ass started towards the house where the party was. We danced and sang along to "Different" by Iamsu!, and I must admit he was growing on me. Khyle said he was big shit in California. I'd never really heard of him, but he had a new fan in me though.

Because we had such a good time dancing to the music, it seemed like we got to the house in no time, even though it was almost a half an hour away from school. Perry found a park after hunting for a few, and once she did, we exited and had her sniff us to see if we smelled like weed. She said no, but we still used some of the body mist Bella had in her purse before walking down the street to the house.

You could hear "Monster" by Problem coming from the house, and could see purple strobe lights going wild through the windows. I swear the whole house was rocking. We made it to the front, and some white guy with sandy brown hair asked us for our school IDs, which was something they did for school affiliated parties, I learned. I guess it was to make sure no random people could benefit. It was only certain functions though, when the host wanted exclusivity.

"She's my best friend, she's visiting," Khyle explained, giving Emery a side hug. The guy stared at her for a little bit, and then stamped her hand.

As soon as we walked in, it seemed like everyone was dancing everywhere. I was sure that someone was fucking somewhere on something. I mean, the couches, walls, the floors, the balcony of the stairs—people were freaking on everything to "Hookah" by Tyga. The five of us moved our bodies subtly to the music as we made our way through, taking in the scenery. I wasn't sure what they were looking for, but I was looking for Anton. I finally spotted him standing by this bar in the home, lighting up the fattest blunt I'd ever seen.

"I'm gonna go over there," I told my friends.

Khyle looked over there and spotted Oden, blowing out a cloud of smoke as big as his curly hair with his eyes closed. He licked his lips, and took another pull as some hoe danced lightly in his lap.

"Go ahead, and text me if you can't find us," Bella said and I nodded.

I nervously walked to where Anton was, as "No Reason" by YG blasted over the house. It was so hard getting through all these people popping their asses and grinding on each other like they were fucking. I hated that every 'excuse me' that came out of my mouth landed on deaf ears. After bumping and nudging a bunch of sweaty muthafuckas in heat, I finally made it to Anton. As soon as he saw me, his beautiful mocha complexion brightened, and his smile lit up the whole room. He had on a white polo, with white jeans, and all white Pumas. A gold link chain hung around his neck, and he had the iced out gold watch to match. His cologne was A1, as usual, and I was smitten… as usual.

"Tasmanian!" he chuckled and I rolled my eyes.

"Hello to you too."

"You look good as fuck, baby girl. Who you all dressed up for?" He looked me up and down, while biting his plump bottom lip and stroking his beard.

"I just like to look good," I shrugged one shoulder.

I took his free hand into mine, as he used his other to continue smoking. Once we got a little closer to the middle of the dance floor, I began dancing on him. He wasted no time touching me and groping me with his strong but soft hands. When I saw his nails were clean, I smiled to myself. I hated niggas with busted feet, chapped lips, and dirty fingernails. That most likely meant that dick was dirty too.

I danced on him until I broke a damn sweat, and by the time I got tired of popping my ass to song after song, I turned to face him, draping my arms over his shoulders. We moved slowly but still on beat to the rap song with a heavy bassline. When his lips crushed against mine, I thought my legs were gonna give out. His hands gripped my ass as we let our tongues dance around each other slowly. His lips were so soft, and I could taste the grape from whatever had been in his mouth earlier.

He started walking me back to the den area that I pulled him from, and we didn't break our kiss the whole way. I felt us bumping people, but neither of us stopped to apologize once. Finally, he sat down and pulled me into his lap to continue our kissing session. Oden was next to us, still smoking and kissing on the girl's neck, who was in his lap, every now and then. Truman was up against the wall, and some girl was crouched down in front of him, so it was obvious what she was doing. It was dark though, so… I guess.

"Hold on, baby, put your number in before I forget," Anton pulled away to retrieve his iPhone from his pocket.

As I typed in my number, I kept thinking, *mission accomplished, bitch.*

# CHAPTER FOUR

# Bella Bacigalupi

Khyle and I danced to "Time" by Fetty Wap, as Perry stood there with her lips tucked in. She was so awkward but the shit was jokes. Tasmine and Anton had disappeared from the dance floor, but not before Khyle and I recorded them kissing like a couple in love. Emery had vanished too, and I was not complaining one bit. She was killing my mood by turning everything Tasmine and I said into something negative. We couldn't say shit to her ass without her taking it like some sort of insult. I really didn't see how she and Khyle were best friends.

"My Check" by Eric Bellinger came on, and people started dancing harder than a muthafucka. As I moved my body to the song, someone came up behind both Khyle and I. The guy behind her was this dude named Huelo, a fine ass Tongan guy on the football team. We both began to dance on the guys and once the song changed, I turned to look at my dance partner and my eyes almost fell out of my head when I saw it was Santino.

Santino, or just Sanz, went to the same high school with me back in Arizona. We dated before I met my fiancé Dean, and I was so in love with him. My parents loved him, and I thought it was cool that we both had Italian and black backgrounds. His father was Italian, and my father was Italian and Black. His mother was Black, and mine was Hispanic… pretty much we had a lot in common.

Everything about us was great. That was until he got me pregnant, and once I told him he broke up with me. I went ahead and got an abortion because I knew my parents would be disappointed, and I wanted to make something of myself. I was depressed about the shit, but I met Dean who was there for me, and built me back up. I loved him for that.

I hated Santino still to this day. I threw up violently when I found out he'd gotten a football scholarship to the same school I'd gotten an academic scholarship to. I wanted to go somewhere else, but my parents didn't have the money, and I refused to let him run me from a school I really wanted to go to. I planned to avoid him, but I was starting to see that he wasn't gonna make that easy.

After staring down into my eyes with his pretty hazel ones, he pressed his lips against mine. I felt the same chills and spark that I did when we were together three years ago. I don't think I ever fell out of love with him, which is why I tried to stay away from him while being here. But it seemed like he was purposely trying to be around me, which pissed me off. Once I came to my senses, I shoved him off and stormed away, ignoring Khyle calling after me.

"Bella!" Santino yelled, grabbing my arm once we got outside of the house. I accidentally stepped on a red cup, so I moved back, but he kept his grip on me.

"Let me go, Sanz, please." I tried to pry my arm from him before the tears spilled down my cheeks. How could he still make me cry?

He was so beautiful, with his caramel skin, short curly hair, muscular tall frame, and sexy demeanor. He was the perfect combo; fine and was good as hell to me. That's why I couldn't believe the way he acted towards me when I said I was pregnant. He was always so caring and understanding, and swore that he loved me yet, he'd hit a complete 180 when he found out about the baby.

"Come here." He pulled me in because he could sense that I was about to cry. That was how well he knew me and I hated it. "I'm sorry, baby." He kissed the top of my head.

"It's too late for that shit, move." I stepped back from him and pulled my compact from my purse so that I could fix my makeup.

"That nigga gave you that ring?" he scoffed.

"Yes, because he loves me."

"I'm sure he did that because he knew you were coming out here to go to school with me."

"Don't flatter yourself, honey. Dean doesn't give a fuck about you, and neither do I. He doesn't need to propose for me to not be involved with you."

"So you don't love me no more?" He flashed that cocky smile of his that I used to love but now hated.

"No, I don't. And you don't love me."

"Yes, I do, Bella. I always have, but when you told me about the baby, I panicked. If I could take that shit back, I would. There isn't another girl that I would rather have a baby with."

"Well, too bad, because if you ever have a kid it won't be with me." I tried walking past him to go back into the party, but he gripped my arm again.

"I love you, Bella."

I had to take a deep breath and close my eyes so that I wouldn't say it back to his wack ass. I didn't understand how I could love someone who treated me the way he did. Where was my pride? Where was my self-respect? He threw me to the side and never called me again, yet here I was two years later feeling the same way that I did back then. Even though he smashed every hoe in our high school, and dissed me on multiple occasions when I tried to talk to him, I still yearned for his touch.

"Let me go, Sanz. I don't care that you love me. I am engaged to the boy I love, and obviously that isn't you. You'll get over what we have soon, just like I did."

"I'm not gonna give up, baby," he called after me, but I just kept walking, despite having the urge to want to run back to him and jump in his arms.

I touched my mouth as I walked through the party, looking for Khyle. I could still feel Santino's lips on mine, making me lick them slowly. To ease my feeling of guilt, I took my phone out to text Dean.

*Me:* I love you, goodnight.

*Dean: I love you more baby. FaceTime tomorrow morning?*

*Me: Of course.*

I smiled down at our conversation, but our moment was interrupted once a familiar cologne traveled up my nostrils. I looked out the corner of my eye and saw Santino slowly walking by me with a smirk on his face. I knew he was on a mission to make me his, but that shit wasn't about to happen. I loved Dean.

I had to love Dean because he was there for me. He could be a bit controlling at times, but I owed him because he helped me when I had no one. I will admit that leaving him back in Arizona was the greatest feeling ever, but it was only because I needed some space. Dean could act like a second father at times, and I wanted a break from that.

"You okay?" Tasmine walked up to me and I nodded.

"Yeah, where is Khyle?"

"Right over there," Tasmine pointed to Khyle talking with Huelo. Perry was just standing by, doing something on her phone; probably playing a video game.

We walked over, but once Santino tried to get in the mix, I gave a signal to my friends so we could walk away. We found a spot on a couch nearby, after getting something to drink, so we just sat there for a little bit, sipping and dancing.

"So what did Anton say?" I looked to Tasmine and she blushed.

"We just talked, kissed mainly, and got even higher than I already was. He's so sweet and fine as fuck. He left though because he said he had an early meeting."

"You get his number?" Khyle quizzed, cocking her head.

"Girl, yes! And he asked me for mine."

Khyle and I both nodded in approval, as Perry smiled, just listening in.

"Where is Emery?" Khyle frowned as she put her phone to one ear, and her finger to the other to drown out the party. "She's not answering." Khyle tried her a couple more times before she stood to her feet, ready to look for her. Her phone buzzing stopped her from searching. She answered it and began talking to whoever it was, as Tasmine and I continued to sip our drinks and dance. "She said she's good. She met somebody and they left." Khyle shook her head and I knew she was irritated.

I hoped Emery knew what she was doing because she was extra as fuck for dipping out alone.

# CHAPTER FOUR

# Oden

*I* sped to the hoe crib with some thot I met at the party in my passenger seat. As usual, I'd already forgotten what she said her fucking name was, but I'd be sure to ask her once we got to the crib. She was okay looking, but her body was out of this fucking world. She was coming to the hoe crib because she was only good for one thing, I could already tell. Any woman that comes out in public with her ass cheeks hanging out, ain't looking for a nigga to treat her right. And if she is, then someone needs to school her on changing her ways.

"Your place is so nice," she beamed as I pulled into the community where my townhouse was located.

"Thank you."

I bobbed my head to the music playing in my car until we made it to my specific spot. Swooping into the park, I turned the car off and hopped out with the quickness. She followed behind me with her shoes clacking against the ground rapidly, since she was trying to catch up to me. Once inside, I took out a bottle of bourbon and some glasses, before filling them up. We both sat on the couch, and I took that damn bourbon to the face before refilling my shit.

I was still a little upset at the fact that Khyle chose to stop fucking with me altogether. I thought I would get over the shit, but every time I saw her ass at a party I felt some type of way. She was so damn pretty, and different than a lot of the girls I ran into. Most chicks out here were like her sister Shayne, but not Khyle. I just hated that she had a nigga because he was definitely in the way of me having my way with her. I knew she would eventually be mine, but this period of us being apart fucked with me.

"So what do you do, Oden?" old girl sitting next to me asked. I had completely forgotten she was here because my mind was on Khyle.

"I do all kinds of shit."

"That's cool, I guess. I'm so happy I met you. I've been wanting to for a long time, so it's almost like I hit the jackpot, you know?"

"How do you know me?" I looked over at her.

"Oh, I've heard things about you."

I swear I was like a damn local celebrity in Vegas, and I guess having a club and liquor line brought even more attention. Because even before I had that shit, people knew who Anton, Truman, and I were. It was rare that we'd meet someone who didn't know us. I'm not sure when I became so damn hood famous, but shit had been that way for as long as I could remember.

"Are you okay?" she lifted my chin and stared into my eyes.

"Don't touch my face, please." I moved away from her.

She kissed the side of my face before getting down onto the floor.

I continued taking sips out of my drink as she unbuckled my jeans too slowly. She loosened the button on my Ralph Lauren boxers, and reached for my dick through the hole. I watched her closely as her thin lips wrapped around the tip and she began sucking me gently, allowing her mouth to get nice and wet. I was high as fuck, and on my way to being slightly twisted, so my sense of touch had intensified.

"Shit, baby girl." I massaged her short hair as she sucked me off like a hardcore porn star.

This girl was definitely not new to anything she was doing to me right now. I felt my head bumping her tonsils, and that shit was driving my twisted ass crazy. A few more slurps, sucks, and tongue swirls, and I was exploding all in her mouth. She swallowed it up like it was a cure to a cancer she had, and then licked her lips as if it was the best thing she'd ever tasted.

"You wild," I smiled lazily and scratched my hair. "Come on." I rose to my feet, catching my jeans so that they wouldn't fall, and led her to the bedroom I used while here.

As soon as we stepped foot in the room, I began unbuttoning her little ass shorts as she pushed my t-shirt upward to caress my abs. Once I had her naked, I undressed myself as she watched with a lustful stare. She was salivating at the sight of my dick as if it wasn't just down her fucking throat.

I made my way over to her, and grabbed a condom from the nightstand drawer to roll down. She tried to pull me on top of her but I nipped that shit in a bud. I didn't do missionary. If she wasn't on top or letting me hit it from the back, it wasn't happening. Missionary was too intimate, just like giving head, so that's why I did neither unless it was someone I was interested in outside of the bedroom. And the last person that had me like that, prior to Khyle, was this chick named Naomi. But she became too jealous and insecure, so I had to tell her ass to go fly a kite.

I put old girl on all fours, and then got on the bed behind her, pressing her face into the pillow. Sliding inside, I could already tell why her head game was so good; her pussy was trash. I gripped her right shoulder, and began slamming into her, hoping I could bust before getting soft. Every time I looked down at her nice round ass bouncing, my dick got harder, but as soon as I threw my head back to enjoy the feeling, I was headed back to Softville.

"Fuuuccck," she cried out as she gripped the sheets.

I felt her explode on me, and then once again before going soft, I finally had to fake my nut and pull out. I was breaking a sweat for nothing. She had some nerve being that fucking thirsty knowing she had that wack ass box between her legs. I wanted to knock the shit out of her for busting that weak ass pussy open for me. I'd never been in something so worn. She was way too young to have such a ran through ass pussy. Pussy had more miles than a damn city bus.

"I'll be right back," I said once she collapsed onto her stomach, panting.

I went to the bathroom, locked the door, and hopped into the shower after flushing the condom. Once inside, I beat my dick to thoughts of Khyle so I could bust before I got blue balls. After getting myself together, I washed my body and then brushed my teeth. I checked in on her, and she was lying on her back, still breathing hard.

"Coming to bed?" she half smiled.

"Yeah, give me a minute." I closed the door and then went to sleep in the extra bedroom we had here. I made sure to lock the door because I was not trying to wake up to abyss pussy in my bed.

***

My 6:30am alarm went off, and I covered my face with both hands before finally sitting up and turning it off. I went to the kitchen to make some waffles and a bowl of fruit, before brushing my teeth and showering. After getting dressed while the chick was knocked out, I finally shook her ass so she could get the fuck up out of my shit.

"Oden!" Anton yelled through the house, so I left the girl alone for a second.

"What's good?" I came out of the room.

"We have to go to that bourbon meeting this evening or tomorrow evening?" he frowned as he went into the fridge to grab something to drink.

"This evening for bourbon. Tomorrow is the other shit," I responded quickly before going to the back to wake the girl from last night up. *Fuck is her name?* I thought. Entering the bedroom, I said, "Aye! Aye! Baby girl, wake up."

She opened her eyes just a little, before smiling at me and sitting up. I stepped back when she swung her legs off the side of the bed, before handing her, her clothes and shit. She pulled everything on, and since I was anxious to get her ass out, I held the door open for her.

"Last night was fun," she smiled and I gave her a fake one, wanting to push her ass out of the bedroom since she was walking so damn slow.

"Oh shit, what's up?" Anton smirked when she sauntered into the living room.

"Hey," she waved flirtatiously. I didn't give a fuck because I planned to never see her ass again. Anton could smash that trash ass pussy all he wanted. "So we should hang out again, Oden. I don't leave until Sunday evening."

"What's your name again?" I questioned. Anton almost spit his cereal out, and old girl had her jaw on the floor. I couldn't care less about her being embarrassed; she could answer the question or not. It was up to her.

"It's Emery, remember?" she smacked her lips and rolled her eyes. "You want my number?"

"My phone is tripping, but if I don't see you before you leave, have a safe trip." I backed her over the threshold and out of my spot before closing the door as Anton cracked the fuck up.

"Aye, can I at least get some money for a taxi or something?" she hollered from outside.

"How you broke with a pussy?" I looked to Anton.

"Right," he chuckled before turning his bowl up to drink the milk.

I let out an exasperated sigh, and snatched the door back open. I wasn't about to give her money for shit, so while she stood there, I called the homie, Truman, so he could take her ass home. I knew he was close by, overseeing the dealership and shit, so it wouldn't be too much of a hassle. Once he said he was on his way, I gave her ass a cold water bottle and closed the door. I didn't want her ass in my house.

***

After Truman picked Emery up, Anton and I left to our real spots to change for a meeting we were having with this commercial director. We wanted to do something classic for the commercial, and since I'd seen his work, he seemed like the right guy to handle it. That took up about three hours of our day, and since we were free which was rare, he and I met Truman at Palace to watch the strippers underground.

"That girl you had me pick up was wild as fuck," Truman shook his head, wearing a smile as he sipped his beer.

"What you mean?" I furrowed my brows, keeping my eyes on this pretty ass stripper named Ice.

"She grabbed my dick while I was driving, made me swerve out my fucking lane and shit. I had to drop her ass off fast because she was way too fucking eager," he shook his head.

Truman, Anton, and I have shared many girls. We've never went in on one like a train because that shit was kind of gay, but we did swap bitches and fuck them on different occasions. It was nothing for us to do that. No girl was off limits unless we said it beforehand; otherwise, it wasn't odd for one of us to mack on a bitch the other smashed prior. I personally liked to have a girl first, but if she was fine enough, I didn't mind coming at her even though I knew she'd sexed Anton or Truman. And honestly, most of the time they would still be sweating me even though I'd seen them with my homies just days before.

"She was cute, but ya boy over here acting like her pussy was horrible," Anton pointed to me with his thumb while laughing.

"Nigga, I have never faked a nut in my life, but I had to." They both doubled over in laughter as soon as the words left my mouth.

"Ain't no fucking way a bitch would have me faking the muthafucking funk. I would've told her to get her loose pussy ass up out in a hot second," Anton shook his head.

"I was in shock, that shit had never happened to me." I'd fucked with plenty of women who were considered hoes, and each and every last one of them had walls. What killed me is that Emery was definitely younger than them, so when did she start fucking? As a toddler? That shit blew me. "Her head game was A1 though."

"Damn, I should have let her have her way," Truman shook his head as we laughed.

Ice finished her set, and came right over to me. We were smiling hard at one another because we both had the same idea. I wasn't really sure what Ice, or Keesha's race was, but she was beautiful as hell with a banging body to match.

"Can I talk to you?" she smirked.

"In my office." I stood up and headed towards it with her following right behind me. If I couldn't have Khyle, I was gonna continue to bang out these hood rats.

# CHAPTER FOUR

*Earlier that morning…*

$\mathcal{E}$mery still hadn't come back yet, and it was now 10am. Bella, Tasmine, Perry, and I had just come from eating in the dining hall, and I'd called her about three times. I didn't know whether to be mad or sad about the situation. I wanted to be mad because she was supposed to be here for me, yet she was doing the most with some nigga she'd just met. Then again, what if he did something to her? That part had me worried as hell.

"Try her again," Bella frowned as she painted her toenails.

"She's not gonna answer," I huffed just as my phone lit up. I looked down to see it was a text message from her, so I immediately opened it.

*Emery: Hey downstairs, come let me in.*

"She's outside," I said before slipping on my Rihanna Puma slides and walking toward the door.

I made my way down to the lobby to see her ass standing outside looking like a two-dollar hoe. I let her in, and she waltzed in past me like she had done nothing wrong. I guess she hadn't done anything wrong in a sense. The scent that came from her was very familiar though, making me wonder where I'd smelled it. But, she was here now so I was gonna try to be cool. I couldn't lie and say I wasn't annoyed by her antics though.

"How was last night?" I quizzed as we stepped onto the elevator.

"Bomb as fuck," she grinned. "Best dick I ever had. I'm hoping to try that shit out again, because I'm pretty sure I'm addicted." We stepped off of the elevator, headed to my room.

"Damn. You just left me and didn't tell me shit last night. It would have been nice for you to at least show me who the hell had you so captivated, Emery. What if something happened to you? I would have no idea who the fuck murdered you." We entered my room.

"Hey," Emery spoke to the room in the driest tone ever. I could tell she wished that they weren't here, but this was Tasmine's room too, so she needed to shape the fuck up. "Anyway, I didn't say anything because when I saw his lap was empty, I knew I had no time to waste," she replied to my previous statement, picking up and dropping her duffle bag onto my bed to sift through it. "Some bitch had been on him all night so when she got up for a second, I slid in."

"Damn, what was his name?" Bella chimed in as she placed her miniature fan close to her feet.

"Wouldn't you like to know," Emery giggled. "I'm probably gonna see him again tonight, so I can get me a little going away present."

"Are you gonna say his name or nah?" Tasmine cocked her head.

Emery smiled to herself as she laid her outfit across my bed, before turning to look at us.

"Oden," she cheesed.

The room fell silent, and I swear I felt my thumping heart fall into my stomach. I could feel Bella, Tasmine, and even Perry staring at me, as I glared at a chuckling Emery.

I'd told her all about Oden, shit that I thought you told your best friend, but maybe she wasn't my best friend. She knew I liked him and how much it bothered me to cut him off, yet she brought her ass down here and fucked him. I hadn't even fucked him and she did! And this nigga, I can't believe the way he was making his rounds within my circle.

"We're gonna go watch TV in my room okay, Khyle?" Bella stood up to leave. I was too angry to respond, but I could see in my peripheral that Tasmine and Perry followed her.

"You slept with Oden?" I quizzed, trying to hold back the anger that wanted to rush to my face.

"Yeah, so what? You said you weren't gonna talk to him anymore so I didn't think it would be a big deal, Khyle."

"Not a big deal? I told you I liked him!"

"You just met him! You don't know if you like him, Khyle! And you haven't even talked to him in almost a month, but I'm supposed to stay away from him?" she palmed her chest with furrowed brows.

"Yes! You are my best friend, Emery! The last person you should have been looking to fuck was Oden. All these niggas up here? All the dudes that were at the party, yet you went for him?"

"You've seen him. He's sexy as fuck, and if you weren't gonna be fucking him, and Shayne wasn't, then somebody needed to. No point in letting such a fine specimen go to waste."

"He wouldn't be going to waste, he has plenty of women, Emery."

"Yeah, I'm sure he did, but now that I put it on him, I'm sure he'll be calling me back, begging for more. Who knows, I may move out here and be closer to you two."

"Emery, he is never going to call you, and if he does, it'll only be to fuck and nothing else. Oden is not the type of guy you can lock down by being a hoe."

"For one, I'm not a fucking hoe. I go for what the fuck I want and since I wanted him, I had him. Secondly, how the fuck would you know what he goes for, Khyle? All you've done is kiss him."

"Maybe because we talked. That's how you get to know people. It's okay to talk to a guy, go get food, do regular shit without bouncing on his dick."

"I think I know exactly what he likes, especially after last night. I loved sucking his dick," she grinned. I had to turn away from her for a few because I was about ready to kill her ass.

"I can't believe this."

"Khyle, you have Brian! It's not fair for me to sit around lonely while you collect every nigga you see. You didn't want Oden so I took him. It shouldn't be any hard feelings. Now, I have to go shower because we're going to the mall today, right?" She didn't give me a chance to answer, she just took her stupid ass into the bathroom.

I left her ass in my room because I was beyond tempted to run up in there, pull the curtain back, and slice her ass up with some scissors. Yes, I was willing to fuck my best friend up over Oden. I wasn't sure if she fucked him to purposely mess with me, or if the things I told her about him had her genuinely interested. Regardless, she should have kept her fucking legs closed, because I was two seconds from rocking her shit.

Listen at me. I was never the type to fight over a nigga… ever, but for some reason I wanted to pound her face in. The sad part about this all was that I would have rather her fucked Brian than Oden. How backwards am I?

"You okay?" Tasmine answered Bella and Perry's room door, and I just nodded before changing my mind and shaking my head 'no'.

"Am I tripping?" I asked the room as I entered fully.

"Hell no! She knew you liked that nigga, especially if you felt the need to tell her about him. I would've dragged her ass all throughout the campus!" Bella snapped.

"Right. I know that's your girl, but she for real did that shit on purpose, Khyle. You shouldn't have to tell her not to fuck with him," Tasmine backed Bella up.

"I had to leave because I was about to punch her ass. I don't fight over guys but I swear I was about to just a minute ago." I glanced over at Perry who was watching us while tearing up a cup of yogurt. I hated yogurt.

"And what about him? Does he know about her?" Bella questioned.

"I think I mentioned her, but maybe not. And I'm sure she told him that she and I were best friends. But I can't expect him not to fuck her, we haven't spoken in almost month. Not to mention, she's the one that's supposed to have my back, not him."

"But still, he already smashed your sister, he could have at least turned your best friend down," Tasmine scoffed.

"Maybe she misunderstood you," Perry finally piped in.

"She didn't misunderstand a damn thing. She fucked him even though she knew I was bugging from having to cut him off. But I'm off her ass too." I turned on my heels and started storming towards the door. I'd made up my mind to whoop her ass.

"Khyle, don't." Tasmine grabbed me. "Just stop fucking with her, that will hurt way worse."

What if this was karma for me hanging out with Oden when I knew my sister had some dealings with him? Yep, this was punishment. I wanted Oden, and since he didn't want my sister, I tried to justify the fact that I hung out with him, by pretending to only want a friendship. I just didn't know karma worked so damn quickly! If this was my payback, then did I really have a right to be mad at Emery?

***

*That evening...*

The five of us had just come home from walking the strip and doing some light shopping at the fashion mall. The stores there were way too damn expensive for my bi-weekly allowance budget, so all we did was do a little damage in Victoria's Secret and Forever 21. I got more of the body mist that Oden liked, and I even bought some sexy panties, which I never did. I usually bought just regular thongs because Brian didn't give a fuck. He was just happy when I agreed to have sex with his ass.

Currently, it was around 10pm at night, and even though it was a Saturday, we weren't going to a party. I wasn't really in the mood, and Bella and Tasmine didn't want to go without me. Emery complained, but I just ignored her like I'd been doing all damn day. It was awkward at times, but do you think I gave a fuck? She was on my fucking shit list regardless of the fact that her actions were my karma. I couldn't wait for her ass to get the fuck up out of Vegas tomorrow evening.

The five of us were watching some show named Wentworth on Netflix, which was just like a more hardcore version of Orange is the New Black. It was cool, but my mind was elsewhere.

"Shit is about to get real!" Emery chuckled and looked over at me.

I ignored her ass and continued scrolling on my phone. I went into my text messages, and reread the conversation between Oden and I. Yeah, I had completely ignored the fact that I had two unread messages from Brian waiting. While scrolling, I spotted the text containing his 'real' address. After pondering for a few moments, I got up and put on my Puma slides before grabbing my purse and keys.

"I'll be back in a little bit," I told the room as I ordered an Uber on my phone. Damn did I need a fucking car.

"Khyle!" Emery yelled down the hallway like an imbecile. "Can I come?"

"No."

When the Uber pulled up, I hopped in and inhaled sharply. I

couldn't believe I was popping up over this nigga's house. What had he done to me? He had me acting all out of character, and I'd only known him a little over a damn month. Brian had never driven me this crazy. Speaking of Brian, I hadn't lost one bit of sleep after hearing about him and Jacqueline. I'd been meaning to get in his ass, but he sadly hadn't crossed my mind.

"Thank you," I said to the driver once he pulled up.

I rushed to Oden's door, and knocked a few times. After some minutes went by, I knocked again. I looked around to see if I saw his Lexus truck, but I didn't. He wasn't here, my Uber was gone, and I was looking dumb as fuck. I walked a little ways from his door so I could sit on the bench, and once I did, I just stared out into the night sky, wondering how the hell I got here. I had fallen off too quickly and majorly.

# CHAPTER FIVE

# Oden

*Meanwhile…*

*Yo' bitches TD, yo' niggas TD. Yo' bitches TD, yo' niggas TD. Don't make us turn it up on you niggas right quick. Don't make me turn it up on you bitches right quick.*

Anton, Truman, and I were throwing our last stack at the strippers in our section, as "TD" by The Game blasted over the strip club. I'd had a good ass time tonight and didn't want it to end, but I had somewhere to be in the morning.

Once the song faded out, I rose to my feet, pulling up my jeans as one of the strippers got into my face. Well, I was 6'4 and she was about 5'5, so she wasn't really in my face, but she was for sure all up on me. I smiled down at her, making her blush, before licking my lips at her thick ass body.

Wasn't nothing like a bitch who had something for you to grab on. I wanted so badly to take her home and dig her out, but not only did I have somewhere to be, I needed to slow up on smashing my employees. I'd just fucked that stripper Ice in my office earlier, which was enough for the day. A nigga like myself had no business running a damn strip club, but it was a lucrative business, especially out here in Las Vegas.

"Aight, I'm out," I slapped hands with Anton. He had one of the girls in his lap, and Truman's ass was fucking some bitch in the cut. He'd better be glad he was my nigga, otherwise I'd dead that shit. "Remind me to bring the cleaners in tomorrow," I yelled out to Truman, but he was in the zone, staring into old girl's eyes as she bounced in his lap.

"Am I invited?" the girl who was in my face questioned.

"Maybe next time, baby girl." I walked past her and went upstairs to the club portion, which was jumping already.

I continued out to my car and hit the alarm to unlock it. I couldn't wait to get home and take a hot ass shower, before drinking some warm almond milk. Whenever I went to sleep without drinking warm milk, I always woke up groggy, or sometimes I would toss and turn all night. That shit was weird to me, but I wasn't gonna stop drinking that shit. If it ain't broke don't fix it.

When I pulled up to my spot, I saw what looked like Khyle sitting on the blue benches we had all around the community. She was texting on her phone, with her legs stretched across the bench. I couldn't lie, I missed her little ass so it had me feeling some type of way seeing her here.

"What are you doing here, Khyle?"

"You're fucking my friends now, too?" she rose to her feet and raised her brow. Her long ass hair was framing her face instead of being pushed behind her ears. She looked upset and sad as fuck, but beautiful nonetheless.

"What are you talking about?"

"Emery!" she hollered loudly as fuck.

"Okay, we're not about to do this out here." I led her to my front door, before opening it for her so that she could walk inside. Closing it behind me I said, "Emery is your friend?" I was kicking myself for smashing that dark hole pussy ass bitch.

"Yes! First my sister, and now her? We really have no chance now, Oden!" She dropped her purse onto my couch before sitting down herself. "You fuck everybody," she whispered before dropping her face into her hands, and then running her fingers through her hair. "Did you fuck someone else today too?" My mind immediately went to Ice aka Keesha.

"Khyle—"

"I swear you fuck every damn body."

"I promise I don't—"

"You're always promising some shit! Talking about you're loyal but you're smashing my fucking sister and my best friend!"

"Aight, first things first, lower your voice. Secondly, I didn't even know yo' ass when I fucked your sister, did you forget that, Khyle?" I made my way over, standing in front of her. "And I didn't know that bitch was your friend! She didn't mention you, so how the fuck would I know?"

"I know," she responded lowly. "But now we can't."

"I didn't know you wanted to, baby girl." I got down on my knees so I could look into her eyes. She caressed my curly hair and gazed down into my eyes. I couldn't help myself so I pecked her softly. "I would have been with you last night and not her, you know that. And I wouldn't have fucked another bitch earlier today either."

"It's too late." She plopped her back against the couch, but reached to play with my chin hairs. I gripped her small waist and yanked her toward the edge. Her pussy was right in my face as I sat her legs on my shoulders.

"Too late for what?"

"For us."

"Nah, you got me fucked up." I reached for the waistband of her tights and pulled them down her smooth legs. She watched me with her bottom lip tucked in. The panties she had on were white, lace, and sexy as fuck.

I kissed her center, making a soft moan escape her lips. I inhaled her scent, and just got hella up close and personal with the pussy before pulling her panties down. It was just as pretty as I knew it would be, and the sight prompted me to kiss it like I loved it. Opening her legs a little wider as they still sat on my shoulders, my kisses became more sensual, and soon enough I was straight French kissing the pussy.

"Mmmm," her voice trembled as she massaged my hair.

Once I felt like I'd had enough of the kissing, I gripped her thighs, pressing them into her stomach, and began sucking her clit. I started slow, with gentle sucks and flicks of my tongue, before attacking her as if I hadn't eaten in days. Listening to her soft moans was like music to my ears, and only motivated me to go harder. My mouth was damn near attached to her shit as I sucked her button like it was a straw.

"Oden," she whimpered as her legs trembled while she gripped my hair.

Her juices spilled over, and I lapped them up immediately. Not ready to stop, I kept feasting on her until she was crawling up the couch. I yanked her back down in order to keep going, and after she quivered from releasing, I let up. I swiped my tongue slowly between her folds while looking up into her eyes, before planting a deep kiss. I loved eating pussy and hadn't done it in a very long time.

Her chest rose and fell rapidly as she inhaled and exhaled sharply. I stood to my feet to pull her shirt over her head, and when I saw she wasn't wearing a bra, my dick got even harder. I could crush a bag of ice with my dick right now. I towered over her as she stared up at me innocently, because I just wanted to take a few moments to admire her body. Picking her up, I carried her to the back as we kissed like two long lost lovers. I placed her on the bed, and she sat up to unbuckle my jeans as I removed my shirt. We kept eye contact as she pushed my jeans and boxers down. Stepping out of my shoes, I pushed my bottoms past my feet, before tossing them onto the chaise in my room.

"You good?" I chuckled as she stared my dick down in amazement.

She simply nodded before taking it into her hand and wrapping her lips around the tip. She wasted no time lubricating the head, and I swear I'd never been more turned on just from watching in all of my life. She was so fucking beautiful with her long dark hair, full lips, glowing cinnamon complexion, and deep brown eyes. Seeing that sexy ass face slob on my dick was a sight like no other. There was nothing like seeing a pretty bitch get nasty.

I was thanking God that I'd showered back at the club after fucking Ice. Otherwise, I wouldn't be enjoying this right now.

"Shit," I grumbled. I could tell she didn't suck dick much, if she ever had at all, but it still felt good. I would get her right over time anyway.

I pushed her hair back so I could see better, and began to slowly hump her face. She took every stroke, allowing her saliva to go crazy just how I liked it. The sloppier she sucked my dick, the sexier she looked to me. I loved freaky shit and especially a freaky bitch.

"You're so fucking beautiful," I panted, biting down on my bottom lip while watching her. I pulled out of her mouth, and then shoved it back in. She didn't slow up at all. Her mouth was perfect for fucking. "Oh, fuck." I felt myself nearing that peak, and soon enough, I was releasing all into her mouth. "Toss it back," I instructed and she did just that.

She sat there, waiting for my next move as I rolled a condom down. I climbed into the bed, on top of her, and in between her legs, as I sucked on her lips and kissed her sensually. I'd been waiting to fuck her for the longest, so I was definitely gonna take my damn time. I positioned my dick at her opening, while keeping eye contact with her. She gasped as I pushed myself inside, and I couldn't help but groan at the feeling of her.

"Oden," she whimpered again, hugging my body as I sucked on her neck.

She was so wet, tight, and warm that it was fucking crazy. To go from getting some trash ass puss to this, was crazy right now. I kept moving in and out of her slowly while kissing her, making her lock her legs around me. That gave me more access, so I pushed myself deeper into her as if I wasn't already in as far as I could go. I was kissing and sucking everything; her lips, shoulders, nipples, ears. I was feeling on everything that I'd been thinking about since I saw her. She came hella quickly, and her eyes bucked because she was surprised that she'd had an orgasm. I guess she'd forgotten about the ones I brought on from eating her.

After getting my fix of making love, I put her on all fours and slid inside from behind. We both let out a breathy moan before I pressed her face into the pillow. I started off giving slow and deep strokes, enjoying her snivels and quivers every time I let it sit inside. Once I'd gotten enough of that, I began pounding into her with force, gripping her long hair into my hands.

"Uuuh, ahh!" she called out innocently, turning me on even more.

I yanked her up by her hair, and bit down on her shoulder, letting her sit on my dick for a bit. Her body trembled as she released again, and after she caught her breath, I put her face back in the pillow to finish strong. After some long, hard pumps, I finally filled up the condom.

I sat there inside her for a few, and then finally slid out, removing the condom once I was to my feet. She turned on her back, but kept her attention on what was out of my window, basically avoiding eye contact with me. I went to get us some warm towels, bringing them to the room so that we could clean up. After placing them in the hamper, we cleaned our hands, before heading back to the bedroom.

"I guess I should go," she started looking around the room for her clothes.

"They're in the living room, and no you shouldn't leave. It's late as fuck. Why would you leave?" I found myself getting annoyed by her statement. I could tell that she was about to be on her bullshit again, saying we should cease all contact.

She was about to speak, but I guess she could sense me getting angry.

"Never mind." She peeled the covers back and climbed into the bed. I did the same, and pulled her into me so that she could lie on my chest.

"What are you thinking about?" I questioned.

"Nothing."

"Don't lie."

"Just wondering why I came over here and did what I did. Not that I didn't like it, or you, but it was a bad decision."

Clenching my jaw I asked, "Bad how?" I knew why it was bad, but I believed some kind of good could come from this, despite where we started.

"Because I have a boyfriend that I promised I would be faithful to. And because you've slept with my sister. Oh my gosh," she groaned and rolled off of me. "Then Emery too."

"Khyle, I told yo' ass that none of that would have happened, had I met you before her, but I didn't. I understand you're upset about me and your sister, but give me a damn break, I didn't know she was related to you. Hell, I didn't even know you. And your best friend, she ain't ya fucking best friend if you told her the deal."

"Maybe I didn't tell her the deal." She stared up at the ceiling with her long hair everywhere, damn near swallowing my pillow.

"Did you?"

She paused for a few before saying, "Yes."

"Aight then, neither of those situations should be a problem baby because it wasn't on purpose. And don't penalize me because your sister liked me first. Doesn't it matter who I want?" She nodded. "Good." I pulled her back into me. Lifting her chin, I gazed into her eyes for a few before pressing my lips against hers. "And I told you I was gonna make you cum," I whispered against her lips, making her smile softly.

"You did."

I got on top of her, between her legs, and she placed her small palm against my pelvis.

"What?"

"I'm a little sore."

"I don't mind." I placed her legs onto my shoulders and slid in before she could protest.

I knew shit was not gonna be easy, but I was gonna give it the old college boy try.

# CHAPTER FIVE

# Anton Nickerson

*A couple days later...*

"How many cars are sitting in the fucking shop?" Oden frowned as our chop shop owners sat in the room with us.

If you didn't know, we ran a very successful car theft ring. Oden and I started out as just the niggas who stole the cars and delivered them to our boss, but overtime we worked our way up. Now, we didn't even touch the shit. All we did was direct and let our young niggas know where to get the cars from, how to get them, and where to take them. We dealt more with the business side, like negotiating the prices with people who wanted them overseas. Them rich niggas overseas paid a lot of fucking money for these nice ass cars, so even though Oden, Truman, and I made bank off of the new nightclub and the bourbon, we had no plans on stopping with this shit.

"It's three cars, but we should have them done by tonight," this guy named Donnell responded, and I could see the lump he swallowed as Oden lowered at him.

"Three fucking cars? The same damn ones that were brought there 48 fucking hours ago?" Oden grimaced, standing to his feet. Holding a whip past 24 was unacceptable, because it increased our chances of getting caught.

"We ran into a little problem, that's why, but I swear they're gonna get shipped out by tonight, Oden."

"They better be, and if not, you and I are gonna have a little talk." Oden ruffled his own hair with his eyes closed, before sitting back down. "Look, we have to get these cars in and out faster. If y'all can't control the workers and make sure that the cars aren't out in 24 hours or less, then maybe I need to get rid of y'all asses."

"Nah, I swear we're gonna have it done," Donnell assured with a repeated nodding of his head.

"You too, your shit been a little slow, man," I pointed to this nigga named Ryan, who already had his eyes bucked. This nigga couldn't even spell poker face. Whenever he was guilty, he looked the damn part.

"I get the cars out in 24," Ryan responded.

"Yes, but you only get one damn car out versus other people who get out three and four. What's the deal?" I frowned as Oden and Truman waited for his response.

"I was having some problems on the home-front, but I'm good now."

"You have one week to improve," I said before standing up.

"Aight, y'all can go," Oden dismissed them.

The whole room cleared out, and once Truman closed the door behind them, we all shook our heads. Sometimes them niggas acted like kids instead of grown ass men.

"Aye, you feeling like Ryan is stable?" Oden quizzed.

"He seems like he's on edge, almost like he'll rat us out if it came down to it," Truman nodded.

"I agree. I'm gonna watch that nigga. Keep tabs on him and see what the fuck he's doing. If I find out some shit, I'll just dead him before he can bring us any harm," I replied. They both shook their heads before we sat in deep thought for a moment.

We discussed a few more details of all of our businesses before finally parting ways since I had class. Yeah, a nigga was in school, but I didn't have much more to go. I was studying marketing at the advice of Oden's grandfather. I enjoyed figuring out ways to cleverly promote our brand, so why not get certified in the shit? It was a long road getting to where I was today, because I had to attend a damn community college before even being accepted into a university. But now that I'd made it this far, I wasn't gonna stop. I was doing this for myself, and my life down the line, but also to honor Oden's grandfather who was like a dad to me.

I made it to my school with about 30 minutes to spare before class, so I decided to go and get some food from the student union. They had a nice amount of variety, but it was shit that skinny bitches on diets liked so it was rare that I frequented it. I'd much rather get some shit off site, but I didn't want to risk being late. I might be a thug, but a nigga was prompt and always on the money. Shit, being late was actually a pet peeve of mine, so you know my ass was always somewhere 15 minutes early, at the least.

After getting my Subway, I found a table in the corner and sat my ass down. My damn stomach was on some other shit and I didn't feel like walking anywhere just to eat a sandwich. A nigga might faint if he did that.

"Tony, what's up?" this girl named… umm… shit… Oh, Marnie sat down across from me. If I knew how to roll my fucking eyes, I would. This was the exact reason why Oden and I went to class and left, because bitches were thirsty and didn't care how busy you were. I could be taking a fucking piss and they would come up in there and try to converse. There were no boundaries in their minds.

"What's good, M?"

"Nothing, just been busy with school. I never see you outside of class, but I'm happy I caught up with you," she smiled.

Marnie was cute, but she was trying to make something out of nothing with me. We used to fuck a lot, but eventually I got over it. Not to mention the fact that she let Oden and Truman fuck down the line. I don't know how she thought that we were gonna be anything more than whatever the fuck we were. Don't get me wrong, I never planned for her to be my girl, I was just flabbergasted that she felt like she had a chance with me.

"Cool."

"So are you busy tonight? Or this weekend? I'm free after class for the rest of the week."

I was about to tell her I was busy as a bee, but that Tasmine chick came into the student union, headed for Panda Express. She was wearing a dress that hugged her filled out body like a damn glove. I had no idea that her ass and titties sat up like that. I knew she had a pretty ass face, which usually meant the body was built like a bag of laundry, but not this time. Fuck, I thought as I reminisced about kissing her fine ass at that house party.

"Tony," Marnie low-key snapped.

"I got a headache right now, Marnie, so I'll get at you later, but let me eat in peace." I kept glancing from her to Tasmine, hoping Marnie would be gone by the time Tasmine needed a seat.

Marnie followed my eyes and then sucked her teeth.

"Whatever, nigga." She finally stood up and switched off just as Tasmine turned on her heels, scanning the area for a seat.

When she spotted me, she flashed her beautiful smile. I waved her over, and she immediately began making her way over to me. Damn, this girl was beautiful as hell now that I was seeing her under bright lights while sober. Her eyes were a pretty honey color, and her dark hair looked so soft, perfect for pulling.

"I didn't expect to see you in here, mingling with the college kids," she smiled.

"I know. I usually don't be hanging around here like that, but a nigga was hungry and had no choice but to eat on campus."

"I don't remember you saying you were in school when we texted?" she cocked her head, holding her plastic fork in her hand.

"I don't really talk about it, I guess, especially when I'm conversing with a woman. And truthfully, I assumed you already knew."

"Why would I know that when I don't know you?"

"I ain't used to meeting girls who don't know me, but it's refreshing as fuck." I watched her place a forkful of food into her sexy mouth. "Can I tell you something?"

"I don't like the way that sounds, but go ahead. I can't be responsible for how I react though."

"Okay," I chuckled. "I didn't know that you looked this bad. Like I knew you were cute, but now that I'm seeing you in the light with a clear head, my dick is on one."

"Umm, okay, I'm not sure if I should be insulted or not. And when I saw you at that backyard barbecue, it was plenty of light from the light poles."

"True, but a nigga was twisted as hell that night. There were so many beautiful women that y'all all kind of just ran together."

"Oh."

"But trust me, had I been in my right mind, I would have been all over you."

"Instead of the girl with the bad weave and no ass?" she raised her eyebrow and I couldn't help but to laugh. Yeah, she liked me because she was insulting other bitches that I entertained.

"Yeah, instead of her. But what are you doing tomorrow?"

"Nothing after 12pm, since that's when my class ends."

"Aight. I'm gonna hit you up, and make sure you answer. I'm

gonna tell you right now that I'm an impatient ass nigga," I stared down at her seriously, making her smile fade.

I grinned down at her to let her know I was only half joking, and she flashed me one back. I was impatient as fuck, which people mistook for having a temper, but I just hated to wait. If I fucking text you, you need to hit me back ASAP or when you do later, I'm gonna be hot. I never had that problem with females because they'd reply to my ass before I even hit send on my text. But my homies Oden and Truman would take a cool minute sometimes, pissing me off. And Tasmine was different from the bitches I usually fucked with, so I felt the need to warn her. She didn't seem like the type to be sitting in her room, waiting for me to hit her line.

"See you soon then." She continued eating her food as I grabbed my shit and left out.

I prayed class went by fast because this day was tiresome already. Also, I wanted to drop by and check in on Donnell's progress before I went home.

***

That long ass fucking class was finally over, and when I stepped outside, I saw the sun was starting to go down just a little bit. It was the tail end of summer so it was still pretty bright, but I knew soon it'd be dark as hell. I made my way to my car, and as soon as I got in I checked my glove compartment to see if I had any pre rolled blunts. After I rolled up on Donnell's hoe ass, I wanted to be sure I had some shit to take straight to the face for the night.

As I checked my phone to pick and choose which texts I wanted to respond to, there was a knock on my window. I slowly turned to look, and it was this crazy stalking ass bitch named Kai. I swear I couldn't stand her, and despite the fact that I felt strongly about not hitting a woman, she'd made me choke her ass one time. That's just how mad the bitch had gotten me. I contemplated getting a restraining order many of times, but I was a hood nigga and only bitch ass ones did shit like that.

"Fuck out of here!" I yelled through the window, not wanting to roll it down.

"Roll your fucking window down before I bust it open!" she barked. I didn't want to do it, but I knew her psycho ass would for sure break my shit, and I would end up strangling her ass in a parking lot full of people.

"What?!" I shouted once I'd rolled the window down.

"TJ is sick, and the shot he needs costs too much. As his father, you should be the one to pay for it."

TJ or Anton "Tony" Jr., was Kai's son that she swore up and down was mine. I'd asked for a DNA test on multiple occasions, and when I did, she would scram. Her being away would usually only last for about two weeks tops, then she would pop up on me like right now.

I knew that little nigga was not my son because I'd never smashed her raw, and the condoms were always intact afterward. Kai refused to tell me the truth, and she was around here telling niggas I was a deadbeat and shit. I had to beat the brakes off of one nigga who came at me foul on her behalf.

This bitch was nuisance and I was starting to see that the only way to get rid of her was to kill her. But then who would take care of little man? I was torn. And the worst part of all this shit was that she wasn't the only one screaming that I was her baby daddy. It was a cool three chicks right now, running around claiming me as their baby's father, and all three of them were lying. I didn't know what it was about me, and why these hoes chose me to pin a baby on.

"That nigga ain't my kid, Kai."

"Yes he is! He's two years old now, you really need to stop being in fucking denial! All this fucking money you got and you can't support him?" she placed her hand on her thick hip.

To say Kai was bad would be a fucking understatement. She was thick in all the right places, had some sexy ass lickable chocolate skin, pretty eyes like Tasmine, and some short cut like Halle Berry used to have. When she didn't open her mouth, she was arguably one of the baddest in Las Vegas. But when you got a glimpse of that attitude, it was a complete turn off.

Like all the women in my life, Kai was some pussy and nothing more. Literally, we only talked when I wanted to fuck and that was it. Somehow she came up pregnant, by another nigga, and that's when our relationship soured. I so wished she had fucked the homies too, because that way they'd be in this mess with me. I laughed lowly at my shady thoughts.

"DNA test, I told you. If he comes back to be mine, then I will be more than happy to assist. But you know he ain't and that's why you won't do it."

"Look, I don't have time for your immature ass games. If you didn't wanna be a daddy, you shouldn't have been fucking me."

"Get up out of here and don't talk to me unless it's about a DNA test."

*WHAM!*

She slapped the shit out of me and tried to dart off, but I opened my door abruptly, which knocked her ass to the gravel.

"Fuck is wrong with you, huh?" I towered over her as she lay on the ground, scowling like she was really about that life. "Stay yo' ass away from me, Kai. If you keep up with this bullshit, I'm gonna have to take care of you, and we know what will happen to TJ if he doesn't have a mother."

"Fuck you, Tony!"

I ignored her, getting back into my car. I quickly rolled my window up, and floored it in reverse so I could get out of that parking lot. If I planned on ever being anything to any other girl, I needed to get all my fake baby mamas under control. Otherwise, Kai, Selinda, and Violet would be the death of me.

# CHAPTER FIVE

*I* sat across from my sister at Red Lobster on Flamingo Road, which was pretty much walking distance from my school. She asked to meet me somewhere, and I told her I didn't want to go far because I had a paper to type. I wanted her to believe that I was mad at her for being mad at me about Oden, but honestly, I just didn't want to face her. I made a big deal about the fact that he and I were just gonna be friends and that she was overreacting, when I knew that I liked him. Now, I'd let the nigga fuck me, multiple times at that, and I felt all the way wrong.

Every time I went home from his place, I told myself that I wouldn't hang out with him anymore. I would tell myself that what I'd just done would be the last time. Then he'd text or call me, asking to go get food, chill, or do something, and I'd be jumping for joy.

While being with Oden, I'd been ignoring everyone except my parents, Tasmine, Bella and Perry. I mean Perry didn't really count because she didn't say or do much, but you know what I mean. Brian was becoming frustrated with me, and I was starting to think he didn't love me anymore. Although I wanted to be with Oden, thinking that Brian was over me bothered me still. For some reason, I wasn't ready to let him go, even though I'd been cheating on him.

"I know you're angry with me about not wanting you to be friends with Oden, and that's why I asked you to come here."

"Go on," I stirred my strawberry lemonade with my straw.

"You told me you guys were just cool, right?"

"Yes."

"So I wanted to know if you'd do me a favor. Oden is a little rough around the edges, I'm sure you know from being his *friend* and all, so he's not being very nice to me right now. I was wondering if you could tell him how I feel, so that he will maybe give us a chance."

I stared into her eyes for a few moments, processing the fuckery that had just come out of her mouth. Was she seriously asking me to put in a good word? I knew my sister, and she knew me, so she was very aware of the fact that I liked Oden. Right now she was testing me, and I wasn't sure if I wanted to fuck with her and pass the test, or just speak my mind.

"You want me to tell Oden how you feel about him, while you have Pierce sitting at home?"

"I don't want Pierce! I haven't wanted to be with him since... since..."

"Since he got dropped from the 49ers?" I raised my brow, a bit disgusted by her.

Before coming here, my sister was my idol. The fact that she was over Pierce because of his failure didn't make me see her any differently. I felt like he lied to her and led her on. I know that was far from the truth because he couldn't control the fact that he'd gotten dropped, at least I think he couldn't, but I would have told myself anything to make my sister sound like a good person. Now, knowing she stopped loving her man because he wasn't Mr. Popular anymore was fucked up in my eyes.

"Yes, since he got dropped. I don't know. He used to be this macho guy with all this confidence and fame, and now he's just a little weasel who complains too much. I wanna be with Oden," she damn near whined, face twisted and everything. She sounded like a toddler begging her mother for a toy.

"Shayne, I told you what he told me. No matter what I say to him, he's not gonna fuck with you. When will you realize that? I've never seen you act like this over a man."

"Because I've never met one like Oden." Her gaze was intense, and I felt like I knew exactly what she was thinking. "I mean, is there another reason why you won't talk to him for me? Cheating on Brian already?"

"Ain't nobody fucking cheating on Brian, aight?"

"Mama told me he came to the house to try and call you from the landline since you weren't answering his calls." She wore a smug expression.

"That's because I heard he was hanging out with Jacqueline, not because I'm so wrapped up in another nigga like you."

Was I really doing this? I was talking to her as if what I spoke was the truth. We were in the same boat, sort of; in a relationship we didn't want to be in, and lusting after fine ass Oden Bishop. The only difference is he didn't want her ass, and he *did* want me. Well at least that's what he made me think.

"Whatever, Khyle. Whether you help me or not, Oden and I will end up together. You know I always get the niggas I want. When have I failed?"

She had never failed when pursuing a guy in the rare times that she had to.

"Good luck; doesn't make a difference to me. I love the man I'm with and I'm happy to be with him."

"Well then you're blessed."

We both signed our receipts that the waitress brought over to us, gave a light hug, and then parted ways. I was starting to feel like I was allowing Oden to tear my sister and I apart. We used to be tight, thick as thieves, and now we were enemies damn near because of his ass. I didn't want to be one of those girls who lost everything behind a man, especially when I'd only known him for a couple months.

I planned to come to Vegas to bond with my sister, make new friends, party, and get my education so I could eventually become a probation officer. Lately, all my time and thoughts had been consumed with Oden. I swear I thought about him from the time I woke up to the time I laid down for bed. I even thought about the nigga during class lectures on occasions. And every time his name was mentioned by a girl in class or around campus, my heart would beat quickly as hell, and my stomach would fall to my ankles, because I was afraid of what they were saying about him, hoping it wouldn't break me. I had it bad and I didn't even know why.

As I waited outside of Fridays for an Uber, since I declined the ride my sister offered, my phone chimed. It was a specific chime that I'd assigned to Oden. Before answering his text, I removed the tone from his name because it was unfair to Brian. I'm sure he would be more upset that I was getting fucked by Oden than him having his own tone, but hey, it was for my sanity.

*Oden: Hey baby, still busy?*

*Me: Maybe, why?*

*Oden: Lol. Are you going to that black party tonight?*

*Me: Yes, with Bella and Tasmine.*

*Me: Perry will drive us.*

*Oden: Let me know when you get there so I can have you all to myself. And leave with me…*

Getting all warm inside, I held my iPhone tightly in my hand as I got into the Uber. I don't even know why I called this shit, knowing my school was close by.

*Me: I can't leave with you. I have a boyfriend and I know what you wanna do when we leave.*

*Oden: Boyfriend lol. I'm your boyfriend out here.*

*Me: Boyfriend #2*

*Oden: Nah you got me twisted baby girl. I'm always number one.*

*Me: He was my man first though… lol.*

*Oden: But I'm the one that makes that pussy cum.*

I gasped when I read his response, even though I really wasn't surprised that he'd sent that. A light throb between my legs surfaced upon reading it.

*Me: Goodbye Oden!*

*Oden: See you later baby.*

I fucking loved this nigga! I wasn't in love with him… but I loved a lot of shit about him… you know what I mean.

***

*Later that night…*

*Me: Staying in tonight, not feeling well.*

*Oden: Cold?*

*Me: Cramps if you must know.*

"So you're sure you don't want me to stay, boo?" Tasmine asked as she looked over herself in the mirror. Her and Bella were really becoming some close friends of mine, especially now that Emery and I were at odds.

"No, girl, go. Anton is gonna be there, and you know despite all that shit Bella talks, she wants to see Santino," I sighed as I thought about the fact that I was gonna miss the party. It was supposed to be at some big ass mansion about 20 minutes away, and boy was I looking forward to it. Not to mention I was ready as fuck to see my forbidden boo.

"True. Well, we won't stay long."

"Yeah right," we giggled in unison.

*KNOCK! KNOCK!*

Tasmine jogged lightly to the door to answer it, and in walked Bella and Perry. Bella's perfume made me smile as she neared me with her bottom lip poked out.

"You better feel better by the next event bitch," she said as she touched my hair.

"Oh, I will. I will walk up in that shit with a cane before I miss it."

"We'll keep an eye on Oden's ass for you."

"Please don't," I chuckled. I really didn't want them watching Oden because if they told me anything bad, I would fucking faint. Yeah, I liked him that much that ignorance was for real bliss right now.

"Okay, bye!!!" the ladies said in unison almost as they strutted out of the room.

Once they left, I turned on the medium sized television that Oden bought me. He refused to take no for an answer, and while I was in class, Tasmine let him and his friend Truman in to set it up. In addition to the TV, he got me a fancy ass Keurig because I told him I loved tea and warm milk. Little things like that made me like him even more. It wasn't the fact that he bought me shit, but that he listened to me.

After making myself some tea and frothed milk, I cut the lights out to watch some stand-up comedy shows on Netflix. My cramps were pretty bad, but the tea was helping me a little bit. In the middle of my relaxing, there was a knock at my room door.

"Tasmine must've forgotten something," I said to myself as I placed my tea on my desk and went to answer it.

"Hey, baby," Oden grinned as he stood there looking sexy as fuck.

His toasted vanilla complexion was so beautiful, and so was his wild curly fro. His eyes were a little low, so I knew he'd been smoking as usual. He didn't smell like weed though, just his Clive Christian cologne. Black basketball shorts were on his bottom half, sagging just enough to see the waistband of his Polo boxers, when his tattooed arm lifted his black shirt to rest against his six pack. I wondered what his parents looked like. They had to be ugly as fuck, because ugly muthafuckas always had some fine ass kids.

"Oden, what are you doing?" I asked as he smoothly made his way into my room, dragging his Nike slides across the carpet as he checked my spot out. He always did that as if he was looking for something.

"I brought you juice, cereal, ibuprofen, heating pads, and cashew milk." He lifted the bag. He remembered the things I clung to when I had cramps. I don't remember how we got on the subject, but I recall telling him. Why was he doing this to me? He was supposed to be a bad guy.

"Thank you."

I made my way over to him, took the bag to set it on my desk, and then draped my arms over his shoulders. He picked me up swiftly, and I wrapped my legs around his waist as we pecked one another a couple of times. He finally let me down, and I cut the light on to make a bowl of cereal. I ate it as we watched Kevin Hart, and when I was done, I took the medicine and put on a heating pad. My pains were worsening, so I eventually just lied down after cutting the light back off.

"You okay, baby?" he questioned as his big hand rubbed my back.

I was only wearing a nightshirt that I'd recently gotten from Victoria's Secret.

"Not really," I whined.

He cut the TV off, and then removed his shirt before getting into my small ass bed behind me. I didn't mind us having to be so close. I faced the wall since my bed was right up against it by the window, and he held me tightly from behind, just rubbing my lower stomach. The pressure from his strong hands along with the heating pad, helped to alleviate some of the pain. I closed my eyes only for a second as he continued to rub me. The feeling of being in his tattooed muscular arms was everything. The fact that he was here taking care of me instead of out partying was doing something to my soul.

Before I knew it, I'd fallen asleep.

Oden was making it really hard for me to love Brian.

# CHAPTER FIVE

# Shayne

"What do you think is going on?" Alanna quizzed as we sat in my living room, chilling.

"I know she's fucking him or at least about to," I sucked my teeth as I thought about Khyle's ass.

I hated that she actually thought I believed she was only friends with Oden. What she failed to realize was that everybody was watching him, and they'd told me how close the two had become. Well, they didn't tell me but I'd heard it through the grapevine. I loved my sister, but she was dead wrong for going after this nigga when I had my claws in him first. I would never do some shit like that to her.

"Are you still blocked?" Alanna pulled me from my thoughts.

"Yeah, that nigga isn't gonna unblock me. He probably can't take a minute for himself to think with Khyle all in his fucking grill."

"Well, I say just keep Pierce until you meet someone else. Or you could just work things out with Pierce. You guys have history and you love him."

"I don't love him anymore, I told you that." I refilled my wine glass.

"So there is nothing he can do to make you come back to him emotionally? When I first met you two, I was almost jealous of how in love you were."

"Alanna, shut the fuck up. I told you I don't love him anymore because he's changed! He's not the man I fell in love with, he's just a sad sap and I ain't with that."

"Try boosting his self-esteem. He loved playing football, Shayne, and now he will never play again. Can you imagine not being able to do something you love?"

"He can take his cry baby ass to the damn park and play catch if it's that serious. I don't want a nigga who is gonna bitch and moan when he doesn't get what he wants out of life. I want a nigga that's gonna get his money by any means necessary, like Oden."

"Pierce is getting money, just not a lot. He works two jobs just to pay all the bills while you audition for Vegas shows and drink wine."

This bitch was about to get a slap to the face in a minute if she kept defending Pierce. I understood where she was coming from, but she needed to realize that it was a wrap.

I wasn't one of those girls who helped their nigga when he was down. It may sound shady but it was the truth. I was the bitch that left your ass if you fell off, plain and simple. If you were on top, you had nothing to worry about, but once you fell from grace, I was chucking them deuces up. If niggas wanted a bitch who was gonna rock with them for better or worse, they'd better look elsewhere because Shayne didn't fit that criteria. I was there for the better and if shit got bad, I was moving on to a nigga who still had it good. I was worth way too much to be chasing behind a nigga who was on the down and out.

"He's getting money but the problem is that it ain't enough money. Look where the fuck we live! I mean it's cool, but I'm trying to be up in somebody's mansion, ringing bells and shit for service," I turned my lip up and we both chuckled in unison.

"That does sound nice. That was the shit I expected too," Alanna stared off, as she brushed her lips lightly with the rim of her wine glass.

"Girl, you really need to forget about Earl Jr. He did you wrong and here you are still missing his ass. I would've blown his damn brains out had he dissed me like that."

"You're still after Oden, and he dissed you too."

"He only dissed me because my little sister got in the fucking way. But there is no way Khyle is gonna leave Brian, and once Oden realizes that, he'll be back on the prowl. I'll be right there too."

"You know his homeboy is having a birthday party in a couple weeks at Palace. I met this girl who is working the door, and she said she could get us in."

"So," I shrugged.

"The club is only for grown folks, meaning over 21. We're 22, and Khyle is only 18, so she won't be there."

"He could sneak her in."

"But what if he doesn't?" she smirked, swishing her wine around the glass.

Suddenly, that same smile covered my face as I caught on to what she was saying. I would have Oden all to myself, with Khyle nowhere around. And even better, Oden would have some liquor in his system, making him a little nicer than usual. Yes, I was going to this party and getting my man back.

Alanna and I drank wine until the spaghetti was ready, and after scarfing that down, she went home. I hopped into the shower because that was when I did my best thinking. I couldn't wait until that party, and I would make sure that every move I made was perfect and calculated. I needed to prove to Oden that I was the better choice for him. Just thinking about being alone with his fine ass, and fucking him that night had me smiling with my eyes closed. Suddenly, I felt some hands wrap around my midsection, causing me to shriek and jump.

"Pierce, what the fuck!"

"Sorry, baby, chill," he chuckled, showing me his beautiful smile. Pierce was so fucking sexy to me, but he didn't have that aura or that bread that I was looking for.

"Get out, I wanna shower in peace," I nudged him, but he gripped my wrists and pinned them to my sides as he kissed on my neck.

Rolling my eyes, I cocked my head to the side to give him more access since that was my spot. I felt myself getting turned on, so I removed my wrists from his grip to massage the beast between his legs. Pierce was fine, and a monster in bed, I just wished he led the lifestyle that I was after.

Once I felt him hardening, I draped my arms over his shoulders, and he picked me up, bringing me down onto his dick. He bounced me slowly up and down as we kissed heavily under the showerhead. For a minute, my feelings for him were strong. As I looked him in the eyes while he stroked my pussy, I placed soft kisses on his full brown lips. Alanna was right, I did love him, but I couldn't be with him because I wasn't happy. Sometimes love wasn't enough, and in our case it wasn't.

"Mmm, uuuh, aaah!" I called out as I exploded on him.

He gripped my ass, tucked his bottom lip in, and pummeled my center until he filled me up with his seeds. I'd stopped taking my birth control when Oden and I started fucking around, so I had to be sure to get a Plan B in the morning.

"I love you, Shayne, and I promise I'm gonna make you happy," he whispered before covering my mouth with his.

It was too late for that shit.

# CHAPTER SIX

# Oden

Khyle told me her morning class was cancelled because her teacher's girlfriend had some kind of an appointment that she needed to go to. I didn't really give a fuck, but I wanted this opportunity to take her to breakfast at one of my favorite spots.

I knew I was playing with fire by spending all my fucking time with a girl who had a boyfriend. Deep down I knew she would be mine in the end, but when would the end come? I hadn't even pressed her about her nigga because I felt we weren't there yet. I didn't want her feeling pressured but then again, I wasn't about to sit around while she kept two niggas. Two could play that fucking game because there were a lot of females waiting for me to hit them up.

I frowned up at my thoughts, but that shit quickly faded when I saw her walking towards my car in some jean shorts and one of those tops that were cut off. Her stomach was out, and so were her sexy legs, which I loved. I paid close attention to her as she moved her long ass hair out of her face and continued over to me. I smiled when I saw she was wearing that platinum bracelet I'd given her.

"Good morning," she slid into the car and immediately got into my face for a kiss.

"Aye, come here." I gripped her neck lightly to stop her from pulling away, and kissed her nastily. I was sucking her lips and everything, getting my dick hard as a missile.

"Oden!" she giggled, moving away to fasten her seat belt.

I let my eyes roam her sexy frame for a little bit, as my teeth sank deep into my bottom lip. Everything about this girl was sexy, and I don't know why that nigga she had back home let her leave the state. But see, the difference between him and I was that Khyle was so into me that she could be over in New York and still not let another nigga get close to her. Emotionally, mentally, and physically, she was my girl; that nigga back home just had the title. I swear on everything I love he would never hit again. Watch.

I sped out of the parking lot headed towards The Egg and I, blasting my music the whole way. I let the windows down a little bit because I loved to see her hair blow. Occasionally, she would glance over at me and smile, while moving her hair out of her face.

We finally made it to our destination on Sahara Avenue, and went inside. I loved this place because the portions were pretty big and the food was of good quality. I hated them restaurants that loaded your plate up with bullshit. I'd rather you give me a little bit of food that's fire, than a gang of weak ass shit.

"Welcome to the Egg and I, my name is Ashley, and I will be your server today. Can I get you something to drink?" the waitress approached our table with a chipper attitude.

"Orange juice, please," Khyle smiled after I gestured for her to go first.

"Same, thank you."

Ashley nodded and walked off to give us time to look over the menu, but returned about 10 minutes later to take our order. Khyle got an omelet, and I got a scramble with a side of pancakes like always.

"This place better be good, Oden. If not, I'm gonna be mad that you wasted my time by bringing me here," she chuckled before wrapping her full lips around her straw.

"It is good, chill."

"I was kidding about wasting my time. My time will never be wasted when I spend it with you." She reached across to take my big ass hands into her small ones. We eventually intertwined our fingers, staring at our hands as if we were watching some sort of magic show. Hers were so pretty, even with them long ass nails attached. "I love being with you and I shouldn't."

"Here you go with this shit," I sighed, taking my hands from her.

"Don't get mad."

"Stop saying that shit. Don't nobody wanna hear you complain the whole damn time we're together, Khyle. I don't even know why you're with that nigga when you don't wanna be."

"I never said I didn't wanna be, I said I was conflicted."

"When was the last time you talked to him? When was the last time you initiated conversation with him? Whose bed have you been sleeping in every night? Whose dick been in ya mouth?"

"Oden!"

"I'm just wondering because you claim you love this nigga yet you all in my grill. You stay hitting me up, coming to my house, and opening your fucking legs whenever I ask you to, so I'm confused." I was hot.

"Wow," she folded her arms and shook her head as she stared off.

I hated to be rude but she had pissed me off with her stupid ass comment. I get that she had a man, but why couldn't she just dead that shit? Ray Charles could see that she didn't wanna be with the nigga. I wasn't about to keep sitting around waiting for her to make a fucking choice. If she wanted to just play house instead of actually building one, I was all for it.

We didn't say much to one another as we ate our food. I immediately requested the bill, paid the shit, and then we left. After I took her ass back to school for her midday class, I went to handle some shit with the chop shops to make sure their progress was up to par. I had other shit to be worried about, and Khyle wasn't about to be one of them.

✱✱✱

I'd been handling business all day with the car ring. There was an event tonight at some mansion, and they were using a valet service. Every expensive car from Bentleys to Maseratis were gonna be parked in that shit. I would have never known about the party, but it pays to have friends in high places. A nigga attending the shit put me up on game about it, and had I not known him for a cool minute, I wouldn't have trusted him. He was too smart to pull some dumb shit like setting me up though. He knew I had a lot of muthafuckas in law enforcement in my pocket, so if he tried to go that route, it would only end badly for his ass, not me.

My hair was still a little damp from the shower I'd just gotten out of, so instead of putting a t-shirt on, I just used a shirt to suck up some of that water. Walking to my living room in just boxers, sweats, and socks, I grabbed a beer from my fridge and sat in front of the TV. I didn't wanna think about shit right now, but chilling, and my boy's birthday party in a couple weeks. As I put the beer to my lips, I heard someone at my door.

"The fuck," I scoffed, getting up. I grabbed my .45 from the coffee table drawer, and looked through the peephole to see the top of Khyle's head. "What?" I cracked the door, setting my pistol down on the end table by it. I discreetly covered it.

"Can I come in?"

"For what?"

"To be with you."

"Fuck you wanna be with me for, baby girl? Go FaceTime with your nigga since you love his bitch ass so much. You feel guilty when you're with me, so just stop trying."

She stared up into my face as tears welled up in her eyes. I'd never seen this girl cry ever in life. I wasn't even being that mean to her sensitive ass. She wiped her tears, and pushed her hair behind her ears without saying anything. I should've slammed the door in her face but I was frozen. Finally, she turned around to leave, and after sighing heavily, I stepped out to grab her little ass and pull her inside. I closed the front door and gripped her pretty face as I backed her into it.

"When you're with me, I don't wanna hear about how bad it feels. I don't wanna hear about your nigga either. And I'm gonna tell you right now, baby, as long as you're with him, I am not gonna stay focused on only you."

"What does that mean?" she sniffled.

"I'm gonna do me. I'll make time for you because I'm feeling you, but don't be surprised if you see me with another bitch or if you hear about it."

She shoved me backwards, forcing me to let go of her face. I was being honest with her ass. I wasn't no fucking sucker and she was gonna stop playing me like I was one.

"So you're gonna fuck other bitches."

"If I want to." I sat down on my couch.

"What if Brian and I break up?"

"Then we'll talk."

There was silence for a few moments, and then she suddenly appeared in my view. She straddled my lap, and my hands immediately went up her dress. I stood to my feet, carrying her to my bedroom before laying her on the bed.

"When I'm with you, I only want you thinking about me," she said in a low tone as I pulled on her panties.

"You don't even have to say that, Khyle," I whispered back.

After I got her naked, I stepped out of my clothing and climbed into the bed with her. As soon as I got on top, I took her nipple into my mouth, sucking hungrily. I switched back and forth between her breasts, while toying with her clit as she cooed. Her body was so soft and smelled so fucking good. I loved that sweet coconut shit she wore. I forced my way into her snug hole, making us both moan softly into one another's mouths as we kissed. I wound my hips into her for a few until she came, and then propped myself up a little bit so that I could look down into her face.

"I wanna be with you, Oden," she whimpered.

"I know." I sucked on her neck as I pumped into her roughly, and pulled out slowly. "I know you do."

"Ju-just give me time."

Wanting her to be quiet about that shit, I gripped her neck with my right hand and began fucking the shit out of her, making her cry out. Pressing my lips against hers, I nibbled and sucked on her full lips as she hollered and came. You could hear the sound of me plunging into her feverishly, which was turning me on like crazy. I loved seeing her beautiful face all balled up as she cried out for mercy. I knew I was about to cum soon, so I pulled out and yanked her up so she could suck me off.

Khyle wasn't a virgin, but she hadn't been turned out either. I knew that she'd only been with that fuck nigga from California, who had never even made her cum.

"Fuck," I grumbled after spilling my seeds into her mouth.

After taking it down, she got out of the bed to go the bathroom and I followed her. We both wet some towels with warm water and soap, before cleaning ourselves. She brushed her teeth, and then we washed our hands before returning to the bedroom. We laid down in the bed together, and I turned my back to her, not intentionally.

"Oden," she whispered, tugging on my shoulder.

Already knowing what she wanted, I turned to face her, kissed her, and then turned her over so that I could cuddle her bratty ass from behind. We stayed like that the whole night, no matter how hot it got. She made sure to hold my hand as it rested on the front of her body, so that I wouldn't be able to pull back. This girl was fucking with my head.

# CHAPTER SIX

*A week and a half later...*

*I* slid my panties up slowly because I was still sore from last night. Oden showed no mercy on me in the bedroom, in the dining room, and on the living room floor. We'd been fucking like animals in heat for the past week or so. I was trying to stay in his face 24/7 because I didn't want him to have time for other girls. I knew he could still do it to them while I was in class, the library, and any other time I was away from him, but I was gonna do my best to prevent that.

I was excited about today because it was Friday and I didn't have class on Fridays. I planned to spend all day with Oden, which had me smiling for no reason, as I slipped on my tube dress. As I spread lotion all over my body, I wondered what we would do today. Every day that we spent together was different, but it usually ended the same: in bed. I felt bad at first because of Brian, but now it'd become so normal that I barely thought about him or the guilt. Terrible I know, but life was short. And if I ever did feel a little bad, I would just tell myself he was hanging with Jacqueline behind my back.

"Are you okay?" Tasmine frowned as she watched some video on her laptop.

"Why did you ask me that?"

"Because you're walking like you're bowlegged or something," she giggled. "You and Oden are getting it in I see. I practically have a room to myself."

"You miss me?"

"Maybe a little," she smiled.

"What's up with you and Tony? You told me he said you guys would hang out, so what's the hold up? Or have I missed something?"

"He hasn't hit me up and I'm not about to text him. I've done most of the damn work already, and I'm somewhat over the hype."

"Bitch, yeah right." We chuckled in unison.

My phone started ringing in my hand, and I answered it without looking because I already knew it was probably Oden. I texted him and told him to call me before I'd gotten into the shower. The voice that came through wasn't his however, and it caught me off guard.

"About time you answer, I haven't talked to you in a whole 24 hours, baby," Brian smiled into the phone.

"I'm sorry, baby. I've been a little busy, you know with school and stuff. You were right about six classes being a bit much."

"Of course I was right, I'm always right." I just nodded as if he could see me, and there was silence on the phone. "I miss you, Khyle."

"I miss you too. I wish I could see you right now, I would kiss you all over your handsome face," I laughed, laying it on thick. I was trying to compensate for the guilt I felt for not really missing him at all.

"Well, why don't you come downstairs to the lobby and do that then."

"Huh?"

"I'm here in Vegas, Khyle. I came here to surprise you, baby, now come down here and kiss me like you said you would."

"Umm, yeah, okay, one second."

I hung up the phone, and when I looked over at Tasmine, she was already staring at me. I slid my feet into my Rihanna slides, and then grabbed my student ID and purse. I didn't know what the hell I was gonna do having Brian here when I was supposed to spend the day with Oden. Furthermore, I didn't wanna be cooped up with Brian, I wanted to hang out with my boo. Pouting, I walked towards the door as if my execution would happen on the other side.

"Who was that?" Tasmine questioned.

"Brian." Her eyes bucked and her eyebrows raised to her hairline. "Same thing I said."

"Good luck."

I made my way downstairs, and as I got closer to the exit of the lobby, I spotted Brian standing there with his tall ass. He had a duffle bag hanging from his shoulder, and he was dressed in jeans and a polo. He looked handsome, and a part of me did actually miss him now that I was looking at him. I spotted some girls staring at him, admiring his tall skinny frame, so I quickly made my way over to him. We engaged in a passionate kiss, and then pulled away to look into one another's eyes.

"Let's take your bag up, and then we can go have breakfast."

"I can eat what I want in the room." He grabbed my ass.

"No, Brian," I chuckled. "My roommate is in there, remember?" Plus, I was sore as fuck from last night, and in no position to spread my legs apart.

"You good?" he touched my lower back. I was walking a little funny thanks to Oden.

"I'm great."

We got onto the elevator and rode it up to my room. I wasn't even sure if he was allowed to stay in here with me, but I was gonna try. College was more laidback than I thought it would be as far as the residential life. I thought I would have some person breathing down my neck about how late I stayed out, and how long I had company over, but it was nothing like that. I was literally just on my own, living in a huge building as if it were my apartment. I loved that freedom.

"This is my room," I smiled over my shoulder at Brian as I used my key card to get in. "And this is Tasmine. Tasmine, this is my boyfriend, Brian."

"Oh," she moved her computer from her lap and got down off of her bed. "Nice to meet you, Brian. Khyle talks about you all the time," she lied for me, making me grin.

"She better." He pulled me close and kissed my temple.

I was about to speak but there was a knock at the door, and when

I answered it, Bella switched into the room like the ray of sunshine that she was.

"So the party tonight, we need to leave around 9:30 if we wanna pregame and still get there before it's too crowded. You know these damn house parties get cluttered…" She turned to see Brian, and let her sentence trail off. "Bella." She reached her hand out.

"Brian, I'm Khyle's boyfriend."

"Oh! Right! Well, nice to meet you." When he turned his back to her, she bucked her eyes at me with her crazy self, making me laugh.

"Well, come on Brian, let's go out." I wanted to get him away from the school because I felt like we'd be safer. In other words, I felt it'd be less likely that we'd run into Oden, Anton, or even Truman if we weren't around.

"Aight, nice meeting y'all," Brian said as I pushed him out of the room lightly. When I looked back at Bella and Tasmine, they were shaking their heads and smiling.

***

Brian and I went to have breakfast at some place Siri found for us, and it was pretty good. It reminded me a lot of the place Oden had taken me to eat, and maybe that's why I couldn't stop thinking about him. All while Brian talked to me about his pre-med classes, I zoned out thinking about my time with Oden, especially the sex. The way we made eye contact as he ate me out… I just loved his sex game.

After breakfast, Brian and I walked the strip for as long as we could since it was hot as hell outside and we were close to fainting. We went into the fashion mall, which was located in the middle of the strip, and filled with all kinds of expensive ass stores. My friends and I only came here when we planned to really shop, and during the week because on the weekends, it was too much of a hassle to come here if you didn't stay in one of the hotels on the strip.

"Let's get some matching shoes, babe," Brian pointed into the Foot Locker we were passing.

"Fine," I chuckled.

He leaned down to kiss my lips as we turned to go into the store. I was actually a little happy that he was here now. Him coming over reminded me of how much fun we had together and why I made him my boyfriend in the first place. I did love Brian, and I wasn't ready to let him go yet. Maybe I didn't wanna be with Oden at all. I was starting to think he was just something for me to do since I didn't have Brian here. Yeah, I thought about him all throughout our breakfast, but now that I was around Brian more, Oden crossed my mind less. Not to mention he never called me like I'd asked him to.

We looked at all the shoes that caught our interest and finally decided on some Nike Huaraches; those were our favorite shoes. As we were waiting for the associate to bring our sizes out, we sat down on the bench holding hands. I laid my head on his shoulder, and then he craned his neck around to kiss me passionately. That made me smile and feel all warm inside.

When Brian pulled away from my lips to face forward again, my heart dropped. Oden, Anton, and Truman walked into the store laughing and talking. There were like five girls with them, but they all seemed to be friends, or at least that's what I wanted to think. Oden finally spotted me, and his beautiful smile faded instantaneously as he walked past me, low-key mugging. He looked so damn bomb, and all the thoughts I had before had been completely erased.

Me not wanting him anymore was a temporary feeling because I wasn't in his presence, but now that I had him and Brian here together in a sense, it was obvious whom my heart beat for. I loved Brian, but he didn't make me feel the way Oden did, and I didn't even love Oden. I could only imagine how I would feel if I actually fell in love with him. My like for Oden was stronger than my love for Brian somehow.

"Here we are," the associate walked out carrying the two boxes of shoes.

Brian and I tried them on and when I went to look into the mirror, he came behind me in his pair to hug me. Leaning my head back onto his chest, I spotted Oden through the mirror, conversing with his crew of people and no longer paying attention to me.

We took the sneakers off and then got in line so that Brian could pay for them. Oden, Anton, Truman, and the girls got in line behind us, and I couldn't help but to pretend as if I was looking off to the side so that I could see him. The way he licked his lips, and then nibbled on the bottom one while running his hand over his wild curly hair had me hot. He was wearing one of those sleeveless t-shirts that had his muscular arms exposed, which were covered in tattoos. His cologne danced around in my nose as I rushed the cashier along in my head. In a minute, I was gonna jump on him and kiss him all over his sexy face.

"Have a great day," the cashier smiled at us as she handed Brian the bag. When we turned around, I avoided eye contact with him, but

I don't even think he was looking at me. What a fucking day.

***

My friends were already at the party, and I couldn't wait to see them. I really didn't want to come but Brian wanted to have some fun. I can't remember the last time he and I partied together; I'm sure it was when we were in high school. I planned to hopefully get some drinks in my system and just have a good time with my man. Liquor would also help keep Oden off of my mind. Ever since we left the mall, I'd been thinking about him, checking my phone to see if he'd hit me up and everything. Of course he hadn't.

"Prolly" by Sevyn Streeter played loudly over the house as Brian and I entered. It was dark, but red, purple, blue, and yellow lights were flashing everywhere as people danced wildly. The wood flooring was already sticky from people spilling drinks and shit too. I rolled my eyes when my stiletto got stuck to the floor.

Grabbing Brian's hand, I led him to the middle and began dancing on him, while scanning the crowd for Bella, Tasmine, or Perry. I wanted to get a drink from whatever they pregamed with, because we didn't trust the shit here unless it was beer. I didn't even drink beer until I moved here.

For the next 15 minutes as Brian and I danced, I hadn't spotted my friends, but I was tired from shaking my ass and needed to sit down.

"So this is how they do it out here, huh?" Brian kissed my arm, since I was sitting in his lap on a couch by the dance floor.

"Pretty much."

I bobbed my head to YG, and as if it were fate, I looked towards the door to see Oden, Anton, and Truman walking in. I watched them as they went into the den area, which had a pool table, some speakers for the music, and people dancing just as hard. I draped my arm around Brian, and then dipped my tongue into his mouth, hoping the kiss would take me somewhere else but it didn't.

I sat there dancing in Brian's lap for about 30 minutes, kissing him here and there, until I watched Oden go upstairs.

"I have to pee, Brian."

Before he even responded, I got up to catch up to Oden. I followed him up the stairs, and down a hall, then watched him walk into a bedroom. If he thought he was about to smash some hoe up in here, he had me fucked up. I rushed down the hallway, bumping two girls who were hanging all over some guy, clearly about to give him the night of his life. I quietly entered the bedroom, and saw someone was in the bathroom, because I could see the light shining through the cracks of the door. I closed the bedroom door to drown out Wale's "PYT", and barged into the bathroom, hoping to ruin Oden's fuck session.

"Damn, baby, what the fuck!" he frowned, shaking his dick after he peed. He kept his sexy screw face on as he buckled himself and washed his hands.

"Sorry," I came in, closing the door behind me.

"Fuck you want, Khyle?" He dried his hands. He looked so fucking good in his hood attire with that beautiful hair all over his head. His low ass eyes screamed that he was high as fuck. He was so blowed that when he ran his hand over his full lips, his eyes were closed. "What's up?" he grinned. God he was beautiful.

"You didn't call me this morning."

"That's what you followed me up here for? Damn, I've only been here for like 30 minutes and you're already on my trail?"

I hated when he acted like I was some thirsty hoe.

"Don't treat me like I'm some groupie that you're tired of."

"I'm treating you like a girl who can't fucking make up her mind. I want you but you want that nigga, so excuse me if I'm confused on why you stay in my damn face," he shrugged, pursing his lips. Everything he did was sexy.

"Oden," I moved closer to him, pressing my body into his. Despite being high as a kite, he smelled so fucking good, like sandalwood and… just goodness. The scent was manly but intoxicating.

I caressed the side of his face as he stared down at me, licking his lips. I pecked him deeply, and in a hot second, we were tonguing it up. His hand went up under my dress, and before I could say anything, he ripped my panties off. Now how the fuck was I gonna explain to Brian why I had no panties on? Lifting me up, he sat me on the sink and we resumed kissing while he released himself. He raised me slightly to place a towel under me, and I knew whoever owned the place was gonna be pissed about their decorative towel getting messed up.

"Uuuh," I whimpered as soon as he entered me. It hurt so bad, but every time he pushed into me I got wetter.

"Pussy feels brand new, baby. You better not be letting him fuck."

I just shook my head 'no' in response since I was in too much pain. The tops of my thighbones were sore from him doing me last night, and his size was adding to that pain right now.

Our tongues danced continuously as he pounded me gently with his long, thick dick, getting me used to his size again. I had my hands all in his hair, pressing his face more into mine. I was sure we couldn't kiss any harder, but I was gonna try. He placed one of my legs on his shoulders, leaned me back so he could look into my eyes, and then went in. We were both moaning as if we were being murdered, and I thanked God the music over the party was so loud.

"Who does this pussy belong to, Khyle?" he groaned, staring down into my eyes with a lustful gaze.

I could barely speak because every time I tried he rammed my spot. I came hard, but that didn't slow up his pace whatsoever; he was murdering my center.

"Tell me, Khyle," he demanded, sinking his teeth into his bottom lip as he held me by my waist, keeping eye contact with me.

"Yo-yours, Oden," I whimpered, sounding like I was about to cry as my body quivered from another orgasm.

"Turn over."

I got down and bent over the sink to face the mirror. We both trembled when he entered me, and I had to grip the sides of the sink. He gripped my neck from behind, and craned his neck around to suck my lips. Once he stopped, we kept eye contact in the mirror.

"Fuck," he finally let out his warning that he was near his peak.

"Mmm," I tucked my lips, attempting to muffle my screams as he beat it up.

Suddenly, we both yelled out, exploding.

"I was supposed to pull out but that shit was too good, baby," he panted.

"I'll take care of it," I replied as he slid out of me.

We both reached for my torn lace panties, but Oden got to them first, stuffing them into his pocket with a grin. I just chuckled at him. We cleaned ourselves up before leaving the bathroom and bedroom, and went our separate ways. When Brian and I got back to the dorm, I went right to the shower so he wouldn't question me being panty-less. I also had to fake my period to keep him from trying to fuck.

Even though tonight's events had taken place, I still didn't know where Oden and I stood. But I guess that was my fault.

# CHAPTER SIX

*The next night...*

Alanna, some bitch she became buddies with named Marisol, and I were on our way to Palace nightclub for Truman's birthday party. We were all dressed to impress, but I was the only one leaving with Oden. I didn't care what these hoes did or whom they did it to, as long as it wasn't with him.

Alanna dipped through the streets as I spread my lipstick over my lips, using the visor mirror. The three of us sang along to "Set the Roof" by Rae Sremmurd, getting in the mood to party. I hadn't felt this good in a long time, and I think it was because I knew what was gonna happen. I wouldn't mess up this time; I would convince Oden he was after the wrong sister. And the fact that I knew Brian was out here helped me out a lot. I was sure Khyle was chilling with him, and I was even more sure that Oden wasn't happy about that.

We finally pulled up, but Alanna had to park all the way in the back. Even though Palace wasn't on the strip, it stayed crowded as fuck. Niggas would much rather come here than go to one of the hotel clubs on Las Vegas Boulevard. Palace was no easier to get into though, and it was just as expensive if you were a nigga or got there too late. Tonight, we planned to get in for free, however, and also get access to Oden's VIP since Alanna said she knew the girl working the door. If it didn't pan out, I might whoop Alanna's ass. There was a lot riding on me getting inside and getting close to Oden.

"Let's go, bitches!" the chick Marisol yelled, making me roll my eyes.

I didn't like girls like her. She was too boisterous, ghetto, and just out there. I always kept it classy, and didn't say too much.

Marisol was very pretty, and reminded me of those Instagram models. She looked Spanish, but she could've been mixed with black too, I didn't know. I wasn't sure where Alanna found her, but after tonight she needed to take her ass back. She was too beautiful and too loud, and I didn't like hanging with bitches that might possibly overshadow me. If I wanted that I would hang with Khyle more.

"How much is it gonna be if the girl can't slip us in?" I asked as we neared the front.

There were two separate lines on each side, one full of guys and one full of bitches in damn near lingerie. "No Shopping" by French Montana was blasting from inside, and you could see how live everyone was whenever someone walked in or out of the huge wooden double doors. I loved the design of this place because it looked like a for real kingdom. It stood out when you drove by it, even in the daytime when it's extravagant lights were off. Oden was smart making this not only a nightclub but a daytime club too, which mainly was a huge ass pool party on the rooftop.

"Hey, is Jenna around?" Alanna quizzed the bouncer as we walked up the red carpet covering the steps.

"Uh! Uh!" some bitch hollered because we hadn't gotten in line.

"One second," the bouncer responded to Alanna, and said something into his mouthpiece. I just continued to scan the crowd, wondering how all of these people were gonna fit into the club, when it was clearly packed already from what I saw.

"Hey, Alanna!" Jenna came from inside of the club in her all black work attire and hugged Alanna. "Are these your two guests?" she eyed Marisol and I as she pulled three gold flaked wristbands from this black bag hanging from her wrist.

"Yes, this is Shayne and Marisol."

"Hello, ladies. So the gold wristband means that you have a VIP area, which includes bottles, and your first three cocktail drinks will be free." She placed the bands on our wrists and led us inside.

People were dancing closely on one another to "LUV" by Tory Lanez. The DJ switched to "Say It" by him, and shit really got nasty, making it harder for Jenna to get us through. We finally were able to get up the winding staircase, which was gold flaked like our wristbands. I hadn't paid much attention to the detail of the club the last time I came, but this shit was beautiful. I had tunnel vision the previous night, but I was happy that I was able to take it all in this go round. The VIP area was even nicer, with couches covered in red velvet, and gold tables that held the liquor, juice, ice and glasses. I for real felt like I was in a palace. The name of this place fit so perfectly. There were even humungous paintings on the walls of the club of African kings and queens.

"Have a good time, ladies, and let me know if you need anything. Just tell the bouncer to ring me," Jenna smiled as we sat down, preparing our glasses for the free liquor. I nudged Alanna so she could do what I'd asked.

"Oh, Jenna, where is Oden?" Alanna questioned.

"The owner?" her eyebrows went up, and Alanna nodded.

"He's in his designated VIP." She pointed across and upward. "It's a glassed VIP. He only chilled in the regular VIP for the grand opening."

"Is there a way we can get up there?"

"I can tell him I have some pretty girls that want to come up and say hi. He, Anton, and Truman usually allow that if the ladies are good looking," she smiled and walked off.

"Don't say our names!" I yelled after her and she nodded without turning around.

"So you know Oden or something?" Marisol leaned forward so that she could see me, since Alanna was in the middle of us.

"Yes, we talk."

"If y'all talk then why do we need that girl Jenna? Can't you just text him or something?"

"No, I can't. He's a busy man and if I rely on a text we may not even get over there for hours. Just let me handle this okay, sweetie."

"No need to get upset, it was just a question." She bucked her eyes like I was crazy and then looked at Alanna as if she were supposed to silently agree.

We danced quietly in our seats while nursing our drinks, and finally Jenna was coming back wearing a smile; that must have meant good news.

"He said I can bring you," Jenna waved us to follow her.

Oddly, she headed towards the back of our section instead of back down the stairs. We trailed her to the back, and then walked through a bright red door. Behind the red door was a gold-flaked staircase with gold rails that had plush red carpet on the steps. A strong but sweet smell of lavender invaded my nostrils as the four of us ascended the stairs. Once at the top, we were met with a big glass door, and I could see my baby inside it looking drunk and high off of his ass. There were about 20 bitches in there along with Anton and Truman, and I was not feeling that. I wasn't in the mood to do too much competing.

"Gentlemen," Jenna addressed the VIP box, attempting to be louder than the club's music. The guys looked her way, except for Truman who was getting danced on by some big booty bitch. "These are the ladies," she gestured for us to walk in.

I kept my eyes on Oden, and thankfully his eyes were on me, well my breasts.

"That's Oden, huh?" Marisol nibbled on her bottom lip. She started towards him, but I gripped her arm tightly and shook my head 'no'. "Y'all *talk*, that don't mean he's your man." She snatched from me and continued over.

Alanna just shrugged at me and put her straw to her lips. She had a little crush on Truman, but she wasn't gonna act on it because her dumb ass was still waiting on Earl Jr., her ex, to come back. Dummy, I swear.

I watched Marisol smile all in Oden's face before sitting next to him, draping her leg over his. She didn't even care that some other bitch was already in his lap. The girl did though, because she stood up abruptly, mugging Marisol who was too busy smiling at Oden. If she was gonna play dirty, then so was I, which is why I made my way over to him, lifted his chin, and kissed his cheek. His eyelids were so low, that I knew he'd smoked a lot of marijuana.

"Fuck is your name? I know you," he grinned, embarrassing the fuck out of me in front of Marisol.

"Shayne, baby, remember?"

He squinted his eyes at me, and then just looked away. Marisol was forward as fuck, rubbing all over his crotch while kissing his neck. I swear I wanted to whoop this bitch's ass, but I wasn't that type of girl. Like I said before, I was classy.

"So Oden—" My sentence was cut short when Marisol straddled his lap, not caring that she was wearing a dress.

I watched Oden's hand go between her legs, and heard a moan escape her lips while he kissed on her neck. I specifically told this bitch I was here for him and she still went after him. She was just like Khyle. I glanced around because I felt eyes on me, and saw it was Alanna's ass. She had the nerve to shrug at me like it wasn't her fault that this bitch was all in my nigga's face. I didn't want to sit there pouting, so I leaned over and began kissing his neck while he touched and kissed on her.

Suddenly, he stopped, and moved her to the side.

"Come on y'all." He stood to his feet, and gripped both of our hands before leading us out of the glass box that overlooked the club.

We walked back down the stairs, and went through another door that was like a red room at a strip club but way fancier. There was a bed on the far right, that was fit for a king. These niggas took the royalty theme seriously. He led us both to the bed, and I swear he looked even sexier under the red light. I didn't wanna sleep with him tonight because I was trying to approach him differently, but Marisol had ruined that. I could either compete with her and just do it, or leave.

I sat on the bed contemplating, as I watched them strip one another's clothes off. They acted like they didn't even know I was fucking here. Once Marisol was naked and Oden was in his boxers, he yanked me up, pushed Marisol onto the bed as she giggled, and then turned me around to unzip my dress. I couldn't find the words to tell him that I was gonna leave so that he'd respect me, so I stood there and let my dress fall to my ankles, exposing my lace bra and panties.

"Damn," he mumbled as he looked from me to Marisol. "Y'all are sexy as fuck," he slurred, due to being cross-faded. I'd never met a man who looked fine drunk or sober, but Oden definitely did, especially when he gave us that lazy grin.

He began kissing on the nape of my neck as he unhooked my bra, and when he dropped down to push my panties to my ankles, I grabbed my iPhone. Once he stood to his feet and groped my breasts from behind, I took a selfie just for my little sister, before locking my phone. Marisol saw what I did, and just shook her head with a smirk.

Oden threw me onto the bed next to Marisol, and once he pushed his boxers down, that bitch had her mouth on his dick like he had candy on it. Once she sucked him off for a minute, I did the same, and we had one hell of a night together. So much so, that he even took us back to his crib to continue the festivities. I guess Marisol wasn't so bad after all.

# CHAPTER SIX

# Jasmine

***The next afternoon…***

"I'm baaccck!" Khyle sang as she came back into the room.

She'd rode in an Uber with Brian to take him to the airport. Her ass used me, making me stay in the room with them so that he wouldn't try to have sex. I don't know why she didn't just break up with his ass, but that was none of my business so I wouldn't give my input unless she asked for it.

"Are you relieved?" I sat up on my bed.

I was bored out of my mind like always on Sundays, because nothing really went down. I mean, there were the occasional kickbacks and shit, but they didn't really pop unless the right person was throwing it.

"Yes, I am, but then I still have that queasy feeling in my stomach."

"Why?"

"Because I don't know if Oden is still fucking with me or not. I mean, yeah, we had sex in the bathroom at that party on Friday, but we haven't talked to one another since."

"You texted him?"

"No, but I think I will. I wanna wait until I figure some stuff out though because I feel like I'm slowly becoming just his fuck buddy and nothing else." She looked down at her phone for a bit, and I could see her facial expression change.

"What's wrong?"

She didn't say anything, she just walked her phone over to me, with a picture on the screen. It displayed her sister, and it appeared to be Oden standing behind her, sucking her shoulder. You couldn't see his face because of all that curly hair, but I knew that fro anywhere, so I know Khyle did.

"So he's back fucking with her."

"Why would she send that to you?"

"Because she's a grimy bitch. That nigga has turned us against each other. I'm not much better because I still pursued him despite her telling me she liked him, but this is wrong on his part. I expect this from Shayne now that we aren't really rocking with one another, but for him to sleep with her… he's really lost me."

I watched her as she paced back and forth, clutching her iPhone in her hands tightly.

"Khyle, just break up with Brian and be with Oden. I'm tired of hearing about your dilemma that ain't really a damn dilemma. The only reason you don't wanna break up with Brian is because you trust him and you think Oden may fuck you over. But you need to take the risk, or cut Oden loose and stick with Brian."

She looked to me, stared, and then nodded.

"That's why I like you, Tas," she smiled and so did I.

My phone chimed, and I was gonna ignore it because I'd given this dude my number on Friday and the nigga was a bugaboo. I would literally tell him I was going to sleep, and he still wouldn't stop trying to talk. Also, he would randomly FaceTime me out of nowhere. I don't know about other people, but you need to get my permission through text to FaceTime me.

When I checked my lock screen, I saw Anton's name on it, which sped up my heart rate immediately. Picking my phone up, I unlocked it to see what his lying ass had to say. He was supposed to take me out like three weeks ago, and the nigga never called, texted, or anything. I was over chasing him because frankly, he should be doing that.

*Tony: Busy tonight?*

*Me: Maybe, why?*

*Tony: Wanted to see if you'd like to come over and chill.*

*Me: Nah, I don't chill. You wanna see me, take me out on a date.*

I chuckled at myself. I usually would've been jumping for joy, but since he in a way stood me up, I was gonna make him work for it. Plus, Khyle and Bella told me niggas like him didn't like girls that were too eager, and since I'd never had a man, I needed to listen. I mean, I had my older sister to guide me, but like Shayne, she was a bit promiscuous and did shit that I never saw myself getting into.

*Tony: Lmao. Damn, okay. You wanna go eat somewhere?*

*Me: That's fine, surprise me.*

*Tony: Be ready by 7:30. You stay in Dayton Hall right?*

*Me: Yep.*

*Tony: K. See you later baby girl.*

I decided not to reply to keep him begging for more in a sense.

I couldn't wait for Khyle to get out of the shower, because as soon as she did, her, Bella and I were going to the nail shop so I could tell them about tonight. I needed all the advice I could get.

***

Anton would be here in just 30 minutes, and I was still trying to decide if I should wear a dress, or jeans and a cute top. I didn't want to be too dressed up, and we go to like a diner or some shit. But then I wanted to look good, show his ass what he's missing by not blowing up my phone like young thirsty that I met on Friday.

"I say do the jeans and a fancy top. You'll still look sexy, and if it's a cheap spot, which I doubt, you won't look overdressed," Bella chimed in, sitting on Khyle's bed.

"True. The shirt is a crop top so you'll be showing him some skin, but won't overdo it," Khyle agreed with Bella.

I quickly changed after spreading lotion all over my body. The three of us listened to music as if we were all going out together, and by the time I was done bumping the ends of my hair, my phone was jumping. I checked my texts and smiled when I saw Anton's name. A part of me thought he might stand me up again, so I was relieved to see he'd made good on his word this time.

"How do I look?" I placed my hand on my hip and cocked my head playfully as if I were trying to be seductive.

"Cute, yet sexy," Bella nodded.

"Yeah, but not too sexy to where he thinks he's gonna smash tonight," Khyle winked.

"Thanks. Goodnight, ladies."

"Don't stay out too late, you have class at 11am!"

I ignored Khyle and continued down the hall until I made it to the elevator. While inside, I checked myself out about one hundred times, making sure I looked good as hell. My skinny jeans were tight enough to show that I had a nice ass, but it didn't look like I was trying too hard. My stomach was showing since I had on a crop top, but it wasn't in a skanky way. Stepping off of the elevator, I made my way towards the front of Dayton where most visitors waited, and since no one was down here, Anton was easy to spot. It's not like I couldn't spot him in the crowd of one million people though.

"Damn," he mumbled as he stood to his feet.

He looked so good in his red polo, with a camel colored blazer layered on top of it. His jeans were a dark blue, and his shoes were some kind of sneakers that looked expensive, and were a red and camel color like his upper attire. He smelled so good, that I had to ask what the hell he was wearing exactly.

"What scent is your cologne?"

"Maison Margiela," he replied, tugging on my wrist to pull me in for a hug.

"Ah!" I shrieked when he gripped my ass in his hands.

"I'm sorry, I had to. I've been thinking about that shit since we talked in the student union," he laughed, and it was too adorable to stay mad at him.

We left out of my dorm complex, and I saw he parked his car right in front of it, which was something you couldn't do. I wasn't surprised by his ass at all though. He seemed like the type of nigga to not follow rules, and then get upset when someone tried to reprimand him for it.

Opening the door for me, he admired my frame from head to toe as I slid into his nice ass red and gold Lamborghini. I didn't know shit about expensive cars, but when I saw him whipping this out the parking lot one day, I had to snap a picture and ask someone more familiar.

"This is nice. I see tan, gold, and red are some of your favorite colors," I said to him once he got in on the driver's side.

"Very observant, I like that."

"Thanks, I try. I can't stand oblivious people." I shook my head as he drove out of the school, pulling onto the street.

"Same, especially in my line of work. I need to be around muthafuckas who are alert at all fucking times, because if not, shit can go left."

"You mean like with the club and the liquor line?" I looked to the side of his handsome chocolate face. He could be a model for real.

He paused for a moment, then smiled while still staring at the road ahead.

"Yep, exactly." He looked to me for a quick second and then back to the street.

The road of Las Vegas Boulevard was clear, so he was able to peel down it and really show me what his car could do. I was kind of scared, but it was also hella cool to see him arrive at what I assume was our destination, in two and a half minutes flat. My school wasn't far from the strip, or the Venetian hotel, which is where we'd arrived, but still that was the quickest I'd seen anyone get somewhere.

"You ever stayed in this hotel?" he asked as he pulled up to the valet attendant.

"No, but I've heard it's nice and that a lot of celebrities stay here."

"Yeah, it is very nice. It's pretty expensive but I think it's worth it, especially if you're able to get a suite and not just a regular hotel room."

He got out of the car before I could respond, taking the ticket from the attendant. He then came around to get the door for me, and helped me out, making sure to look at my ass. Walking inside of the hotel, my jaw hit the fucking floor. This place was beautiful with clean ass marble floors, and tall ass pillars. I felt like I was in a Greek castle of some sort.

"This is beautiful, Tony."

"It is."

After walking around the hotel, we ended up on the casino floor. One of the attendants were trying to press me for ID, and Anton almost whooped his ass so I had to step in and explain that we were just going to dinner at the restaurant we were standing right in fucking front of named AquaKnox. I hadn't been in Vegas that long, but I learned that if you were under 21, you couldn't do so much as put your big toe on the casino floor without them having a fucking fit.

The attendant eased up, not because of my explanation but because I think he realized Anton was two seconds from breaking his face. It was obvious he was a hot head, so I made a mental note on that. I'd never dealt with a guy who was a thug, then again, I'd never had a man to compare him to. I just hoped he wasn't too much for a girl like me who was a virgin to relationships. I'd had sex before, but never had a boyfriend. I wasn't exactly happy about that.

"This is nice," I nodded.

They just didn't have all this extravagant ass shit over in Kentucky, so excuse me if my mind is a little blown by this hotel and its amenities.

"They have good ass food too," he nodded.

The waitress didn't take long to come at all, so we put in our drink order and then Anton ordered us the filet mignon since I said I wanted what he thought was best. He got it medium well, and although I preferred well done, I was up to trying new things.

"So how is it that you can afford so much when the liquor line just came out, and so did the club?" I questioned.

I didn't want to seem too forward, but I had to know. When I came to visit he had a Maserati, and that was in the summer before he and Oden even had the club or the drink. I had a love for numbers, so in my mind shit wasn't adding up.

He swished his drink around in its glass for a second as his strong jaw tightened. He was the handsomest man I'd ever seen, and I wished we had niggas like him back in Louisville.

"I think that I will tell you more about my finances when I get to know you better. I have to know that I can trust a person before I go into any detail about my life, Tasmine. If this goes any further, then I will be more than willing to open up, but for now that's gonna stay a secret." He spoke with so much authority, that even though he low-key told me off, I was turned on.

"Understandable."

"What are you in school for? I saw you had a math book with you, but that's just general shit so I couldn't really tell." He tucked his full lips in, letting his brows dip in the middle. *Focus, Tasmine. Don't get lost in his sexiness.*

"I'm a math major, but you're right, that was just undergrad math. I plan to be an accountant. I wanna work with people who make large amounts of money, and assist them in keeping track of it."

"Like celebrities, so they won't become MC Hammer?" he grinned, and we chuckled together.

"Exactly. I've always been into managing money, and because of that, my parents let me get a credit card before I came to school here."

"So they trust you, that's good. I don't know if I could have a daughter as beautiful as you and allow her to go away. Where are you from? I get the impression that you're not from Vegas."

I was still cheesing at the fact that he'd called me beautiful.

"I'm from Kentucky. And thank you."

"For what?"

"Calling me beautiful."

"I mean you're welcome, but I'm just stating facts, baby girl. It's a given how beautiful you are, you know that and I'm sure you hear that shit all the time."

"No."

"Well, get ready, because if we spend more time together, you're gonna get tired of me saying that shit."

"I don't think I will get tired of hearing it, especially from you."

We gazed into one another's eyes somewhat lustfully for a few seconds, but our moment was interrupted by the waitress setting our plates down. We thanked her, and then held hands to pray. My hand felt like it belonged in his, and I didn't wanna let go.

"You were right, this is good, and the medium-well factor made it much more tender," I nodded my head as I cut my steak into more pieces.

"I told you," he chuckled.

"Were you born in Vegas, Tony?"

"I was born in Texas, but when I was five my parents moved here. They broke up when I was in tenth grade, and my dad moved back to Texas."

"You still talk to your mother?"

"I do. She's sick so I make sure to spend a lot of time with her."

"May I ask what she's sick with?"

"She contracted HIV from my father, who got it from some prostitute he slept with out here. He found out he had it and didn't tell her, so she kept getting sicker and shit. I don't really fuck with my dad you know. I felt like the least he could have done was let her know he caught the shit instead of taking care of himself on the low."

"I agree, that's fucked up." I shook my head. I didn't know what to say. I wanted to say that I hoped she got better but we both knew she wouldn't. It was so crazy learning about all these new people and their backgrounds.

"It is."

"I don't have a fucking reservation!" some female yelled. I looked towards the entrance of the restaurant, and some chick was storming over towards us. I know this nigga doesn't have a girlfriend and didn't tell me.

"Fuck," he sighed, dabbing his mouth with the cloth napkin. By the time he rose to his feet, old girl was approaching the table with her face twisted up.

"Oh, so you're on a fucking date, Tony!" she screamed.

"Selinda, do not do this shit right now. Take your ass home, girl, on some real shit."

"Fuck that! You need to be spending this money on your son!" *Son? The fuck? I guess the rumors were true.* "Who are you? If you think you're about to be his next bitch you have me fucked up." She looked me up and down with disgust.

"That ain't my damn son, Sel."

"Okay, I have no idea who the hell you are, and I was under the impression that he was single." I scooted back from the table. "Tony, have a good night. I will Uber back."

"Tasmine!" he yelled after me but I kept walking. "Tasmine!"

"Let her go, Tony!"

After a few moments, he followed me all the way through the hotel until we made it outside. His alleged baby mama was right behind him, bumping her damn gums, and loudly might I add.

"Tasmine, come back inside so we can finish."

"I'm good," I waved him off.

"Aight, then let me drive you home, please?"

"Tony, are you—"

That nigga got up in her face, well towered over her, so damn quickly that she almost choked on her spit from being cut off. I could see his jaw clenching as he panted lightly while staring down at her.

"Take yo' muthafuckin' ass home before I knock the shit out you in front of all these people. And with my connects, do you think anybody will tell, bitch?" he gritted. "Your kid is not mine and until you can prove it, you need to stay the fuck out of my face before I make yours unrecognizable." Even I was scared so I was sure she was.

She nodded repeatedly and wiped the tear that traveled down her cheek before rushing off. He stared straight ahead for a few moments before turning his attention to me and smiling shyly. Yeah, he was crazy, but it was sexy.

"Let me give this ticket to the valet guy," he smirked and walked away. I cancelled my Uber because I was scared to go against his wishes, but also, I still wanted to ride home with him.

This would be the last time we hung out though. The night had gone from wonderful to horrifying in literally a matter of minutes. Looks like the fairytale I'd planned in my head was never going to happen.

# CHAPTER SEVEN

# Bella

*A couple days later...*

It was a regular Tuesday evening, and I was in the library trying to type a damn paper. I'd been in here for at least two damn hours and only had two fucking paragraphs. School was killing me, and I wished someone had told me about the multiple 10-page papers that professors were gonna be handing out. For some odd ass reason, I felt like me not declaring a major would make my freshman year an easy ride. What harm could six undergrad classes do? A lot, and I was getting tired.

However, I was determined to finish college and make something of myself. My parents weren't rich by any means, which is why I had to come here since this school gave me an academic scholarship. I wanted to make them proud, and not stress them out like my older brother, Brandon. Sometimes I wanted to whoop his ass for all the shit that he put my parents through, from bailing him out of jail, to having to deal with him crashing their cars. I wanted to be the child that gave them a break, assuring them that they didn't have to worry about me.

I watched the girl next to me massage her eyes after pulling her glasses off, and I just shook my head because I felt the same. She'd been here since I got here, but at least she had more than two paragraphs. How in the hell was I supposed to write a fucking 10-page paper on Greek mythology? That shit wasn't even real, I don't think. Now give me a subject like how weak these fuck boys are and I'll have that shit to you by tomorrow, with a little extra.

"Want some tea?" I saw a hand come into view, wrapped around a Starbucks hot cup. I recognized that hand, and wanted it to go away, leaving the tea with me.

"Thanks, I hope you didn't poison it." I threw my pen down gently, and sat up straight as if I was about to get my word count up on this paper.

Santino sat down at the computer next to me, and I could hear his football windbreaker making all kinds of sounds, as he got comfortable. Inhaling sharply, I closed my eyes for a moment to enjoy the smell of his cologne. He'd been wearing that men's Chanel cologne since tenth grade, and I hadn't gotten tired of it yet.

"I would never poison you, baby. Drink it, it's your favorite."

"What's my favorite?" I turned to look at him.

"That vanilla tea, with soy milk, no water, and vanilla syrup added." I hated him because he knew me so well. How could he not? We spent every waking moment together until he knocked me up.

"Thanks," was the only thing I could say in response before sipping that heaven in a cup.

"You're welcome. Are we allowed to get on Twitter in here?" he frowned, pointing to my screen.

I admired his pretty short curly hair, full lips, and caramel skin for a second before turning to see what he was pointing at. It was my boyfriend, Dean. Dean usually only texted me 'goodnight', or 'I love you', but if he wanted to talk, he would inbox me on Instagram or Twitter. I hated it, but he said I answered quicker on there.

"Yes, we can get on Twitter, and any other social media that we want. Mind your business."

"You are my business, and that's never gonna change. I don't give a fuck about him." He scooted his chair closer to me, making me feel uncomfortable yet turned on.

"I ain't been your business since we broke up, Sanz. And move back, you're way too close." I sipped my tea but that only made me hotter.

"You coming to my game? I got a t-shirt for you with my number and I want you to wear it, Bella."

"Let me explain something to you, Sanz. You and I are not friends. We aren't anything to one another, meaning when you see me, don't talk to me. I don't care that you still like me; I have a fiancé. I haven't wanted to be with you for years, and I won't magically love you now."

"You think about me all the time, Bella, just like I haven't stopped thinking about you. I would give anything to bring the baby back and have you as my girl, I swear. I'm for real, Bella," he tried to explain, as I laughed as loudly as I could in such a quiet library. It was the only way to mask the pain. His words were getting to me.

"Even football? Because I remember that being the reason that you broke up with me. You didn't wanna mess up your future, and me getting pregnant was doing just that, right?"

"I was 15, I was stupid."

"And what happened in the years after that, Sanz? You didn't say shit to me, and now that you want me, you expect me to just be with you? You only love me because I'm in your face."

"Not true. I wanted to get back together but my parents told me to stay away from you or they would kick me out."

"So what's the difference now?"

"I don't need them for shit. I'm here on a football scholarship, so they aren't paying for anything. And I'm for sure going to the NFL after this. I want you to be my wife when that happens," he whispered the last part. *Don't fall for it, Bella.*

"You see this?" I lifted my hand so he could see my engagement ring. "That means I'm gonna be someone else's wife, so you'll have to look elsewhere."

"Bella, I'm not asking you to leave that square just yet, all I want is a fair chance to show you that we belong together. Once I do that, it's up to you to figure out who you want to be with."

"No, Sanz."

"Let's go get some food. I know your brain is fried, and there is an Italian place I wanna take you to. This is just a friendly dinner, baby, nothing more."

I stared into his handsome face, pondering, before finally sighing and agreeing. What the hell was I doing?

***

I tried to quietly enter my room as Santino kissed on my neck while hugging me from behind. I know, I shouldn't even be allowing him to touch me, but I loved him and he offered to give me some head. As soon as he was done, shit would end there because I wasn't about to let his ass smash after what he'd done to me. But, I was horny as fuck and wasn't trying to fuck a dude I just met, so why not let a guy I knew eat me out? Dean would be upset, but that would only be if he found out which he wouldn't.

"Shhh!" I told Santino, not wanting to wake Perry.

The room was dark, but the blue light from my fish tanks kept my side of the room lit. We walked past Perry to my bed by the window, and Santino immediately began pushing my tights down. He tried to lift my shirt but I smacked his hand away.

"Just head, remember?" I raised a brow, causing a smirk to form on his face.

"That's all I want."

He took his jacket and slide-ins off, before climbing into the bed with me. I looked over towards Perry's side, by the door, and made sure she was still knocked out. Santino pecked my lips making me jump, and I was so mad that I did because he smiled over it.

"Hurry up!" I spat.

He just chuckled and dipped his head under the covers. Feeling his strong big hands spread my legs and press them towards my stomach, was enough to make me cum on its own. After kissing my pussy through my panties a couple times, he gripped the waist of my underwear and pulled them off.

"Just as pretty as I remember." He tucked his bottom lip in. My comforter was sitting on top of his head so that I could see his face whenever he looked up at me. I hated how good looking he was, and how much I still loved him even years later.

"Mm," I moaned softly once his lips met my lower ones.

His kisses soon became licks, as he let his tongue travel the length of my vagina. Pulling my clit into his mouth, he sucked gently while caressing my thighs. I bit down on my lip to muffle my screams; yes bitch, screams! Santino's sex game was always bomb as fuck, that's probably why he had my 15-year-old ass sprung back then.

As he licked, slurped, sucked, and moaned, I gripped the sheets, scratching them up with my freshly done nails. My breathing became shallow as I tried my best not to yell as if I had caught the Holy Ghost. My body jerked as I came, causing Santino to slow down a bit, giving my body time to come back. I thought it was over so I tried to let my leg down, but no, he dove right back in, feasting on me like a maniac. I pressed my chin into my chest to see that his mouth and my middle were one. I didn't know where one ended and the other began.

"Fuck!" I cried loudly as hell as he brought me to the greatest orgasm I'd had in years.

"Bella, are you okay?" Perry sat up. I could see her figure patting the bed for her glasses.

"Yes, I'm fine," I panted as Santino lapped up my juices.

I'd never cum that hard in my life.

"Oh, okay," she replied before hesitantly lying back.

Santino came from up under the covers, lied between my legs, and slipped his tongue into my mouth. I didn't want to kiss him; well I shouldn't have wanted to kiss him.

"Just let me put the tip in," he joked, and we both laughed lowly.

After kissing some more, we got out of the bed and went to the sink to clean ourselves with warm towels. He lived in this dorm too, so before getting here we'd stopped by his room because he had to get his toothbrush so that he'd be able to brush his teeth after. This was the one time I hated that the sink was outside of the damn bathroom, and in the room. After we quietly got ourselves together, we got back into the bed. I should've made him go home, but feeling his muscular arms wrapped around my small frame felt like old times. It felt good… great.

"We can't do this again, Sanz," I whispered, staring at the wall.

"Shut up, Bella. You know me, and you know a nigga ain't gon' let up until I have you back."

"I have a—"

"Fuck yo' fiancé." He hugged me tighter against his chest and moved my hair to kiss the nape of my neck. The bed was small, but I liked that; it forced us to be closer. "Wanna get breakfast before your first class tomorrow?"

"Yeah."

"Goodnight, Bella. I love you." He kissed from the side of my neck to the corner of my mouth, before laying his head back on my extra pillow.

"Night."

This was a disaster waiting to happen…

# CHAPTER SEVEN

## Oden

"Nigga, did you think I was fucking around?" I grimaced, pressing the barrel of my gun deeply into this nigga Donnell's temple.

"Oden, I swear I'm gonna have it together. It wasn't my fault though, them niggas were slacking and shit," he whimpered, snot coming out of his nose and shit. His face was bleeding from getting fucked up.

"And what the fuck are you supposed to do when niggas ain't acting right, dummy?" Truman sneered, sucking his teeth and pacing the floor. The homie was hot. I just stopped him from raining blows on the nigga.

"I tried, man, I swear I tried, but them niggas said they weren't listening to nobody but you." Donnell looked up at me with his swollen eyes.

"And look where they are," I pointed to them muthafuckas dead in a pile. "I actually liked you my nigga, but I can't have no bitches on my team. You're too scared to show some muthafuckas under you that you're running things, I could only imagine what you'll do if the police come knocking."

"Oden, I—"

*POP! POP!*

I sent two bullets into his head like I always did when I murked someone. I never shot a nigga only once in the dome, ever since some dude lived from a head wound some years back. I remember seeing that shit on the news and thinking if I ever shot a muthafucka in the head it would be twice for good measure. All it took was popping the nigga at the wrong angle, missing that vital organ, and his ass may live.

Donnell's body slumped over, blood pouring from his head. Truman whistled for the clean-up crew to come in so they could pack his ass up and take him to my human chop shop I had in the warehouse. When would niggas learn that if they couldn't do their fucking job, they would die?

See, I was a reasonable ass nigga; if you felt you couldn't do this shit anymore, I would gladly let you go. And as long as you kept it pushing and didn't open your mouth to law enforcement, you would stay alive. People liked to let this light skin and curly hair fool their asses, and that was fine with me because wasn't nothing like surprising a bitch ass nigga with a loaded .45. This 'pretty boy' would light yo' ass up in a second if you didn't come correct.

"Ryan stepped his shit up, but I'm still watching him," Truman came back into the basement, pulling a blunt from his pocket. This nigga was the only muthafucka in Vegas with a mouth full of gold slugs. Bitches loved that shit though, so I couldn't hate.

"Good, and don't stop. If his crew can't push out three cars every 24 hours, I want him brought to me. I can't have stolen cars piling up in my shops. I plan to promote Doobie and his crew to take over Donnell's space immediately. There ain't any time to let shit slow up. Call him for me, Tru."

"Fasho," he nodded, taking a deep ass pull on his blunt. The nigga was so damn skinny that I was sure all that shit would have him floating in a minute. "You smashed old girl with the pretty eyes yet?" he looked to Anton who sucked his teeth.

"Man, nah. I might would have, but Selinda's weak ass showed up and showed the fuck out. I swear I had to say a silent prayer so that I wouldn't smack the shit out of her ass, dawg."

"Nigga, you need to get these fake baby mamas under control. What is it about you?" I burst into laughter along with Truman.

A cool three or four chicks were currently claiming Anton to be their babies' daddy. Most of them only said the shit to get his attention, so they didn't fuck with him too much, but Violet, Selinda, and this hoe named Kai were persistent. At first I low-key believed their asses because of how tenacious they were, but I began to notice that every time he asked for a DNA test, Selinda and Kai's asses would scram and be MIA for a good couple of weeks. In my opinion, if you really wanted the nigga to step up and do right, you would agree to a test. My boy was even willing to pay for the shit, but them thirst buckets weren't having it.

"I've been wondering the same thing. All three of us smashed Selinda, but she chose me to be her so-called baby's father. And Kai's damn baby is pale as hell! I'm dark as fuck, and she's brown skinned, so how the hell is he mine?"

"Aye, but she for real named that nigga Anton Jr.," Truman blew out smoke as he and I cracked up at Anton's expense. Kai was bold for that one, knowing her baby didn't belong to my homie.

"I'm glad y'all find this shit funny. I can't wait until y'all get a baby pinned on y'all asses."

"Ain't gonna happen, I stay strapped," I half lied. I fucked Khyle more than a few times raw, and she was the only girl that I'd done that to outside of my ex, Naomi, which was years ago. Neither were pregnant, so I was gravy.

"So do I, but somehow these hoes don't let that stop them. I swear I'm gonna have gray hair on my balls in a minute," Anton sighed, taking the blunt from Truman.

"Well, if a bitch tries to pin a baby on me, I'm straight murdering her ass. Pilar will kill me if a girl comes yelling about she's having my baby," Truman shook his head at the thought.

Pilar was his girlfriend of like six years or some shit. She didn't play, and to her knowledge Truman was faithful as they came. It was crazy because that nigga cheated from sun up to sun down when he wasn't working, but he kept his shit tight. No girls approached Pilar, and they knew not to speak to him if they saw him with her.

We all had these women on their best behavior, but Kai and Selinda just didn't know how to act. Violet was calmer, but I think it was because she actually had love for Anton. Personally, I would've just dropped their asses already, but I understood that Anton had a heart and didn't want these hoes' kids not having a mother.

"Alright y'all, I'm gonna head out. A nigga got class tomorrow, and then that meeting. It's three cars that we need to get, and have them shipped out by tomorrow," I said and they both nodded.

The three of us went our separate ways, and by the time I got home it was already 9pm. I was a night owl, but I'd been forcing myself to go to bed early on Mondays and Wednesdays since I had class the next day. That shit was weak because I wanted to catch up on shows and play video games, but I knew the sacrifice would be worth it once I got that degree. Yeah, I switched to the degree program.

I hit the alarm on my car, walking towards my door, and out popped Khyle's pretty ass. I wish I'd never told her to come through whenever because she for real did that shit. I hadn't seen or talked to her in weeks though, ever since I smashed her in the bathroom. She didn't text me and I didn't text her. Had I thought about her? Hell fucking yeah, but I wasn't with the bullshit games that she liked to play. I was the king out here, and I wasn't about to let some little girl play me like a hoe every time her daddy long leg looking boyfriend showed up.

"I need to talk to you." She folded her arms across her chest.

She was wearing some little ass shorts that made me bite my lip as a reflex. Her top was one of those short ones, and I could see that she didn't have on a bra because her dime-sized brown nipples were showing through the white top. Fuck, man. Her extremely long hair was all over the place, and I just wanted to pull it while hitting it from the back one time. Memories of her bouncing on my dick while I groped her body and sucked her nipples, flashed before me. I was horny as hell, but for her specifically.

"I gotta be up early. I wanna shower, and go to bed. I really ain't got anything to talk about right now, baby girl, but if it's important, come back through tomorrow."

I unlocked my front door, walked in, and tried to close it, but she barged in with her face twisted like I had her fucked up. I loved when she got feisty sometimes, because it made me want to fuck her into submission. It was an ego boost knowing I could make a girl like that scream my name and shit. Not to mention the fact that she stayed sweating me, and I knew she wasn't the type to sweat niggas. She was bad than a muthafucka so she didn't have to; I knew it.

"I wanna talk now."

"Make it quick." I closed and locked the door, then headed to my bedroom with her right on my heels. I began pulling out my drawers for some fresh boxers and socks as she started.

"Oden, do you want to be with me?"

"Next question."

"I'm serious!"

"I don' told yo' ass a million fucking times what I wanted and I'm not gonna repeat the shit again! Quit asking me before I change my answer, Khyle."

"Then what is this?" she held her phone up, and all I could do was shake my head. That snake ass bitch, Shayne. I almost kicked her out of my glass box, but I used the wrong head to make decisions that night.

"It's me about to fuck your sister. Baby, I was twisted as fuck, you and I weren't talking, and there was another girl there. You keep complaining about shit that I've done, and every time, I tell you that it could have been prevented."

"How?" she wiped the tear that had fallen from her eye. I moved closer to her but she backed away.

"If you would just quit playing games, you would be my girl, and I wouldn't have been with them! Damn! Every time you push me away, you get mad at who I fuck. Do you want me or not?"

"Because you fuck everyone around me! Who's next, Tasmine and Bella?"

"No, because I know they're your people. Baby, I didn't know Shayne was your sister the first time, and I didn't know that garbage pussy was your best friend." She looked away, shaking her head slowly. "Come here." I pulled her into me, and she wrapped her arms around my torso. Gripping the sides of her wet face, I leaned down to peck her pillow soft lips. "Be my girl." I kissed her again, but more sensually. She hugged my torso tighter. "You gon' be my girl, Khyle?"

She nodded her head slowly, before I kissed her again.

"You have to be everything that I think you are," she said lowly.

"What's that?"

"Perfect… for me."

"I'm gonna do my best, I promise. You said you want loyalty and I can give you that, you know that. I know you do."

"I do."

I kissed her again, sliding my tongue into her mouth and pushing her face further into mine. She was hugging my body so tightly, that I never wanted to move. I could feel how scared she was of her decision, but I was happy she'd made it.

"Call him."

"Who?"

"Your nigga, well your old nigga. Call his ass and tell him the deal right now."

"Oden, it's almost 10 o'clock."

I just leaned up against my dresser, with my hands clutching the edges. I wasn't playing. She needed to call his ass and tell him it was a wrap. I prayed that he was awake, but if he wasn't, she was gonna try bright and early in the morning.

"Put it on speaker," I cleared my throat when I saw her put the phone to her ear.

"Baby, is everything okay?" his voice came through.

"No Brian, I have to tell you something. I love you, I really do, but—"

"Hurry up!" I shouted, being petty as fuck. I usually was the last nigga to be petty, but she was mine now and needed to dead her old situation ASAP.

"Who is that, Khyle?"

"Brian, that's Oden. Umm—"

"Who is Oden—"

"He's my boyfriend. We got close when I moved here, Brian. I'm sorry, I really tried to—"

"Good enough." I took the phone from her. "Glad we have an understanding now, Brian. You have a goodnight."

"Wait—"

I hung up the phone and she just glared at me.

"You could have let me do it how I wanted! You made me be rude about it."

"Why you care? Only nigga's feelings you need to be worried about are mine. Unless you've changed your mind."

"No, never." She came closer and I picked her up, wrapping her legs around my waist. "I missed you, Oden."

I carried her to the bathroom while kissing her neck. I couldn't wait to tear her pussy up all night. A nigga had finally won. That's corny as fuck but it's true as fuck too.

***

*BAM! BAM! BAM!*

I beat on Shayne's door repeatedly until I heard someone unlocking it. I didn't give a fuck who answered, I was gonna put this bitch in her place. And if her blind ass nigga had a problem with it, he could get the business too.

"What the hell are you doing banging on my door like that, Oden?" she frowned, tightening her robe. "Excuse me!" she shouted when I barged into the house.

"You think you're funny, sending pictures around and shit, bitch?" I hissed.

"Hold up, who the fuck are you calling a bitch—"

"I'm calling you a bitch, bitch! And you gon' be a dead ass bitch if you keep trying to keep your sister and me apart! I know you're used to mousy ass niggas like the one you lie next to at night, but you don't want to fuck with me, Shayne, I promise you don't. I'm begging you to save yourself before I have to drop you, baby girl." I was so close to her that she could easily kiss me if she were tall enough.

"She has a boyfriend!"

"She does, me. And unlike her last boyfriend, I'm not afraid to fill yo' ass with some heat if you don't straighten the fuck up. Your sister is my girl, and I'm her nigga. It's gonna be that way for the rest of our lives, so get used to it."

"How do you know that you'll always be together? Look how she did Brian."

"Now, we both know Brian and I are damn near two different species. Khyle ain't going nowhere, and neither am I."

She just stood there, shaking her head 'no' as her eyes became glossy.

"I had you first, Oden!" she whined.

"Shayne, kill that shit and save some of your man's pride. Do what the fuck I said or we're gonna have some damn problems, period, point, blank."

And with that, I left. I would hate to kill my girl's sister, but I would. I fucking would. Her and anybody else that wanted to come between us.

# CHAPTER SEVEN

*Thanksgiving Break...*

$O$den and I had been together for a little over a month now, and I must say that I was so happy I chose to be with him over Brian. In hindsight, I'm also happy that he made me call Brian right then and tell him the deal. Knowing me, Brian would still be my boyfriend, but getting neglected like crazy.

It wasn't that I didn't know who I wanted to be with, it was just that Brian was the safer choice. I knew he loved me, I knew he cared for me, and I knew if anything he would marry me. Oden was a bit more unpredictable, and his reputation for switching bedmates as much as his underwear didn't help. But, I decided to take a leap of faith and I'm so fucking happy that I did.

On the flip side, a little tiny part of me knew Brian was messing around, even before I left for college. Shayne would always tell me to keep an eye on him before she moved away, but I just thought she was being paranoid. Now that I look back, I feel like he'd been doing some shit all along. And the worst part of it all was that I didn't know why. I was a good girlfriend from what I knew, prior to coming here, and it wasn't like I wouldn't give him sex, so I really didn't know why he would cheat on me. I just hoped I'd been paranoid all that time, because if he was being unfaithful, that would fuck with me regardless of whether he was my ex now or not.

I'm probably not one to talk because Oden's and my relationship was and still is forbidden in every way, but I can't help who I want to be with. I refuse to be with Brian, while yearning for Oden. And who knows how I may react if I see Oden with another woman. So to prevent all of that, I just decided to be with the man I felt so strongly for, despite my reservations. Yeah, I didn't like that he fucked Shayne *and* Emery, but sadly, it wasn't enough to make me lose interest.

"You sure you don't want to come, Tasmine? My mom is gonna have plenty of food, and it's only gonna be her, my dad, Oden, and I."

"No, I'm good. I'm just gonna chill here. Plus, I don't like long car rides and you said it takes about four hours to get to California, right?"

"To Los Angeles, yes."

"Then, no thanks. I have a weak bladder and I can't sit still for too long," she chuckled. I could tell she missed her family, and I would too if I were that far away, I guess.

"And Bella flew to Arizona, so you couldn't have gone with her."

"Nope, but I will be fine. Text me and let me know how your parents react to Oden."

"Oh, I will. And if Perry invites you to her home for dinner,

Tasmine, you better go."

"I'd rather not. That would be the quietest damn dinner ever," we both laughed in unison, as I threw my duffel bag over my shoulder.

"It sure as hell would be. Oden is downstairs so I better go, but see you later." I hugged her, and then she opened the room door for me so that I could leave. I really wished she would come, but I wasn't gonna force her.

Making it off the elevator, I spotted Oden standing right outside of it instead of over by the lobby. When we saw each other, we immediately began smiling, before he took my bag from me and kissed my lips. Being with him just felt so right, way more right than it did when I was with Brian. Taking my hand into his, we went outside to get into his deep burgundy colored Ferrari. I'd been wanting to ride in it for the longest, and since we hoped to get to California quickly, this was the best way for me to experience it.

"It smells expensive," I giggled once he got in behind the wheel.

"It better smell that way."

He pulled out of my school, and once we got on the freeway, I opened the box of Teddy Grahams he'd gotten me, and a bottle of water. Oden remembered everything about me that I told him and I just loved that. When my mom and dad called, I told them about it and my mom even said I'd found something good. She and I weren't the best of friends as you know, but she did have her moments and that was one of them.

"Saved" by Ty Dolla $ign came on, so I turned it up and let the window down to allow my hair to blow for a little bit. Oden placed his tatted hand on my exposed thigh as he drove, and I just admired how sexy his hands were, along with black diamond watch that he loved to rock. The whole ride we just listened to YG's Pandora station, ate some snacks, talked, and even kissed when we could. I despised driving from California to Nevada and vice versa, but I didn't want this ride to end. I just loved being in his presence. It didn't matter where we were, I would enjoy myself.

By the time we got to L.A., it was around 6pm, and we left Vegas at 3:20pm. That damn car was fast as fuck, and had my adrenaline pumping every time he sped through a clear road on the way here.

I directed him to my home so he could drop me off, and then go to his hotel. I really didn't want to sleep at my parent's home, but I came here to see them so I kind of had to. I knew they'd allow Oden to sleep here, on the couch, but he said he was too grown to be sleeping on someone's sofa, so he booked a hotel room.

"Oden, please remember to come back by 10am."

"Dinner ain't gonna be ready that quickly, is it?" his brows dipped.

"No, but I'm gonna miss you and I want you to spend time with us before we sit at the table."

"I will do what I can," he flashed me that sexy grin he always gave me.

"Oden!"

"Baby, I'm gonna be there. Where the fuck else am I gonna be? I don't know many people out here to be doing too much shit. I will be here by 10am, ready for your dad to pull me aside and grill me." I didn't want these L.A. bitches seeing him because I was sure they would be on him like white on rice. I'd never been this possessive, but I couldn't help it.

"Thank you, baby," I caressed his chin hairs, and then his wild hair, before leaning over to kiss him hungrily.

"Hop on it real quick," he mumbled against my lips before kissing me deeply again.

Before I could answer, he was unbuckling himself. I glanced over my shoulder to make sure no one was looking because my mother had a tendency to look out of the living room window when someone was in the driveway. Then I remembered Oden had tint so I removed my jean shorts and panties before straddling him.

He gripped my waist with one hand, and guided me down slowly making me whimper. I bit down on my lip while just sitting there, allowing myself to get adjusted to his girth and length. He was blessed below the waist, and he never let my poor vagina forget.

"You're so pretty, baby," he pulled my lip into his mouth, while moving me up and down slowly as I trembled. I was damn near paralyzed so he had to do all the work.

Placing my legs onto his shoulders, he leaned me back so that I was lying on his steering wheel, and stared me in the eyes while stroking me deeply. I watched his eyes look down, as he tucked his bottom lip in at the sight. He loved to watch himself go in and out of me with his nasty ass.

"Oden, uuuh, uuuh," I cried out, gripping his strong biceps as he sped up, pounding into me with force. I came but he didn't slow up one bit, he just kept hitting my spot feverishly.

He kissed and sucked on my inner thighs since my legs were still on his shoulders, before making eye contact with me again. A high-pitched scream escaped my mouth when I came for the second time, and he was right after me, panting like he'd need an oxygen tank soon. We finally caught our breaths, so he removed my legs from his shoulders and gently lifted me off of his dick. I stood to my feet while still crouching down so that I could climb back into the passenger seat, and he gripped my waist to peck between my legs.

"Stop, nasty," I hurried away as he laughed. I slipped on my panties and shorts, and then had him pop the trunk so I could get my bag. "See you tomorrow." I sat in the passenger seat with the door open. I was about to get up, but he hooked the waist of my jean shorts with his pointing finger to pull me back. Gripping my chin, he forced his tongue into my mouth to kiss me nastily. I was into it until I remembered we were outside of my parents' home.

"Bye, baby."

"Bye, Oden," I smiled and rushed into the house, going straight to the shower before I spoke to my parents.

***

"It was nice meeting you, son," my dad shook Oden's hand for the hundredth time tonight.

"Likewise, Mr. Luke. Mrs. Luke." He hugged my mother. "I will be out in the car, baby." He pecked me right in front of them, causing me to look over at my dad as he left.

"So do you want my verdict?" My dad folded his arms across his chest as my mom hugged him from behind, wearing a smile. She'd had a few glasses of wine, and thought everything Oden said was so smart or hilarious.

"Yes, that's why I'm standing here," I giggled to lighten the mood.

"I think he's a very mature guy with a strong grip handshake. He's a bit brash and frank, but there is nothing wrong with that, especially if you can still be respectful. I like him for you because I feel like he would protect you and take care of you, but he gives me a womanizer vibe."

"He does?" my mom looked up at my dad with furrowed brows.

"Oh yeah. That's my only reservation, sweetheart, but other than that, I like him much better than Brian. I told you Brian's balls hadn't fell yet."

"James!" my mom squealed.

"Daddy!"

He just shrugged and laughed.

"Where are you guys going tonight? You better not be having sex. I know a guy like him is asking for it 24/7."

"We're not having sex, Daddy. I have to go, though. We will come back by tomorrow before we head back to Vegas, okay?"

"Okay, sweetie, and tell Shayne to call me," my mom replied, as my dad opened the door for me.

"Ferrari? Did he rent that?" my father frowned.

"No, it's his. He has a Maserati and a Lexus truck too."

"Didn't he say he just opened his club this year? And the liquor is pretty new too I'm sure. I guess money comes in fast. I'm in the wrong business."

"You sure are. See you later." I hugged and kissed both of my parents before darting out. I didn't want to keep talking about Oden's finances because I had the same suspicions. I felt like I should know first before anyone else.

I placed my bag in his trunk, got in, and then we took off to his hotel. He booked a suite at the Beverly Hills Hotel, which was an upscale spot that only rich people stayed in. The cheapest fucking room you could get was almost $700. His suite in particular was more comparable to a really clean and beautiful one-bedroom apartment. A man's money didn't matter to me, but I'd be lying if I said I didn't enjoy the finer things in life.

"How much was this, Oden?" We'd taken a shower together, and we were now lying in the bed half naked in the dark. The moonlight gave us enough light so that we'd see one another though.

"Too much, but I told the guy when I called that I needed something nice with a minibar and living room. And when I got here, this is what I was assigned to."

"Damn, I've only stayed in this hotel once, and it was when our bathrooms at home was being renovated so my parents put us up in a suite."

"The perks of having two lawyers for parents."

"I know. I never felt like we were rich though, we were just comfortable. They never spoiled us, but they weren't cheap either, especially my dad. My mom is stricter with me, but she has no problem buying Shayne whatever."

"Why?"

"I don't know. We just never clicked like that. She's a great mom, but I feel like her and Shayne are friends on top of being mother and daughter. I want that too, but we just don't mesh well, I guess. She's my mom and nothing else. She takes care of me, but we don't bond."

"Damn, I never had parents to know what you mean, but my grandpa was cool. I don't think we were friends though, he just kind of kept me on the straight and narrow… well, he tried."

"What do you mean, *tried*?"

He sighed and then turned to face me, pushing his curly hair back, only for it to come flopping back into his handsome face.

"I'm only telling you this because I know deep down that you and I are gonna be in this for the long run. Anton, Truman, and I run a high-end car theft ring. We send niggas out to steal like two or three cars a night, and we have them brought to a chop shop in order to prevent them being found, and then we ship them overseas to people who pay large sums of money for them. Car registration overseas is nowhere near as strict as it is in U.S., so once the car goes over there, it's a wrap; the owner couldn't find it for any amount of money in the world."

"How much do you guys make?" I was surprised, but then again I wasn't.

Oden was too famous, too rugged, and too rich to be all legit. I assumed he sold drugs, but it was kind of cool to see him into something different. Did I like that he did illegal shit? No, but I would be lying if I tried to pretend like I thought he was legit all the way. I may not know how to cook crack, but I could spot a thoroughbred thug from miles away, and Oden, Anton, and Truman were definitely it.

Thug dudes just had a certain demeanor, different from straight up and down businessmen. Not to mention the fact that they were all under thirty and balling out of control. The only time a dude was young and rich was if he invented some shit, was a musician, had an inheritance, or did some illegal stuff that brought fast money.

"Per car?" he raised a brow and I nodded. "Depends on the vehicle, but sometimes it'll be as much as $300,000 we charge for it. I started as just a thief, working for this African cat, but he passed it down to me. My homies and I struggled at first to run shit smoothly, but I eventually got the hang of it."

"Is it dangerous?"

"It can be. I've gotten close to getting caught but that was years ago. It's gotten bad before, especially when a nigga feels like he can go toe to toe with me, but they always learn the hard way."

"You beat them up?" I played dumb, because I already knew what he meant.

"Yeah," he chuckled. "Something like that."

"I don't like that you do that for money, but it is sexy, I won't lie," I grinned.

"So you still wanna be with me?" he half smiled, already knowing the answer.

"Are you crazy? I never wanna see you again." I pretended like I was gonna get out of the bed, and he yanked me back, wearing that adorable crooked grin.

"You got me fucked up, Khyle." He got on top of me, in between my legs. I had panties on, and he had on some boxers, but it was still an intense feeling. "Once you agree to be my girl, there's no backing out," he whispered against my lips.

"No, once you agree to be with me, there's no backing out." I locked my legs around his waist.

He just chuckled and rolled onto his back, so I got on top of him. His hands wandered all over my body, stopping to grope my breasts gently for a few moments, before gliding back down to caress my thighs.

"Why did you tell me that you wanted loyalty?" he cocked his head, brushing his big hair against the pillow.

"I felt like my boyfriend at the time wasn't being loyal to me, but I had no proof."

"Do you feel that way now?"

"No. Even with your track record, I don't feel that way. I wouldn't leave one thing to go to something else that was the same. I left him for you because I knew you were better for me."

"I got something for you." He reached into the drawer of the nightstand on his side of the bed. He removed a blue velvet box, and handed it to me.

"What is this, Oden?"

"Open the shit and see, baby." He laughed in a way that said he shouldn't have had to tell me that. I lifted the top of it to a see a gold chain necklace, with *Bishop* on it. His last name was covered in diamonds, sparkling even in the dark. "You like it?"

"Yes, but why your last name and not your first?"

"So that even before we get married, you will have my last name. I want you to wear it until it's official. It won't be tomorrow or some shit like that, but in like 20 years fasho."

"Oden, 20?" I squealed as we chuckled in unison.

"I'm fucking with you. Put it on though. I want everyone to know you're my shorty and that you're fuckin' with a real one."

I removed it from the box and fastened it around my neck. It hung perfectly, prompting me to rub my fingers over the diamond-encrusted name. His reasons behind it made me melt inside like ice cream in the sun. I never expected to meet someone who I felt so close to when I went off to college, but I'm so thankful that I did.

# CHAPTER SEVEN

*Anton's Thanksgiving... Earlier that day...*

asmine hadn't talked to me in a little over a month, and I knew exactly why. I'd never dealt with this shit before, ever. Selinda and Kai have both popped up on a chick I was fucking with, but the girl would never stop talking to me like Tasmine had done. Oddly, that only attracted me more, because I saw that she wasn't into me just because I was Anton Nickerson.

Most women would put up with any bullshit I threw their way, no matter how fucked up it was, all because they wanted to be the girl that Anton wifed. Little did they know, that shit was never gonna happen. But Tasmine, I don't know, I liked that she wasn't having that shit.

I pulled my hoodie over my head, grabbed my keys and phone, and then left out. I stopped by the grocery to pick up some shit that my mother advised me to get, with a little twist. I'd spent the morning with her, but she got tired fairly soon and wanted to just rest. I hated seeing her so fucking sick, but I couldn't cry about the shit anymore. And plus, I didn't want her feeling bad because for some reason every time I got glum over her condition, she felt like it was her fault. It wasn't though, it was that fuck nigga she called her husband.

After checking out with the shit I needed from Von's, I drove right across the street to UNLV, parking in front of the Dayton dormitory. I wasn't about to park all far and shit, and I wish somebody would say something to me on this here holiday. Lucky for me, I saw a girl I recognized, carrying her basket of laundry from the laundry room, so I beat on the glass door so that she'd let me in.

"What are you doing here, Tony?" Erica smiled.

"Coming to visit somebody. Why didn't you go home for Thanksgiving?"

"You know I'm vegan, I don't eat all that shit and I really don't fuck with my family like that so no need for me to show up, ya know?"

"I guess so," I chuckled as we walked to the elevator.

"Who are you here to see?"

"Girl named Tasmine, you know her? Pretty as fuck, dark hair, sexy eyes, and a body to fucking die for."

"Umm, I probably do but I don't see her that way. You and your horny ass friends will never change, Tony. See you later," she shook her head playfully, stepping off of the elevator.

Getting off, I exhaled heavily, hoping Tasmine was here and that she wouldn't be mad at me still. As I was about to walk down the hall to her room, I saw what looked like the back of her head in the common area. She was watching some movie, wrapped in a bright ass blanket. I smelled kettle popcorn, so I assumed she'd popped some.

"Want some company?" I sat next to her. She was lying on her side, so when she saw me she sat up. I couldn't help but notice that pretty smile upon seeing me.

"No, I was doing just fine. You better leave before one of your children's mothers show up."

"I deserve that, but I swear I don't have any kids. I've been asking for a DNA test, but they never wanna cooperate so, here we are."

"You need to handle that, Anton, if you plan on dating. Especially if you plan on dating me, because I'm not about to be dealing with them girls."

She was right as hell, I did need to handle Kai and Selinda, but the only way I saw to fix things was sending a bullet through their domes. I've done everything in my power to keep them bitches away, but it never worked, and like I said restraining orders were for bitch niggas.

"I know and you shouldn't, you're too good to be dealing with some shit like that. But since you're not doing anything for Thanksgiving, I was thinking we could cook some food together."

"Where the hell am I gonna cook? Only thing Khyle and I have is a fancy microwave."

"I have a full on kitchen at my condo."

"You want me to come to your house? I don't know about all that."

"So you'd rather sit your ass here alone, watching some movie that looks wack as fuck, while munching on some stale ass popcorn, than go to my house where I have a gang of channels and food?"

"Yep," she glanced at me and we shared a laugh. "Fine, let me get my shoes and purse."

I sat there, watching her walk away, looking good as hell. I had to adjust myself and pray that I could be on my best behavior tonight, because as bad as I wanted her, I knew she had no plans on giving that pussy up tonight. But what if she did?

***

"Nigga, these are chicken wings, where is the turkey?" Tasmine frowned as we unpacked all the shit I bought, spreading it on my granite top counters.

"My mama said a turkey would take all fucking day, so I decided we should go with fried chicken," I smiled widely down at her, making her blush.

"Be glad you're cute as fuck, because otherwise I would be ready to go home."

I leaned up against my steel fridge and just watched her wash her hands before seasoning the chicken. I kept quiet as she prepared the other shit because I didn't want her to realize that I wasn't helping. The only thing I ended up doing was putting cheese on the macaroni because in my opinion nobody put enough for me. Since I was like 14, my mama always let me do that because otherwise I would complain that it was just macaroni no cheese.

"Did you really use a whole block, Tony?" her hazel eyes lit up as she stared down into the glass pan.

"You damn fucking right! Can't never have too much cheese on my macaroni and cheese, you'll learn. Now you know for when you make me some, that I use a whole block on that bitch."

"What makes you think I'll be cooking for you past this time?" she laughed lightly.

"I just know." We held eye contact for longer than either of us had intended, before she looked away and went to wash something off of her hands.

About an hour later, the food was ready, and I had my plate piled up like it was gonna be my last. The chicken she fried smelled good as hell, which gave her some brownie points with me. A nigga loved to eat, so I had to be with a girl who could cook more than top ramen, cereal, and microwaved quesadillas. Maybe her chicken was so good 'cause she was from Kentucky. I mean KFC is based on their chicken, right?

"We need to pray first," she stopped me from ripping the damn chicken wing to shreds.

"I ain't never prayed over my food."

"When we went to dinner, you did. When you're around me, you need to always pray first."

Sucking my teeth, I allowed her to place her soft hand into mine, and closed my eyes as she prayed. As soon as she finished, I dug right in, eyes closed and everything.

"I will be honest, Tony, this is probably the best macaroni and cheese that I've ever had. It'll give you a heart attack if you eat it all the time, but it is good," she half smiled, staring down at her plate.

"Told yo' ass. I wish I could eat it every damn day, but I work out too much, and shit like this will make me sluggish."

"Thank God, because your ass would be fat and lonely."

"Nah, I'd have you still." She snapped her neck to look at me like I was crazy. "Yep, I will have you even if I was out here looking like the Nutty Professor."

# CHAPTER EIGHT

# Tasmine

"Nah, you definitely won't see me at all," I responded to his wild ass.

It was funny to me that he actually thought he already had me in the palm of his sexy, strong hands. I mean, he kind of did, but he would never know that. That's why I purposely cut that ass off after that bird popped up on our date. Khyle had Oden in our room and he explained everything to me, but I still wasn't about to hit him up. I didn't like drama, but despite me being turned off a little, I still thought about him and got butterflies when I heard his name.

"Whatever." He set his empty plate on the coffee table, and then downed his water bottle in just a few short gulps. I caught myself staring, so I quickly turned away before he realized it.

"It's cool, I know I'm a good looking ass nigga baby girl." *Asshole.*

"Where is the bathroom?" I rose to my feet. I saw his eyes admiring my body, before he finally stood up too, to lead me across the living room and down the hall. "Thanks."

After relieving myself, I looked around the very well cleaned bathroom, and knew he couldn't be doing this shit himself. I'm sure one of his hoes had been cleaning up for him, because even the cleanest niggas weren't clean enough. I washed my hands with the generic Dial like liquid soap, and looked around a little more as I dried my hands.

"So who cleans this place for you?" I walked out and almost choked when I saw him sitting on the couch in his wife beater. Damn. That beautiful dark skin, which was adorned with a plethora of tattoos, was too fucking much for me. Not to mention the fact that he had just the right amount of muscle, not too buff at all but not even close to being skinny.

"I have a maid who comes through every Monday and Friday to get my shit right. I need her Monday to start the week, and then Friday to come back and spruce shit up." I was happy he didn't have a girl coming through here who was comfortable enough to be cleaning up and shit.

"So do I need to worry about that girl Selinda showing up here?"

"Nah, she doesn't know where I live."

"How? You had a—" I stopped myself when I remembered that this wasn't the same spot he'd had the backyard barbecue at. "Wait, whose home was it that you, Tru, and Oden threw the party?"

"That's our shit," he cheesed, so I knew there was more to it.

"So whose place is this?"

"This is mine too. That other spot on Buffalo is just a place where we turn up, have parties and shit. That's where most people think I live."

"So basically that's where you bring the bitches you wanna fuck and never see again." Before I could even finish he had his balled up fist covering his mouth as he cracked the fuck up. "Wow, I have never heard of anything like that."

"I mean it's the best thing for me and the homies. I could only imagine if half of the hoes I smashed knew where I actually laid my head. I'd have to murk their asses."

"I guess you have a point. I wouldn't want that girl who fucked our date up knowing where I lived either."

"You think the date was fucked up?" His eyes were squinted, and his strong jaw was clenched, really standing out under his sexy mocha complexion. I realized that was something he did when he was upset or in deep thought.

Anyhow, I wanted to say *hell yeah nigga the fuck*? But instead I replied, "I mean, before she got there it was really good, but she just kind of ruined everything."

"I feel you. At least it was good before. I wanna take you out again, but not somewhere close because them hoes be watching me like a fucking hawk man." His mouth was so foul. I didn't care for men who called women bitches and hoes, but as a wise woman once said, 'he ain't talking about me so'…

"Against my better judgment, I'm gonna go on this date with you."

"I know you are." He frowned as if I had him fucked up. I enjoyed his cockiness, a lot. "Aye man, what the fuck are you doing?" he almost jumped out of his skin when I put my feet into his lap.

"I want a foot massage. Standing in that kitchen has them

throbbing a little bit. Please?" I pouted, poking my lip out.

"Hell no! I fucking hate feet, even pretty ones." He stared down at my feet in his lap with his hands up and his screw face on.

"Please, Tony."

"Maaaann, you better be glad you're pretty ass hell. And don't fucking tell nobody about this shit or you and I are gonna have some damn problems aight?" I just nodded, enjoying the feeling of his massage. "Where yo' nigga at?"

"I don't have one."

"What your last one do? You seem like the type to not deal with any nonsense, so I'm sure it was something small," he joked, or at least I think he was joking.

"I umm, I've never had a boyfriend before," I held my breath like a weirdo, waiting for his response. He slowly lifted his head and turned to me with furrowed brows.

"You a virgin?"

"No. I was stupid enough to let some senior in high school convince me to give it up when I was a freshman. But after it happened, he never talked to me again. I haven't had sex since because I'm kind of paranoid."

"Sound like some shit I would do." He paused. "I mean not to you, because I like you, but to these other bitches, yeah, all the time."

"So you lie to get what you want?" I tried to pull my foot from his big hands but he grasped the shit out of my small foot.

"No, I don't lie, I tell them straight up what my intentions are because I don't wanna hear no bullshit when I don't want to converse with them anymore."

"Then that means you've been straight up with me?"

"Hell yeah. I like you. I love the fact that you don't try to please me; you just be yourself and I fuck with that. Too many girls focus on trying to be the girl they think I want, instead of just letting me see who they are. If you approach me on some hoe shit, that's what category I'm gonna put you in. Can't expect me to wanna fuck with you the long way, if the first thing I see is your pussy.

*He likes me!*

"I like you too…" I couldn't quite explain why because I didn't want to sound thirsty. I could go on and on about how sexy his ass was, and how although he was *that* nigga, he didn't have to go around telling everybody.

"I also like that you have rules, you ain't gonna just deal with any damn thing. Men are like kids, whether we want to admit the shit or not, and if you don't set rules for a kid, what do they do?"

"Act a fucking fool."

"Exactly, and us niggas are the same way. If you don't say shit, we're gonna do what the fuck we wanna do until we find a girl that isn't gonna play that bullshit."

"And you think that's me?"

"I know it is."

"Oh okay, good." I played it cool, but I was tap dancing on the inside.

"I ain't never kissed you before." Was he serious?

"Did you forget about that party? The night you got my number?"

He looked into my face with confused eyes, before finally softening his expression and flashing his pretty ass smile.

"I kind of remember, but come remind me." His top of row of perfect teeth dug into his bottom lip, as his eyes roamed my body, making me slightly uncomfortable.

He reached for my arm, and pulled me into his lap so that I was straddling him. Visions of the last time we kissed invaded my mind. I got chills when his hands rested on my waist, holding me tightly. I pressed my lips against his, starting off slow and innocent. Soon enough, we were kissing like we were about to fuck, so I pulled away. The confusion in his face was comical.

"That's all for now."

Climbing out of his lap, I tossed him the remote and he reluctantly turned his TV on. This was hands down one of the better Thanksgivings.

# CHAPTER EIGHT

# Bella

*Bella's Thanksgiving...*

My mother and father cooked a huge ass feast for Thanksgiving; Italian, Cuban, and regular old Thanksgiving food all stirred up into one. That's what you get though when you have parents with different cultures and shit. My daddy wanted his black side and his Italian side to come together, and my mom had to have some Spanish flavor.

After helping my mom clean the kitchen, my fiancé, Dean, and I went to my bedroom to chill. I was stuffed and kind of just wanted to knock out, but I knew he missed me. I was sure that he would be spending the night, and I wasn't gonna say anything even though I wanted my bed to myself. As soon as I kicked my slippers off and laid down, he was on top of me, kissing my neck.

"Dean," I mumbled, but just stopped because I knew he wouldn't listen to my protests.

Dean was gorgeous with his deep chocolate skin, scruffy facial hair, tall muscular frame, and deep brown eyes. I loved him because of how he picked up the pieces when Santino left me high and dry. He became one of my best friends during that time, and for that, I felt like I owed him this relationship. The only problem Dean had was his need to control me. He was two years older, and felt like whatever he wanted was what I was gonna do. Everything was all about his needs in this relationship, even the engagement. He wanted to get married in my senior year so he proposed before I left. I wanted to marry him because I felt like I should, but deep down, I still loved Santino.

Why is it that us women yearn for the niggas who do us dirty? There was no damn reason why I should feel so strongly for Santino when I had a somewhat good man in front of me. But even now as he kissed on my neck, I thought about Santino D'Stefano.

"I'm thinking we should work on a baby, Bella," Dean whispered as he kissed on my neck, forcing his way in between my legs.

"Dean, no. I'm only a freshman—move out of the way." I nudged him back, but he just gripped my wrists and smashed them above my head. As a football player for ASU, he was very strong and very intimidating, especially when he didn't get his way. "Dean, my parents are awake." I tried to wiggle away.

He was now holding both of my skinny wrists with one hand, and releasing his dick with the other. My complaints fell on deaf ears as he sucked my neck and collarbone as if I was into it. Once he had his dick out, he pushed my underwear to the side and forced himself inside of me, not caring that I was dry and not into this. It hurt like hell as he pumped in and out of me, grunting and shit. Tired of wiggling and struggling, I just laid there until he got tired of humping dry pussy. I couldn't get wet for anything.

"Seriously?" he sucked his teeth and rolled off of me.

I was sore as fuck just from that small ass encounter, but I hurriedly got off the bed, ready for him to leave.

If you're wondering why I'm not mortified by his actions it's because it was nothing new. You didn't say no to Dean Wallace, the star football player at Arizona State University. I felt so caged when I was with him, but when I thought about all the shit he'd done for me when I was going through it over Santino, I knew I had to stay with him. But he was another big part of why I went to school in Vegas instead of here in Scottsdale. Being away from him made me feel free. I was a different person when I was with Dean; quiet, reserved, and shy. When away from him, I was myself; fun, feisty, and colorful. I don't know, something about him drained me.

"Dean, I'm not in the mood, and I hate when you just do what you want." I paced the cold laminate floors, rubbing my fingers through my hair. As always, Santino danced around in my mind.

"I put that ring on your finger so that means I get it when I want to. Shit, I've been away from you for months and this is the first time I've seen you."

"I know, but damn, can't we talk a little bit before we get to all that? I don't want our relationship to just be all about sex."

"It won't, come here," he waved me over. I hesitantly made my way back over to the bed where he was, and sat down. He pulled my body into his strong arms, planting kisses all over the side of my face. "I'm sorry for not having a little conversation with you, but you have to understand that I'm the man in this relationship and what I say goes." He caressed my exposed thigh. I just wanted him away from my throbbing vagina. "Now if you wanna talk we can talk about the baby I want."

"Maybe after I graduate and work for at least two years in my career of choice."

"How are you gonna work if I'm in the damn NFL?"

"What do you mean? I'm gonna wake up and go every morning like regular people do. Your football doesn't have anything to do with that."

"If I have to move it does. It's best if you just stick by my side, Bella. And I thought you were gonna study sport's medicine?"

I'd wanted to study sport's medicine since I was a freshman in high school, and it seemed like an even better idea when I started dating Santino. We had it all planned out; he would be a football player and I would be a sports' medicine doctor. But when we broke up, I kind of lost my love for it. So when enrolling in UNLV, I just went undeclared.

"I'm in college, Dean. Why would I go if I was just gonna be a football wife who popped out babies every damn year?" I stood up but he yanked me back down.

"Calm yo' ass down! I just thought you were going so you'd have something to do while I played football. And I knew it would be a free ride for you. Had I thought you were trying to be on yo' independent woman shit, I wouldn't have let you go."

*Wouldn't have let me go?*

"Dean, I'm sleepy. We can hang out tomorrow or something, okay?"

He stared at me angrily, and then scoffed. "Hit me as soon as you wake up. Don't forget, because all that's gonna do is piss me off."

I watched him get off of the bed and slip his shoes on. He looked at me once more before pulling my bedroom door open to leave. I couldn't wait to get back to Vegas.

I powered my phone on as soon as Dean left, since he'd requested that I keep it off earlier, and as soon as my service was up and running, my phone blew up. One person's text in particular caught my eye, Santino.

*Sanz: You should come see me and spend the night.*

*Me: What about your parents?*

I prayed that my response wasn't too late and that the offer still stood.

*Sanz: Overseas, come on. I will leave now to get you.*

*Me: No, I wanna drive myself.*

*Sanz: Yo' ass. Bring me a plate of your mom's food, anything will do.*

I chuckled at his text, before rushing to my bathroom for a quick shower. After slipping into this dress with a hood and my Nikes, I went downstairs to the kitchen to make him a plate, and took my mom's car to meet him. I was way more excited than I should have been.

# CHAPTER EIGHT

## Santino "Sanz" D'Stefano

I stayed seated at the bottom of the steps inside my parents' home, waiting on Bella to get here. I was anxious as fuck, and a little too fucking excited to see her. I know I did her dirty but she needed to understand that I was a 15-year-old kid, who couldn't make decisions about my life like that. What my parents said was what I was supposed to do, and I did. I didn't want to break up with her, but they insisted and if I didn't, they were gonna send me up to Illinois to live with my grandmother. I had too much going for me out here, as far as my football career, and I just couldn't jeopardize it. But I was still in love with Bella and never did fall out.

Knowing she was dating that cat Dean pissed me off every time I thought about the shit. He'd had his eye on Bella since before we broke up, and when we did, he swooped his ass right in. And now they were engaged which was hilarious to me because that damn wedding was not gonna go down. I bet my life on that shit.

As soon as I found out Bella was going to Vegas for college like me, I knew that would be my chance to get her back. My parents no longer footed the bill for my lifestyle, and I was grown, so they couldn't ship me off anywhere. Dean and Bella had better enjoy their last few months—shit, weeks together, because in a minute, she was gonna be right back with daddy.

I heard the doorbell, so I hopped up and jogged lightly across the marble foyer to get it. My parents were rich as hell, and got even richer when they moved from California to Arizona since the cost of living was much cheaper. They were interior designers, so they could work from anywhere and still ball out.

Opening the door, my dick immediately got hard upon seeing Bella in this little dress contraption she wore. It wasn't meant to be sexy, I guess, but the shit was sexy as fuck to me. Anything she wore was sexy as fuck.

"Hey," she half smiled and walked in, her hands deep in the pockets of the dress.

She tried to walk by me but I stopped her and hugged her tightly against my chest. Pushing her hood down off of her head, I stared down into her sad eyes, which made me frown. I didn't know why she was bothered right now, but I hoped it wasn't because she was here with me.

"Happy Thanksgiving," I pecked her lips softly as I shut the door behind her with my free hand.

"Happy Thanksgiving. Why did you come home if your parents

are overseas?" She pulled out of my embrace and began scanning the large foyer with her eyes.

"I think you know why."

"For me? You see me at school."

"Yeah, but I wouldn't have seen you at school during this little holiday, so I came home. Plus, I have a couple homies that wanted to see me and shit too."

"Oh," she reached down into her small duffel bag. "Here is your food?" She handed me the plate, which was wrapped in saran wrap, and tightly too.

"Thanks, baby, follow me."

I went to the kitchen and warmed the food up a bit, before taking her to my bedroom and turning on the television. We were sitting on the bed in there, while she searched for something to watch on HULU.

"I remember this room," she sighed.

"I bet you do. We had some good times in here, some real good ones." I squeezed her leg and put my plate to the side before downing my drink. "Yo' parents can still throw down."

"I know, I was stuffed."

"You had that nigga over?"

"My fiancé? Of course I did, that's one of the people I came home for. I didn't come home for your ass."

"Yet, you're over here instead of with him."

She didn't say anything and just started trying to find something else to look at like she always did when she got nervous. She shifted slightly, and I just chuckled because I knew her like the back of my hand.

Bella and I were meant to be and I was determined to show her that. All my life I've had tunnel vision, focusing on football and making it. Now that I was on my way to the NFL, I was realizing that there was something missing and that was a bonafide relationship.

I wasn't like other niggas who busted in their pants at the thought of smashing different bitches every day. I was the monogamous type. I preferred being in a relationship and building with someone versus having 100 different hoes in my bed who only wanted me because I was NFL bound. Bella was it for me, and I'd have to be in the grave for her to marry this nigga Dean.

"Come here, B," I draped my arm over her shoulders, and tugged her closer to me. I then cut the lamp off, leaving only the TV to illuminate us. Once we made eye contact, her eyes darted away as she frantically used them to search for something else to look at. "Why so nervous, baby?" I hooked her chin, forcing her to look at me.

Bella was so beautiful with her full lips, small nose, golden hair, and big brown eyes. She was skinny but not too much, but even if she were, I wouldn't care. She had a big heart. She loved me still, even though I did her dirty unwillingly.

"I'm not nervous, I'm just…" she sighed, running her manicured nails through her hair. My baby stayed with her feet and hands done, ever since I'd known her, and had me turning my nose up at the sight of chipped polish and shit on other bitches.

I got off the bed, and then moved her to the edge, pulling her dress over her head. Kissing her soft neck, I tugged her underwear down, before reaching behind her to unsnap her bra. Once she was completely naked, I stepped back and got undressed myself.

"Are you serious this time, Sanz?" she questioned as I stood her up so I could pull my thick comforter back.

"I was always serious about you, Bella, I was just immature before and now I'm not," I shrugged, moving her hair behind her shoulders. "Just let me try, and if you ain't fucking with it, cool," I lied. She wasn't getting away from me for a second time, but I'd say anything to get her to fuck with me when we went back to school.

"I can't break up with Dean right now, he—"

"No need. I'll give you that, but once you realize that you wanna be with me exclusively, you have to let that go. Deal?"

She nodded.

Dipping my tongue into her mouth, I kissed her until we fell back onto the bed lightly. I got in between her legs, and had to fight the urge to slide up in her raw. If she got pregnant again, I wouldn't mind one bit, but I knew she had goals and I wanted her to be able to achieve them before having my kid.

I kissed from her lips to her collarbone, before making it to her nipples and sucking gently. Hearing her moan as I groped her small frame, only motivated me and got my dick harder. I missed her so much. I sucked on her flat stomach, while toying with her clit just the way she liked.

"Santino," she whispered.

Standing on my knees, I rolled a condom down and lowered my body onto hers. Our lips met again, and we kissed hungrily as I positioned myself at her opening. I hadn't felt her in so damn long, but I remembered how good the pussy was, even at such a young age. Pinning her hands to the bed, I made eye contact with her as I pushed myself in. She resisted me a little bit, but I was relentless with my attempts to get inside of her, so I eventually got in.

"Fuck, man," I grunted against her ear as she let out soft, broken moans.

Her arms wrapped around my neck as I sucked on hers, moving in and out of her body. With every pump she got wetter, and I could tell that, that nigga Dean wasn't hitting it right at fucking all. She was so tight, almost like she hadn't been touched since the last time we made love. Raising myself up, I held her wrists to the bed and pummeled her feverishly while she cried out, cumming for the second time. Her pretty face was twisted all up, and I just admired it along with her perfect breasts moving about. Feeling her soft thighs against my sides had me reaching my peak, so I gripped her waist and fucked the shit out of her until I filled the condom up.

"I love you, Bella," I panted, pecking her lips gently.

"I love you, too," she *finally* fucking said.

"You gonna spend the night or what?"

"Okay," she half smiled, chest still rising and falling like mine.

After kissing for a little bit longer, we cleaned ourselves up, and got back in the warm bed to talk until we dozed off. This was just the beginning.

# CHAPTER EIGHT

## Oden

Truman and I sat across the street from this little club that was jumping. It was a mediocre spot that I would only expect broke niggas to be at, but that wasn't the case.

We got word from one of the many valet companies that we worked with, that there would be a lot of luxury vehicles in the house tonight. Truman and I weren't doing the robbing, because that shit wasn't our job anymore. But I was here because I wanted to keep an eye on the niggas on the job tonight, Jacob and Ray, to make sure they're getting the shit right. Some niggas acted like a 24-hour turnaround was too much, so I was gonna show them that it wasn't if they used some fucking elbow grease.

"I just knew tonight was gonna be a bust, but I see some nice ass whips up in there." Truman took a pull on his blunt, blowing the smoke out the window.

"Same. I don' seen every muthafuckin' type of car pull up in this bitch. This must be a private party because I'm sure the shit would have been held somewhere else otherwise."

"Right," he nodded.

I lit my own blunt, and took a nice pull on it as I watched the last few people pile into the club. Once it was pretty clear in the lot, the valet guy pulled his phone out to call my people. Ray and Jacob ran up about ten minutes later, and took two sets of keys. I waited with my blunt to my lips to see which cars they belonged to, and finally took a toke when I saw them hit the alarm on a black Wraith and a silver Panamera.

Ray was quick with it, hopping into the Panamera and peeling out, but Jacob was conversing with the valet guy still for some reason, pissing me off. He finally walked to the car, cheesing like the job had been completed, when all of a sudden, some nigga rushed out with two buff guys behind him.

"Shit, come on!" I told Truman, ashing my blunt and getting out of the car. I pulled my gun from my waist and removed the safety as Truman and I booked it across the street.

The two buff niggas had Jacob hemmed up, as the smaller guy punched him relentlessly.

*POP! POP! POP! POP!*

Truman and I sent off some bullets, dropping the two buff niggas instantly. As we ran up, the smaller guy turned to us making eye contact, and I realized he was a worker for Billz Montgomery, one of the biggest drug dealers in La Vegas. I ain't know his name, but I'd seen him one night when Billz paid me top dollar to host a party at my nightclub Palace.

"Oden?" the guy frowned.

"Yeah, nigga."

*POP!*

I dropped him immediately.

"Drive the fucking car!" Truman hollered into Jacob's beat up face.

I didn't give a fuck if he could barely see, he'd better work it the fuck out. And the car better not have one damn scratch on it either, or he was getting killed. Shit, who am I kidding, he was dying tonight either way. He fucked up royally, and I was gonna make an example out of his ass like the niggas before him.

"Oden—" Jacob tried to say.

"Drive!" I got right in his face, making him jump and fumble with the keys a little bit.

I turned to leave with Truman, stopped, and then turned around to smoke the valet guy since he contributed. He knew the job and what he was supposed to do, and it didn't include politicking with Jacob.

Truman and I rushed back across the street to the car before the people inside processed all these damn gunshots. I was in such a rush that I didn't have time to get my silencer, so there was probably gonna be pandemonium in a moment.

We waited until Jacob sped out, and then followed him to meet with Ray at one of the chop shops. We got there about twenty minutes later, and pulled into the underground part of the shop.

Ray's car was already being worked on, so I nodded in approval as I got out my whip. Truman rushed the Panamera, yanked Jacob out, and slammed him into the wall, gritting in his face. Like me, Truman had a temper, which is why it was best for Anton to come with us so he could balance everything out. Because once I got mad, all sense and rational thoughts went out the fucking window. All three of us had short fuses really, but Anton was better at controlling his… most of the time. Maybe because he was used to dealing with Selinda, Kai, and Violet.

"Take him to the back, Tru. Wait for me." Truman did as he was told, escorting Jacob's bitch ass to the back. "Nice job, Ray. Be ready for tomorrow night. You won't be working with Jacob though." I patted his shoulder, cashed him out, and then dapped him up before he left.

I conversed with the shop manager for a little bit, letting him know these cars needed to be out by tomorrow night, and no later. Once he assured me that what I wanted would happen, I went to the back where Truman had Jacob. Jacob was sitting down whimpering due to the injuries that Billz' flunky had given him.

"Fuck was so important that you needed to talk to the valet guy about instead of doing your fucking job, Jacob?" I closed the door and pulled up a chair in front of him.

"I'm sorry, Oden. I just got caught up—"

"On the fucking job!" I barked making his hoe ass jump again. I was mad as fuck and trying to keep myself calm so that I wouldn't beat this nigga to death. "How in the fuck do you get caught up while working, man?"

"It wasn't even that long, Oden," he sniffled.

"Oh, so I'm tripping?" I palmed my chest, raising my eyebrows as if I was hella offended. Shit I was offended.

"No! No, hell nah you're not, I'm just saying it wasn't that long that I was conversing with old boy."

"Those both can't be the case. Either I'm exaggerating or you were talking with him longer than you should have. You talked long enough for someone to run out whoop yo' ass, dummy!"

He couldn't say anything, he just sat there crying and shit, looking ugly as fuck. I was disgusted at how weak he was and at the fact that I even had this nigga on my team. I didn't even wanna waste my bullets on this nigga. I gave Truman the look so he knew to off his ass, and then I left.

***

Walking into my spot, I smiled when I saw Khyle on the couch eating snacks and watching *American Horror Story*. She loved that damn show, but only watched it at my crib for some reason. When she saw me, a sweet smile covered her face, the same one she always gave me. That shit boosted a nigga's ego because you could literally see her light up at the sight of me.

"What, you in love or some shit?" I frowned, pulling my jacket and shirt off. I watched her eyes dance all over my chest, tattoos, and abs.

"In love with this burrito," she lifted it to show me.

"Yeah, aight. I saw you get all happy and shit when I came through the door, baby, it's okay." I leaned over her, and kissed her soft lips so hard her head tilted back. "You love this dick though, huh?" I groaned against her lips before kissing her again. She just nodded subtly, biting her lip in between kisses.

Her head was back against the couch, as I continued to tower over her while kissing her hungrily. She caressed my face for a little bit, before I finally pulled away.

I took a hot shower, and then returned to the living room with her so I could get some of her burrito. I got a fork from the kitchen, some water, and then cut the lights off before plopping down next to her.

"Almost made me drop it," she giggled.

My girl was pretty as fuck. Damn, a nigga was lucky. She wasn't that stuck up pretty girl either, she was dope, which only made her look even better. Not to mention the sex was phenomenal, and she knew how to have a fucking conversation, but also be silly when she wanted to. I had no plans of letting her go, and I had a feeling her ex nigga wasn't about to be over her that easily. Granted it'd been months, but I think that was only because we were in different states.

"Anybody got a problem with us being in a relationship?"

"No, maybe Shayne, but who cares. My parents love you, especially my mother. My dad… he likes you too," she nodded.

"Why did you pause after saying 'my dad'?" I stuffed a forkful of the bomb ass burrito into my mouth, awaiting the answer.

"He umm, he just thinks you're a womanizer, but I would kill your ass and I'm sure you know that so I'm not worried."

"I wouldn't cheat on you, you know that. And if you don't, we have a problem, don't we? But your dad is right, I am a bit of a player, but I would never do you like that," I spoke honestly. I was never one to play the role, not for anybody. Her pops was right, I had all kinds of women, but that didn't mean I was gonna cheat on my girl. Her dad peeped that too, and that's why he still liked me.

"I'm aware, so we don't have a problem." She scooted closer to me, so I draped my arm around her as we continued to attack the burrito in silence. It was a thinking silence; you could tell we were just muddling over all kinds of shit.

"Anybody else tripping?" I finally asked.

"I blocked someone, but I'm sure you know who that is."

"Ex?"

"Yeah."

"Well, let's hope it stops there because we don't want shit getting out of hand, right?" She shook her head no, glancing up at me for a few before turning back to her burrito. I kissed her temple a couple times to lighten the mood, because I could tell she was feeling some type of way.

I was a dangerous nigga, and I wanted to keep her away from that side of me, but when I got mad that was it. I already knew if I even thought that nigga Brian was trying to push his way back into her life, I was gonna kill him; same goes for Shayne. I really didn't wanna do that shit though because I knew Khyle would look at me differently.

"Brian is like a little fly, and he'll get over me in no time." She pecked me, placing the empty plate onto the coffee table. She straddled my lap, and ran her fingers through my big ass hair as much as she could. "Have you been deep conditioning like I told you to?" Her pretty ass face was now all balled up.

I shrugged with a half-smile, so she began pinching at my ribs because she was the only person who knew that I was ticklish there.

"Aye, stop that shit!" I barked, trying not to smile as I gripped her small wrists.

"Okay, okay, I'm not gonna touch you if you answer the question." She was grinning, and as usual, I got lost in her beauty.

"Nah, baby, I haven't been. Shit, give me a break. I just started putting conditioner in after I wash it."

"I will fix your hair tomorrow."

"No."

"Please, daddy?"

I tucked my bottom lip in, and brought her body closer into mine so she could feel how hard my dick was through my boxers. It was the only thing I was wearing since I'd just gotten out of the shower.

"What I tell you about calling me daddy?" I moved her pajama shorts and panties to the side, and stuck my fingers inside of her.

Her facial expression was filled with pleasure as I plunged my two fingers in and out of her tight hole. She was whimpering lightly while holding onto my shoulders. Her sex faces always took me there, so I just gaped while fingering her pussy.

"Damn, babe, you're about to cum," I stated versus asking. I could feel her muscles tightening around my fingers so I sped up.

"Ahhh, uuuh!" she called out, trembling a little and panting. "Oden!"

Taking my fingers out of her, I put them into my mouth one by one to suck her juices off, as she continued to quiver a little bit in my lap. Once I was done sucking her juices off, she shoved her tongue down my throat so we could get the party started.

273

# CHAPTER NINE

## Shayne

*I*'d just come home from an audition, and even though it went great and I was sure I would get the part, I felt glum. Something was wrong with me, and I couldn't quite pinpoint it. I hate when I'm sad and don't know why, and unfortunately, that was my current situation. I knew it was a combination of things, but it was shit that shouldn't have really mattered to me.

"Bitch, pass the bottle," Alanna snapped me from my pity party.

I was lying on the couch, staring up at the ceiling. Alanna brought over some wine, and she said that Marisol was coming too. Marisol and I were cool for like a week after our threesome with Oden, but we soon realized that was the only thing we had in common. He wasn't calling her, and he damn sure wasn't calling me, so there wasn't shit for us to bond over.

*KNOCK! KNOCK!*

"Here she is," Alanna stood up, fixing her jeans. Opening the door, I saw her smile widely and hug someone. Marisol finally appeared with another bottle, dressed bomb as usual.

"I was thinking after we polish off this bottle we should go meet with these two *bosses* I met. They both were bomb as hell. The one that got my number is cute, but his boy is way fuckin' cuter. I was a little pissed that I'd already chose up," Marisol rolled her eyes, speaking in her heavy Spanish accent.

"How the hell you know these niggas are bosses? The only way they can be is if they're part of Billz or Oden's crew, and I know everyone that Oden fucks with," I sat up, irritated that she'd met some niggas for some reason.

"Because I checked their attire out. Robin jeans, crisp ass white t-shirt, iced out jewelry, and some wheat colored Timbs. His finer homeboy was dressed better, but again I had to keep my eyes on mine," she explained, popping open the wine.

"Only two?" Alanna rolled her eyes.

"Yeah, I asked if they had a homeboy and I think they thought I was looking for a train to be ran on me, so I nipped that questionnaire in a bud."

The three of us laughed at her response.

We downed that whole bottle Marisol brought over, and by that time I was feeling like having some fun, so I decided to go along. I couldn't sit and mope about Oden anymore, especially when I should be more upset at the fact that my sister wasn't fucking with me. It's kind of bad that we let a nigga get between us, but hopefully this wouldn't last long at all.

"Let me just put my shoes on," I said, getting up and rushing to the back.

As I was fastening my heels around my ankle, in walked Pierce. I just rolled my eyes and kept doing what the fuck I was doing. We were just living together at this point; well, in my opinion we were. To him, we were still in love and working on our relationship, but I'd been over it.

"Leaving?" he raised a brow, setting his keys on the tall dresser next to the bedroom door.

"Yeah, gonna celebrate the new gig I booked. It's a permanent one; shows all year round," I half lied. I was sure I'd gotten it, but I hadn't gotten the confirmation yet. And tonight's festivities had nothing to do with my work, but I couldn't tell him that.

"That's great, baby. I'm gonna have to take you out next Thursday when I get paid."

"Mm hmm." I stood up and the nigga got right in my face, wrapping his muscular arms around my waist, and pulling me close. He smelled good and looked even better like always, but I just wasn't into what we had anymore. I wanted Oden.

"Let me holler at you for a second before you go."

"Okay, move back." I stepped out of his embrace, and walked to my dresser to spray on my Escada perfume.

"My boy from work, Alvin, was telling me he saw you at Palace Nightclub. You were up in the glass box VIP, all over Oden Bishop."

"And you believe him?" I was sweating bullets. Why was I sweating bullets? I didn't want this nigga, so who cares if he found out?

"Nah, I don't know, which is why I'm asking you. If I believed him I would have come at you very differently, you know me. So tell me, were you at the club and up in the VIP with Oden?"

"Yeah, he invited Marisol up, and since we were with her we came. He remembered me from the barbecue, so we did exchange a few words, but that was it, Pierce."

"Shayne, I love you and I know it's hard out here for a pretty girl like you with niggas all in your face, but I don't want you hanging out with Oden and his crew. I don't care who gets invited to his shit, unless it's me."

"What? Why? I thought y'all were cool?" I turned to face him, frowning. I really wanted to know because they seemed to be old friends at the barbecue.

"We are. I fuck with him but I know how he is. He, Tru, and Tony fuck anything pretty with a pussy, and I wouldn't be surprised if one of them tried to get at you. And if that happens it's gonna be a fucking problem," he stated sternly, turning me on a little bit.

"Okay, baby, I won't hang around them anymore, no matter what." I leaned my head back and he kissed my lips.

"Thanks, have fun tonight, but not too much."

"Okay." I almost wanted to tell Alanna and Marisol to go ahead because Pierce was so attractive to me right now, but I was halfway interested in who these niggas were that Marisol had bragged about. "Let's go, ladies."

The three of us piled into Marisol's Range Rover truck, which had me wondering how the hell she'd gotten it. I didn't know what she did, and she clearly didn't have a man, so I had to ask her ass.

"When and how did you get this?" I quizzed.

"Couple months ago. I was fucking with this dude and the nigga was so sprung he bought the shit for me. He paid it in full, and got it in my name. I stopped fucking with his ass right after," she smacked her lips, checking her lipstick in the rearview mirror at the red light.

"Do you ever meet men that you actually wanna build with?" Alanna's hopeless romantic ass asked.

That nigga Earl Jr. really did a number on her. His game came on the other day and she had to excuse herself so she could cry in the fucking bathroom. And I'm pretty sure he just proposed to some bitch he's been sporting around with him.

"Nope. These niggas ain't shit so all I wanna do is use them for dick and/or their money. Oh, but damn that Oden, I would definitely give that relationship a try," she giggled. "The dick was so bomb, huh. Shayne?" she looked to me through her rearview smiling.

"Yep." I put extra emphasis on my P.

"Mm hmm. It was bomb when I shared it with you, but when he and I did it alone a couple of times, girl, I almost said 'I love you' during." My heart stopped when she said she'd gotten him alone. I thought that after our threesome, that was the last time.

"Bitch, you're lying!" Alanna laughed, clapping her hands.

"No I'm not! Girl, I had to change it to 'I love *this dick*' with the quickness. And we did it three damn times that night."

"I thought you said he wasn't answering your calls?" I frowned.

"And he wasn't. But I'm very persistent, so I waited a week or two then hit him with that goodnight text. Nigga text back 20 minutes later with that 'what you doing?' and it was on and popping!" She stuck her tongue out and popped her ass in her seat to the song playing in her car, as Alanna cracked up. They hi-fived one another as I glared at the back of Marisol's head.

"When was the last time?" Alanna inquired.

"Couple months ago. He got him a girlfriend or some shit. I saw her picture on his Instagram. She's cute, kind of favors you, Shayne, that's crazy."

"I'm sure it's Khyle, Shayne's little sister," Alanna replied. I wanted to slap Alanna's ass.

"Damn, your baby sister stole your nigga?" Marisol covered her mouth, dying laughing as she pulled up into the Caesar's Palace Hotel.

"She ain't stole shit, I have a nigga. Oden was only good for one thing, and I got it on multiple occasions. Khyle has nothing special, that dick is for everybody in Vegas."

"Clearly that dick ain't for everybody because neither you nor me can get it anymore," Marisol shot back. I just decided to be quiet because she'd ruined my mood.

She pulled up to the valet guy and the three of us climbed out. I grabbed the ticket from him since she was too damn busy texting on her phone. We entered the beautiful ass hotel, and just stood there as Marisol waited for the niggas to answer the phone.

"Okay, come on."

We took the elevator up, and ended up on a quiet ass floor. I wouldn't mind sleeping out in the hallway because it was just that nice. When we arrived to their suite door, you could faintly hear music coming from inside. Marisol knocked and as we waited, she swayed her hips to the song. I wanted to beat her ass but I had no valid reason, and I didn't wanna beat on someone who'd eaten my pussy so good.

"What's good?" some sexy dude answered the door. His accent was screaming that he was from New York.

He was wearing jeans, and a white t-shirt that wasn't too tight but showed his muscles, and Timbs like when he met Marisol. His skin was a nice caramel shade, and his dreads were long with blond tips. He was fine, but he had no facial hair, which was a turn off.

"Hey, Roone," she hugged him, and then the three of us entered the beautiful but smoked out suite. "These are my girls Shayne and Alanna."

"Nice to meet you," Roone nodded, and then turned back around to lead us further in.

When we got to his room of choice, a living room, there was another guy sitting there texting away on his phone. He had deep chocolate skin, a long scruffy beard, and I could tell he was tall from his long torso, arms, and legs. His curly hair was freshly lined up, and I almost wet my panties when he rose to his feet, eyes lower than a whip with hydraulics.

His jeans were a deep blue color, and like Roone, his shirt fit nicely, allowing his muscles to bulge through a bit. His arms and neck were covered in tattoos, and despite the large blunt hanging between his fingers, he smelled like a million bucks. He hiked up his somewhat baggy jeans, letting his teeth sink into his lip, and I saw he had some gold slugs in the front. I hated them fucking things but on him, it was sexy as hell.

"How y'all ladies doing? I'm Lloyd," he spoke, his southern drawl apparent as fuck.

"Fine," the three of us said, almost in a trance. Poor Roone, he was no match for his fine ass homie.

"Where are y'all from?" I cocked my head.

"Roone is from Queens, and I'm from Birmingham, shawty," Lloyd responded.

"Alabama?" Alanna raised a brow and he nodded slowly with his sexy ass, licking his full chocolate lips. His eyes were so low that if he weren't standing up and talking, I would think he was asleep.

"Have a seat. Do y'all smoke? Drink?" Roone quizzed as Lloyd and I kept eye contact. Every time he ran his tongue across his bottom lip, my clit throbbed.

"Yeah, we do both, what y'all got?" Marisol spoke up for us, as everyone except Roone took a seat.

"Vodka, Tequila, Rum, and we have all kinds of juice," Roone answered.

"Rum and coke for me," Alanna ordered, and Marisol and I ended up just getting the same thing. I thought it would be nasty, but since the rum was that Malibu brand, it was a little sweet and bomb.

"See, I told you the homeboy was finer," Marisol whispered to me, while eyeing Lloyd. She was right.

The five of us went on to smoke some strong ass weed they had, drank, and listened to music. A lot of the music they played was Gucci Mane, not really my style, but after a few drinks, he was sounding good to me.

About two hours into us getting live, Roone and Marisol went to the bedroom of the suite, leaving Alanna and I with Mr. Fine as fuck. He and I kept making eye contact, and although awkward every time, I couldn't stop looking at his sexy ass.

"Come over here," he mouthed under the music, patting the seat cushion next to him. I glanced over at Alanna who was next to me, and that bitch was cross-faded as hell, swaying in her seat with her cup slightly lifted as if this were a club. My poor friend.

I got up and walked over to him, and noticed he was checking my body out. He wasn't shy at all, and I loved that about a man; it reminded me of Oden.

"Hi," I smiled, giggling like a weirdo. I was high and drunk, and feeling a little warm all over.

"Hey," he grinned. His smile was so beautiful despite the slugs on the few front ones.

"Can you take those out?" I frowned.

"What, these?" he pointed to his slugs and I nodded. "Yeah, but I only take them out when I have to."

"And when is that? When you go to church?"

"Nah," he chuckled in his deep raspy voice. "When I'm eating pussy."

He spoke so seriously, which meant he wasn't joking. I was gonna laugh at first but since he didn't even crack a smile, I kept my laughter inside.

"Oh well, that makes sense."

"You from Vegas?"

"No, I'm from California."

"Oakland?"

"Ugh, no, I'm from the Southern area."

"Why you say ugh?" He was cheesing widely, showing me the deep dimples in his cheeks.

"Because Oakland bitches are hood as hell, and I'm not like that at all."

"Southern Cali got some hood ones too, from Compton, Long Beach, Watts, shit, all of South Central. There are hoods and hood bitches and niggas everywhere, shawty." I would have to get used to that 'shawty' shit.

"I guess," I shrugged one shoulder, knowing he was right. I didn't expect him to be so familiar with Los Angeles. As I sat there sipping my drink, I felt something cold in my lap. When I looked down, I saw it was his iPhone and the screen was shattered. "You need to get your shit fixed." My lip was turned up.

"I don't give a fuck about that, but put your number in."

"I ain't slicing my damn fingers up, I will read it off to you, and you can type the shit in. My hands are too precious for such a thing."

"Nah, you gon' type it in."

Seeing he was dead serious, I picked the phone up and typed my number in as he'd demanded. Handing it back to him, he looked it over and nodded.

"You out here for good?" I quizzed, not wanting him to return to Alabama anytime soon for some reason.

"Yep, got some work here so I'm staying."

"Cool."

I brought the cup to my lips to cover the smile breaking through my face. I was feeling this nigga, so this would surely be interesting.

# CHAPTER NINE

*One week later...*

This weekend was my parents' anniversary, so they paid to fly Shayne and I home. Oddly, I didn't see Shayne on my plane or at the airport, so I didn't know if she was really coming. My parents had no idea that we'd gotten into it, and I wanted to keep it that way. Them finding out that Oden was the center of our argument would have them not liking him.

I didn't want to lose my sister over a man. She needed to move on *and* she needed to apologize for sending me that damn picture before I forgave her. I was wrong in some areas too so I would be happy to apologize, but only after her.

The plane ride was short as hell, and I only had to stand outside for about two minutes before I saw my dad's Porsche truck pulling up. He and my mom hopped out of the car, and my mom hugged me, surprisingly. When I pulled back, I searched her eyes to see if she was drunk or something. She never hugged me, and when she did show me affection it was usually because of liquor.

"You okay, Mom?"

"Yes, I'm fine. I didn't realize how much I missed having you around until you left for school." She rubbed my hair back before kissing my nose.

"I missed you, too," I half smiled.

My father placed my suitcase into the trunk, and then hugged me way too tightly like always. After planting a few kisses on my forehead, he opened the back door for me, and then got in on the driver's side. It felt good to be home, but I of course missed my boo.

We got to our home in Torrance in no time, and I saw Shayne's car parked outside. Rolling my eyes, I hurriedly hopped out of the backseat and grabbed my bag from the trunk. Shayne met me at the door smiling, and even though I didn't want to smile back I couldn't help it. As soon as I set my bag down in the living room, she tackled me onto the couch to rain kisses all over my face.

"Move, Shayne!" I screamed. She always did this shit, and I hated it.

"Do you forgive me for trying to push up on Oden?" she whispered right into my face, still hugging me. My parents walked in, ignoring our awkward embrace and my screams because this was normal.

"Do you forgive me for talking to him even though you told me you wanted to be with him?" She nodded her head 'yes'. "Okay then, I forgive you too—Ah!" Before I could finish, she was pecking my face all over again.

"I think I met the love of my life," she let me go and stood up, running her hand down her long ass ponytail.

"Oh Lord, Shayne, who is this person?"

"I don't want to jinx it, but once I know for sure I will tell you. I just met him, so I have to feel him out some more, you know?"

"Well, once it's for sure I would love to meet him then." I fixed the pillow that we messed up. "Why didn't you take the plane like me?"

"I wanted to drive and clear my head."

I nodded in response.

We chatted for a little longer, and it felt good; it felt like old times. Afterwards, we ate the dinner my mom cooked in the dining room, and then went into our old bedrooms to nap before the anniversary party for tonight. My life was getting back on track finally, and boy was I thankful.

*The next day...*

To my surprise, that anniversary party was fun as hell. The music was good, so was the food, and my parents let me have a little champagne. I hadn't had that much fun with family in a long time. Everyone was there, including our cousins from Seattle, and it just felt great to laugh and enjoy my sister again. My cousin, Delaney, applied to UNLV so she hoped to come there next year. I was happy to hear that because I loved her and hated that she lived in another state.

It was around 10am, and I'd just gotten out of the shower. I missed having my own bathroom, and didn't realize how much of a luxury it was until I moved on campus. All the bedrooms in my parents' home had a bathroom in it. Tasmine was clean, but we shared a bathroom with the girls next door, one of them being that bitch named Raquel. She was like the biggest Oden Bishop groupie in life, but that's another story for another day.

After brushing, flossing, and rinsing, I slipped into something cool because the shower still had me hot. It was getting colder outside since it was early to mid-December, but I hadn't planned to go anywhere today.

I checked my phone, blushing at the cute messages sent to me from Oden, which prompted me to FaceTime him. I was definitely the jealous type if you didn't know, so I wanted to do this random face call to make sure he was on his best behavior. I knew deep down that he was, but there was nothing wrong with checking. He answered on the third ring, running his hand over his big curly fro like always.

"You deep condition?" I smiled.

"Maaaan," he groaned as I chuckled. "I'm gonna do it tonight. That shit better not smell all fruity and shit either or I'm gonna fuck you up."

"I may like that."

"Well, shit then," he bit down on his lip as we laughed in unison. His eyes were slanted, so I knew he was high off his ass.

I talked to him on FaceTime for two fucking hours and didn't even notice until we hung up. And the only reason we did was because he said he had a meeting. I made myself a snack and some iced tea, and as I was about to go upstairs to my bedroom, I heard the doorbell.

I blew out hot air, and then went to look through the peephole to see Emery. Setting my food on the table next to the door, I snatched it open and stood there with a blank expression.

"Can I come in? It's cold as hell!"

"Fine, but whatever you're here for it better be quick!"

"Can I come up to your room? I wanna have some privacy."

I slammed the door after rolling my eyes, and then grabbed my food to take it upstairs. She walked in my bedroom after me as I texted my parents to let them know she was here. They always wanted to know when someone was over and who it was.

I sat down on my bed, and started going in on the fake ass chipotle bowl I made, waiting for this bitch to talk.

"Well," she cleared her throat, taking her gloves off and sitting down on the loveseat in my room. "I'm pretty sure I'm moving to Vegas."

"What? Why? How?" Emery lived with her mother who I knew had no plans on moving. Also, she didn't have money like that, shit she didn't have a job, so how was she moving to Vegas?

"You know I've been wanting to move out of my mom's home and shit, but California is too expensive unless you move to like Hesperia or Victorville, and that's too far from everything. I looked up some homes in Arizona and Vegas, so it's between those two. I also applied for a job in a call center, and the lady is gonna interview me here. I told her the Arizona or Nevada locations were fine."

"Great, but why the fuck are you here?" I hated to be rude, but she fucked my nigga and I wasn't fucking with her because of that.

"Khyle, for real?"

"Fuck do you mean for real?"

"You're still mad over what happened months ago?"

"Have we talked since then? No the fuck we haven't, so why would you think that I wasn't mad anymore, baby girl?"

"I don't know, Khyle. It just seems nonsensical to be so upset over a guy who has slept with your sister, and then your best friend. I mean, you could do better in my opinion."

I held tightly onto my bowl of food so that I wouldn't deck her ass between the eyes.

"I can do better, yet you specifically came over to Vegas to fuck him. Okay, Emery. You're just upset because he smashed and passed your ass."

"I couldn't care less."

"Right, well he's my boyfriend right now so that means anything negative you have to say, keep it to yourself if you're ever around me." Emery's eyes bucked when I said Oden was my boyfriend.

As soon as I finished, there was a knock at the door. Emery stood up to let them in, and when Shayne saw her she rolled her eyes. Shayne never liked Emery because she always said she was a sheisty hoe.

"Can I get your nail polish remover?" Shayne questioned, obviously irritated by Emery's presence.

I pointed to it since my mouth was full. Emery spoke to Shayne, but like always, my sister pretended that she didn't hear her, leaving without replying.

"Your sister is a bitch."

"Okay, Emery, is there anything else you wanna talk about?"

"He's like for real your boyfriend? What about Brian?"

"Brian and I are a wrap. And yes that's my real boyfriend, like on some spend every damn moment together shit." I pointed to my necklace bearing his last name.

"You bought that? A little overboard, don't you think?"

"No, bitch, he bought it. Now let's go so I can work on some of my assignments."

"Khyle, I just want us to be cool again. I miss you and I'm gonna need you when I move out to Nevada. You know you miss me too. Them bourgeois bitches from your school are already getting on your nerves, I'm sure, especially Bella," Emery whined as we descended the stairs.

"No, they actually know the meaning of friendship, goodbye." I pulled the front door open, and slammed it behind her hoe ass as soon as she crossed the threshold.

I ran back upstairs to finish eating, and to start on my final paper for Freshman English, before passing out, enjoying a little nap.

***

I woke up around 6:30pm with my laptop, notebooks, textbooks, and highlighters sprawled all across the foot of my bed. I could never nap with all of this shit back at the dorm, since my bed was much smaller, so this was new for me. I went downstairs to make myself some tea with whipped cream, and then went back to my room to work some more on my paper. As I was typing away, my phone buzzed and I saw it was a text from Oden.

*Baby: Getting home around 1am, down for FaceTime?*

*Me: Of course, you better not forget either.*

*Baby: I couldn't forget about you even if I tried.*

I got warm all over like always, and reread the text a couple more times. It was crazy to me how bomb of a boyfriend he was. I didn't expect it I must say.

*Me: Same baby. Talk to you tonight.*

Smiling like a Cheshire cat, I continued typing my paper and ended up finishing around 8:30pm. As I prepared my shit for a nice hot bubble bath, my phone rang. I looked down at it to see Brian's name, and contemplated on whether I should answer or not. *I should have never unblocked him.* I decided not to, but when the ringing stopped, he called again. Blowing out hot air, I picked up my iPhone to answer.

"Hey."

"What's up, beautiful?"

"Brian, what?"

"Damn, why are you so fucking rude? That nigga got you tripping and not remembering who the fuck you're talking to."

"I'm about to hang up on yo' ass because clearly you forgot who the fuck *you're* talking to. If you don't tell me why the fuck you called me in a few seconds, I'm hitting the end button." This nigga had me pissed off that quickly.

"Calm down… feisty ass. I called because I'm outside and I wanna talk to you for a little bit, that's all. We broke up over the phone, with that nigga talking all in the back. We need to discuss some shit."

"Fine."

I hung up on his ass and slipped my big jacket and UGGs on. I knew I should have changed out of my pajama shorts and tube top, but this was about to be quick. I walked out of the house and spotted Brian's car sitting in my parents' big ass driveway. Getting into his car, I stared straight ahead, sucking on a jolly rancher and toying with my necklace.

"You smell good," he chuckled.

"Thanks."

"Still wearing Very Sexy Now by Vicky Secrets?"

"Yep."

"I love that shit. What, you got the lotion and soap too?"

"They don't make a soap for this fragrance, it's part of the more expensive lines. Brian, you need to talk, I didn't come to discuss my perfume."

When we broke up, he went in on me on Twitter calling me a hoe, had his homies amping him too, and I was still a little upset over it. I didn't like people in our business, and this nigga gave everyone some tea to sip.

"Honestly, I just want to know what happened, Khyle? I mean, I came down there and we were cool, then not even two weeks later, you hit me in the middle of the night on some bullshit and got another nigga with you." His handsome face was balled up.

It did sound shady, and it was shady. I couldn't blame him for being confused because anybody who wasn't aware of what I had with Oden would be confused.

"Brian, I'm gonna be honest, okay?" I glanced at him and he nodded. "I was happy with you before I left, I guess, but when I got to school I met someone. Literally the day I touched down, I met someone at a party that night. I don't know how or why, but we clicked, more than I expected us to. In fact, I didn't expect to click with anyone."

"So you ended a two-year relationship with a nigga you love because y'all clicked?" he scoffed, shaking his head. It was cold so he turned his car on and blasted the heat.

"No. I tried to just be his friend, and when I saw I couldn't be, I ended that. I did what I could to stay apart from him, but I couldn't, Brian."

"You sure didn't say shit when I visited."

"I know, and I'm sorry. I should have told you then that I'd met someone that I wanted to be with. But when you came, I got confused because we were having such a good time."

"So then how do you know you want him?"

"Because when I had you two in the same room, it became obvious where I wanted to be."

"So you're for real with Oden Bishop," he flicked my necklace and laughed. I snapped my neck to look at him, surprised he knew his full name.

"How do you know him?"

"I don't *know* him, I know *of* him. Nigga is some hood from Vegas, into all kinds of shit. I heard he has thousands of bodies under his belt from muthafuckas he's murdered and from bitches he's fucked."

"Well, as his woman, I'm letting you know none of that shit is true."

"So he ain't fuck your sister and Emery? So you ain't never seen a gun locked in his waist? Or seen one around his spot? Fuck out of here."

"Goodnight, Brian." I pulled on the lever to get out of the car.

"I hope you made him wait as long to fuck as you made me."

"Not even." I slammed the car door, but I could see him scowling through the window at me.

I don't know what his motive was, but the shit didn't work. Nobody was gonna convince me that Oden wasn't the one, nobody. That's why I was gonna take my bath, eat the dinner my mom cooked, and FaceTime with him until I fell asleep. Hating ass niggas.

# CHAPTER NINE

## Tasmine

*I*'d been studying in the library for fall semester finals all day damn near, and now that it was getting dark I was hungry as fuck.

Since Khyle introduced me to In-N-Out, I'd been addicted to it. I didn't even like burgers like that, but their buns were off the fucking chain. And the meat, you could for real taste that they cooked them in a skillet or grill and that they weren't freezer burgers. On top of the fact that they were exquisite, they were located damn near on campus so it was convenient as fuck.

Instead of walking to my dorm in Dayton, I cut through by the upperclassmen dormitory so I could make it to In-N-Out. I spotted one of my classmates, Reuben, who grinned widely and stopped in his tracks upon seeing me. Reuben was a cute sophomore who played on the basketball team. According to everyone who went here last year, he was the Santino D'Stefano, Bella's crush, of basketball. Basketball season hadn't arrived yet, but I was anxious to see if he was really as good as they said he was, because Santino was a beast in football.

"Hey, where are you going? Don't you stay in Dayton?"

"Going to get a burger. And while you're questioning me, don't you stay in Tonopah?" I cocked my head, giving him a light smirk.

"Yeah, I was coming from a study session up over there," he tilted his head towards the South dorm and I nodded. "But damn, I could eat. Mind if come with you?"

"I guess, just in case someone tries to mug me you can distract them while I get away."

"Damn, that's fucked up," he replied as we chuckled in unison. "But since you're fine as fuck I don't really mind being your bodyguard."

Pushing my disheveled brown hair behind my ear, I gave him a shy smile.

Since Thanksgiving break, Anton and I had been getting extremely close. We talked every day, and usually tried to hang out if I didn't have to study and he didn't have to work. I expected him to be this thugged out fool who could only talk about his bank account status and getting some ass, but he was deeper than that. We had a lot of things in common, surprisingly.

I mention all that to say that I didn't feel too comfortable flirting with another man right now, because I didn't want Anton to take it the wrong way. Yes, he was nowhere around us, but everybody knew Anton Nickerson just like they knew Oden and Truman.

"Thanks, Reuben," I finally replied to his compliment.

We made that semi long walk to In-N-Out, and after ordering we decided to eat there. The only negative I had about this place was that your food got cold fairly quickly. I think it was because it was so fresh and not sitting under a light or microwaved. I appreciated the freshness and authenticity, but I just wish I could get to my dorm with some hot food.

"Ketchup?" Reuben asked me once I slid into one of the booths, close to the window.

"Yes, thank you."

He grabbed a handful with his big ass hand, and walked over to me. He was so tall and skinny, but he wasn't unattractive. I usually went for muscular dudes or even guys that were a little heavy set, because skinny ones weren't my thing, but Reuben was cute. He was no Anton though.

"I'm surprised you haven't met anybody since being out here," he took a huge ass bite out of his burger.

"Who says I haven't?"

"Shit, my bad, I just assumed. Every time I see you around campus, you're always with your friends and shit. But I guess I should ask, have you met someone?"

"Maybe."

"Okay. How about you give me your number then since you want to play games," he smirked.

"I have met someone, his name is Anton." I chose not to use his nickname Tony, because most people were familiar with his nickname.

"Nickerson?" he frowned, surprising me.

"Yeah, you know him?"

"I mean I don't know him know him, but I know about him. He's a cool dude so I've heard, very much into fatherhood, if you know what

I mean."

I rolled my eyes at his hating ass response and he just laughed.

"Well, we can talk about something else, because that conversation will ruin the mood." I began scarfing my food down because I was ready to end this little outing.

Reuben was about to speak, but when his mouth opened nothing came out. He was staring at something behind me, and when I looked out the window, I saw Anton outside, sitting in his Lamborghini. He was on the phone with somebody, and the conversation looked heated as hell. The way his jaw clenched every time he shook his head and pinched the bridge of his nose was so sexy. I watched him until he hung up, and then he began typing. As soon as he stopped my phone buzzed.

*Anton: Busy studying?*

*Me: Not anymore, eating inside In-N-Out.*

He read it and then looked around the establishment as if he were inside. As he climbed out, I watched him walk around until he reached the entrance. He scanned the place, and when he saw me he made his way over. Reuben blew out hot air, and slurped up some of his drink as if he was really mad and about to do something. He knew full well he didn't want them problems with Anton.

"Aye player, let me sit here," Anton looked down at Reuben, slipping his hands into his hoodie pocket. His chocolate skin glistened under the light in the restaurant,

"Come on man, how you just gon' walk up in here like that and ask me to get up. Tasmine asked me to come here with her."

Anton chuckled lightly before subtly checking his surroundings. My heart began beating fast because I wasn't sure what was about to happen, and I knew Anton was no weasel.

"Get yo' ass up… please." He raised his shirt a little to expose the handgun sitting in his waist.

Reuben's lips parted, before he slowly slid out of the booth with his hands raised. Anton watched him until he left, and then sat down across from me, smiling, like he was innocent.

"Why do you have a gun, Tony?"

"I always have a gun, baby." He grabbed some of my fries and shoved them into his mouth. "Let's go to my homie's kickback for a little bit."

I stared at him with my head cocked, before finally nodding my head in agreement. This nigga was psycho but I kind of liked it.

***

*Almost two hours later…*

This kickback was pretty popping and a little wilder than I was used to. Everyone was here, including Truman and Oden, but Khyle and Bella were back at our room studying. I planned to keep an eye on Oden for Khyle. If he was smart though, he wouldn't do shit in front of me. As for Truman, I knew he had a girlfriend and I was sure the chick he was currently tonguing down wasn't her. His actual woman had him all over her Instagram. He never posted her on his page, but she stayed tagging him. That was the only reason I knew what she looked like.

"You good?" Anton whispered into my ear. I was sitting in his lap, and his muscular arm was wrapped around my midsection. It felt so good to be in his arms and shit like we were a couple.

"I'm great." I looked over my shoulder at him, and we kept eye contact as he sunk his teeth into his bottom lip. Before I knew it, we were tonguing it up, not giving a fuck who was watching.

"Let's go to my crib," he pecked me, making my clit throb.

After thinking about it for a little bit, I finally nodded my head 'yes'. I didn't even know if I was ready to have sex with him. I mean, I wanted to, but I didn't want this situation to be the same as the last one. I would feel so stupid if I got duped twice.

"Aye, I'm about to go get your home girl," Oden walked up to me.

"Good," I smiled and so did he. He dapped Anton up, and the three of us left the party.

We made it to Anton's crib about 15 minutes later, and once inside he cut the heater on. Grabbing some champagne from a glass cabinet, he got two glasses and a carton of strawberries from the fridge. For some reason, seeing him grab the fruit made me laugh.

"Fuck is so funny?" he furrowed his brows.

"It's just weird seeing your thug ass pull out some strawberries."

"Real niggas eat fruit too," he half smiled. "Come on." I followed him to his big ass bedroom, and took a seat on the small couch in there. He joined me after removing his hoodie and shirt, allowing me to admire his chocolate tattoo covered chest.

He filled our glasses after popping the cork, and once I took a sip, I knew I would be helping finish the bottle. I hated champagne usually, but this shit was crisp and refreshing.

"I usually don't like champagne."

"You ain't been drinking the right kind, that's why."

We kept pouring and pouring until the bottle was empty. Plopping back against the couch at the same time, we made eye contact. He scooted closer to me, and bent to down to bite and suck my inner thigh. I usually would've been annoyed but that shit was a turn on.

Dropping down onto the floor, he reached under my skirt and pulled my panties down with the quickness. It was too late to stop now, or maybe I just didn't want to. He got comfortable on the floor, before yanking me to the edge of the couch and kissing my lower lips. I got so much wetter instantly, over such a small gesture. I'd never gotten head before so maybe that was why.

He tugged my clit into his mouth and began gently sucking on it with his soft lips and tongue. Pressing my legs into my stomach, he got all in there, eyes closed and everything. I tried to muffle my moans, but they were so hard to control with liquor in my system, not to mention the shit felt phenomenal.

I bit down on my lip as he sucked, slurped, and flicked his tongue over my button, and finally I was releasing. Throwing my head back, my chest rose and fell as I tried to catch my breath. I guess he had other plans because he went right back in, feasting until I exploded two more times. He licked me slowly as if he was cleaning me, before rising to his feet to remove his bottoms. He was hung for sure, and I hoped I could hang with him. If I embarrassed myself tonight, I would go home to Kentucky and change schools.

"Get up," he demanded, licking his lips as he held my hand to help me up. It was almost if I didn't know what to do unless he told me. He undressed me completely, and then led me to the bed to lie down.

Climbing on top of me, he kissed my neck, collarbone, cheeks, and then my lips. The way he touched me was so gentle, and I admit I was surprised because he was everything but, outside of the bedroom. Securing a condom on his dick, he placed my legs in the nooks of his arms, and pushed his head into me.

"Fuck," he grunted, pausing in the middle. I had the sheets clutched into my fists, anticipating feeling the rest of him.

Finally, he made it all the way in, and began wounding his hips slowly into me. It was painful at first, but the pleasure quickly took that over. Groping my breasts and playing with my nipples, he continued to stroke me with precision, prompting my juices to cover his pole in no time.

Obviously done with making love, he pulled out of me and put me on all fours, sliding in as soon as my ass got in the air. Grasping both of my cheeks in his strong hands, he moved in and out of me slowly. When I looked back, he was watching himself work, bottom lip tucked in, held by his perfect teeth. Sweat was covering his beautiful dark complexion.

"Ahhh, uuuh, mmm," I tried to whimper lowly, but it just felt too damn good to do so.

Speeding up, he pounded into me from behind feverishly, while running his hands all over the back side of my body. I had his soft ass, thick pillow, squeezing it for dear life, as he went in on me. I exploded again, and not even two minutes later, I'd had another orgasm. I could already tell I was gonna be sprung, and in this moment I wasn't regretting it.

"Damn," he groaned again, pummeling me from behind and holding onto my left shoulder.

A few moments later, we were both yelling and releasing. My body dropped onto the bed as I tried to catch my breath, and he just chuckled, sliding out of me. He left the room and returned with some towels so we could clean ourselves up, and once I was finished, I stood up but he stopped me.

"Where you going?" he furrowed his somewhat bushy brows.

"Home."

"Nah, stay." He patted his huge bed, and I happily obliged.

Not only did I wanna stay here with him, but his bed was much more comfortable than my dorm one. Maybe this would be the start of something… at least I hoped so.

# CHAPTER NINE

# Bella

It was the last football game of the school year before everyone went home for Christmas break. My friends and I pretty much went to every game, but Santino begged me to get here early this time so I could be sitting as closely as possible. I pretended like I didn't want to but I was excited that he and I were getting close again.

After having sex back in our hometown, we only did it once more when we returned to school. I felt a little bad so I didn't want to keep it up, and funny enough, he didn't mind. I had a feeling it was because he was getting it elsewhere; I mean he was the star football player. But could I really be upset? I had a controlling fiancé that I wouldn't leave alone.

"You went all out with these signs, girl," Khyle chuckled as she looked down at my glitter-filled sign I created.

"I know I got a little carried away. Perry helped too, though." I turned to my right to look at her and smiled. Perry was kind of cool now, but she still needed to break out of her shell some. We had a lot of time to help her with that though.

"This shit needs to start, I'm cold as hell," Tasmine complained. The four of us were wrapped up in our biggest jackets, scarves, and tallest pair of UGG boots.

"Relax, mami, it'll start in a second."

About 20 minutes later, the game was on and all of the stands were packed. I saw so many people with signs for Santino, but none of them were as extravagant as mine. That was exactly what I wanted, which was why I went in with all that damn brightly colored glitter.

Although a lot of people were cheering when Santino made a touchdown, I couldn't help but notice a group of loud ass girls doing the most for him and yelling his name. I made eye contact with my friends, and the next time he scored we got louder than them. Their group looked at us, as we looked at them, and then the one with Santino's number sixteen painted on her face shook her head and laughed. For the rest of the game, we continued on with our unspoken competition, and when it was over I was ready to go. I felt dumb for even stooping to their level.

"You gonna wait around for Sanz?" Perry quizzed.

"Nope."

"Why not?"

"Because I'm tired and I still have a lot of packing to do before going home for Christmas break," I half lied. I did have to pack a few things, but that wasn't why I was choosing to leave the stadium early.

Glancing over my shoulder, I spotted the girl and her friends still seated, as the place cleared out. A part of me wanted to stay and see if she was gonna push up on Santino, but I decided against it.

Before going to the room, Perry drove us to Starbucks right across the street from the school so we could get some hot drinks. I made sure to get mine extra hot because I didn't want that shit being only warm by the time I made it back to the dorm. As the four of us rode the elevator up to our floor, I got a text, two actually.

**Dean:** *What day and time are you landing? I wanna pick you up from the airport.*

**Santino:** *Where are you?*

I ignored them both because I just wasn't in the mood. I felt bad for doing Dean dirty, and then I was irritated that those bitches were on Santino tough. Also, I knew she just wasn't some groupie. Well, I didn't know for sure, but my gut was telling me that she wasn't… she knew him and well.

"Goodnight, ladies," I half smiled at my friends. We hugged one another before entering our rooms, which were right across from one another.

Since my tea was still piping hot, I brushed my teeth and took a steaming shower, washing my hair and everything. By the time I was out, a bitch was tired as fuck, so I downed my tea and passed out with Netflix still showing.

*A couple hours later…*

*KNOCK! KNOCK!*

"Okay!" I hollered, climbing out of the bed.

Perry's ass was snoring like fucking always, with her mouth wide open. She didn't do much at all but study and finish assignments early, so I don't know why she slept as if she'd cured world hunger.

I approached the door, and when I looked out, I saw it was Santino. He was so fucking sexy in his gray sweats and a simple white t-shirt. I loved the way his face frowned up when he scratched his short curly hair, and how his hazel eyes looked glazed over because he was tired. I swore I could smell his cologne through this thick wooden door.

That was something I loved about him, he never smelled like… man. You know the musty feet stench that niggas get to smelling like after chilling all day and playing video games? Santino never got like that. Even after practice, he smelled scrumptious.

"It's… 1am." I had to glance at the clock on the microwave in the room.

"Fuck you leave after the damn game for?" he sneered, walking in like he stayed in this room too. He was so tall and muscular. Fuck, I loved him.

"I had to finish packing." I closed the door.

"You don't leave for a week, baby, and you were pretty much packed this morning."

"Well, I remembered I had some things I didn't put up."

He flashed me that pretty smile of his, the one I'd fallen in love with three years ago. It was dark in the room, but I could still see his caramel ass anyway, thanks to my miniature fish tanks. Licking his lips, he stroked his chin hair, eyeing me like a piece of moist lemon cake. He loved lemon cake, and he had that same look in his eyes when a slice was in front of him.

"You know I know you too well, so don't fucking lie." He moved closer to me, and picked me up, causing me to yelp. I covered my mouth as if that would take away what I'd just done, hoping not to wake Perry.

"Who was that girl up front, a little ways down from me?"

"Excuse me?" he frowned, still holding me. My legs were wrapped tightly around his waist, and my arms were draped around his neck.

"Light skinned, long, curly hair, and had your number on her cheek. She was screaming for you with her three friends."

"Don't know," he answered shortly before pecking me.

Carrying me over to my bed, he sat me down on it, and then removed his hoodie and slides before climbing in.

"I don't want company."

"You probably don't but you want me, and I want you. You need to quit playing fucking games and get rid of Dean. We're both gonna be in Scottsdale for this Christmas break and if you think I'm gonna spend that whole time without you, you're crazier than I thought." He spoke sternly to me, staring me deeply in the eyes. I knew him like he knew me, so I was sure he meant every word that had just left his lips. "I love you, Bella. What do I have to do to make you see that shit?"

I opened and closed my mouth, unsure of what to say. Before a clear thought could be made though, his tongue was down my throat and he was on top of me. Shit was about to get real.

# CHAPTER TEN

## Oden

It was around noon, and I'd just got done working out so I wanted to come out and do some skateboarding. I used to do this shit all the time, but after breaking too many limbs from doing stunts and shit, I kind of stopped. These days, I only did a little bit at the skate park, since it was right next to the basketball court that I planned to play on once I was done.

I was that nigga that played all kinds of sports but never wanted to go pro. Them professional sports players be fucking their bodies up and don't be worth shit by the time it's over. I ain't want no parts of that; plus, the car, club, and liquor industry had my heart.

"Bishop!" I heard someone call out to me, so I stopped after coming up one of the slopes.

Looking toward where the voice was coming from, I saw one of my security people named Abram, standing in front of someone, patting them down. After he moved from the view, I saw it was Billz Montgomery.

"This nigga," I mumbled, hiking my black joggers up a bit as I made my way over. I made sure my piece was intact as I neared him. "What can I do you for?"

"Just wanna have a chat with you."

"About?" He looked to Abram, so I signaled for him to go ahead and chill off to the side. "Talk, I have shit to do, and it doesn't include chatting with you." Billz and I were cool, but I could sense that he was here for some bullshit ass reason.

"I came to talk to you about my boy Smitty."

"Fuck is that?"

"One of my… people that I found with his brains blown out, outside of my party. Not only that, but my Wraith was gone, nowhere to be found. And by the time I tried to get some people on it, it couldn't be located."

"And how does that have anything to do with me?" I frowned, nodding my head up to my homeboy Kiel, who was waiting on me to come play ball with him and a few others.

"The only other ruthless nigga in Las Vegas who would have killed one of my right-hand men, is you. Not to mention we both know what funded that club and liquor line, so you're no stranger to getting cars across country in no time."

"Can't help you."

"Yeah you can, you—"

"Nah, I said I can't. If your homeboy got smoked he probably deserved that shit, but don't ever in yo' life roll up on me, bumping yo' gums about some bullshit, nigga. If you were really balling like you claim, one bitch ass Wraith wouldn't be shit to you."

Sucking his teeth like a bitch, he looked off as if he was trying to calm himself down.

Billz knew me before I was thee Oden and vice versa. He and I went to high school together and he was a bitch ass nigga then too. He got pulled into the drug game because his father was a notorious kingpin at that time, who eventually passed his shit down. I guess now that he had the reigns on the shit, he thought niggas forgot that he used to get hung in the school's coat closet by his drawers.

"It ain't shit to me. I just came to let you know that you need to keep your shit away from my shit. I don't care how many cars you steal, just don't let it be one of mine."

"Can't promise you that. Fuck outta my face," I hissed, bumping the fuck out of his shoulder as I walked past him in the direction of Kiel.

I could feel him looking at my back but I didn't give a fuck.

I played a bunch of rounds of basketball with the homies, and then took my ass home because I needed a shower. I didn't sweat as much because the weather was hella brisk, but I definitely felt gritty as hell. I made it to my townhouse and when I went to check my mail I saw it was already removed from the box, which meant Khyle was here. Entering, I spotted her to my left in the kitchen cooking. Whatever she was making smelled good as fuck, and had the house feeling nice and toasty.

"What you making?" I walked up to the bar, leaning on it and scanning her small sexy frame.

"Chicken, cornbread, string beans, yams, and macaroni," she half smiled. "You said you hadn't had a good home cooked meal in a while, excluding this past Thanksgiving."

That made me smile, and I wasn't a mushy ass nigga believe me.

I walked around the bar into the kitchen, bent her head back, and kissed her deeply. My feelings for her seemed to get stronger and stronger over time. Pulling away, I looked into her eyes for a second, and she nervously did the same before I pecked her again.

"Thanks, baby girl." I kissed her once more, squeezing her ass in the process, and making her squeal and laugh. "I'm gonna shower."

After cleaning up, we ate dinner together, and I wasn't surprised by how good the food was. She'd cooked for me before, but not a feast like this, and boy was I thankful. Niggas could lie all day and say the single life was popping, but having that one girl by your side would always be better. Khyle was proving to be the whole fucking kit and caboodle.

We were stuffed, so we went to the bedroom to lie down and 'watch TV', but in no time she was straddling me in only a pair of thin crotch less panties. Her body was so beautiful, and I swore to myself that another nigga would never be able to enjoy it.

"So how are we gonna do Christmas break?" I quizzed.

"I'm gonna stay with my parents for the first half, and the day after Christmas, I'm gonna come back to Vegas to be with you until school resumes late January."

"Damn, I can't see you for Christmas?" I bit my lip, admiring how pretty her pussy looked. I couldn't help but to trail my fingers over it. Shit.

"Mmm," she moaned very subtly, moving against my fingers. We made eye contact, and she gasped when I plunged them inside of her. Gripping her small hip with my free hand, I made her grind against my fingers as if it were my dick. Seeing her bite down on her lip in pleasure was the shit. "I c-can c-come back on… in the middle of Chrisss… Christmas day," she stammered as her body tensed up. She released soon after, and I cleaned my fingers off with my mouth.

"That's better. I'll buy your ticket," I replied, lifting her a little bit and bringing her down onto my dick. Her face twisted up as she just sat there on it, pussy throbbing like a heartbeat.

Realizing she didn't have the strength to ride right now, I flipped her onto her back and began beating it up while sucking her nipples. I pinned her hands above her head as I moved in and out of her sopping wet center, and damn, she had me ready to cum already.

Leaning up off of her, I pressed her thighs into her stomach so that her knees were by her ears, and slowly slid in and out of her. I watched my dick disappear and reappear, and licked my lips at her glistening center. Her whimpering and sniveling was such a fucking turn on, not to mention her sexy ass faces. I watched her body quiver as she coated my dick, and kept my movements slow and steady, letting it sit inside every time I was all the way in.

Keeping her thighs pressed against her body, I lowered myself onto her, pressing my lips against hers. We weren't quite kissing, but our lips were touching.

"Tell me it's mine," I ordered.

"It's your pussy, Oden," she cried out against my lips as I sped up, tearing her middle to shreds.

I kissed her inner thigh, before pulling her lips into my mouth to suck on. We then graduated to full on tongue kissing as I pounded her mercilessly, causing her to holler. In no time I was cumming all inside of her.

We caught our breath, cleaned up, and then got back into my huge ass bed to lay up. She laid her head on my chest, so I shifted her long ass hair out of the way. Lifting her head and pressing her chin into my chest, she looked up into my eyes innocently. I moved her hair from her face, and pressed my lips against her pillow soft ones. She had me out of my element for sure… but I fucked with it.

# CHAPTER TEN

*Two nights later...*

*What you mean nigga? Gettin' money is a fuckin' routine nigga. Huh? This ain't nothin' new it's what we been doing. This ain't nothing new it's what we been doing.*

I was on the bottom floor at the underground strip club of Palace nightclub, watching the strippers shake their asses to "What We Been Doin'" by B-Legit. There were plenty of strip clubs to hit up, but I preferred me and my boys' shit. The girls were finer, and could really work their bodies. Most of these clubs out here in Vegas either had a gang of white bitches with no moves and no body to match, or thick black bitches that could barely swing around the pole. Not at Palace, though. We had everything from Asian bitches to Black ones, and not only were they stacked, but they could get your dick hard without even touching you. And believe me when I said my dick didn't respond to every bitch with a pussy.

I accepted the blunt from Truman, and took a long ass pull on it, letting the smoke fill my body. We had access to some good shit, thanks to him and his connects, so getting high was never a problem.

"I'm definitely taking Chiina home tonight," Truman nodded his head at her. A big ass smile covered her pretty face as she gave a lap dance to some nigga.

"And what does Pilar think of that?" I chuckled at him.

"She won't know, and plus, I know where home is. I'm gonna bang old girl out and then head home to my woman. That's where niggas mess up, y'all spend the night and shit."

"Nigga, I never spend the night, but I have let them sleep over at the hoe crib."

"And you shouldn't. I kick their asses out as soon as I bust, unless I wanna smash one more time. But after round two, they get the fucking boot." He took the blunt from me.

"Visitor," the VIP bouncer walked up to me, pointing to Kai's crazy ass who was standing there with her arms folded across her chest.

I shook my head at her, before doing the same to the bouncer so he knew not to let her in. He delivered the news, and I swore I could hear her going off over the music.

"Get me that DNA!" I hollered out as security escorted her out the back exit. "That bitch gon' make me kill her ass on everything I love."

"Bitch would have *been* dead fucking with me," Truman scoffed.

"Thanks, Tru." I looked down at my phone to see I had a text.

***Violet:*** *I have a doctor's appointment next Monday.*

***Me:*** *Aight.*

Violet was still pregnant, so I couldn't get a DNA yet. I knew the child wasn't mine, but just in fucking case, I didn't want to miss shit. However, as soon as that baby took its first breath, I was getting a test. Violet didn't protest… yet.

Truman and I continued to admire the women, and once Chiina was done with her customer, she strutted over and sat right in Truman's lap. I scooted down because this nigga was not the shy type and had no qualms about fucking in the club. Oden and I tried to tell him about that shit but he was part owner, and always made sure he paid to have the place cleaned out, so it wasn't much we could say.

"How Many Drinks?" by Miguel spilled through the speakers, and when I looked to the stage, I saw this stripper named Amethyst. She was sexy as hell, with deep mocha skin like me, and not a blemish in sight. The outfit she wore didn't leave much to the imagination, and I didn't mind.

I leaned back, lighting up another blunt to enjoy the show. Taking my bourbon to the head and nodding for the waitress to get me a refill, I kept my eyes on baby girl. She was moving her body sensually, flinging her hair around in the process. Before I knew it, the stage was covered in money, and she had only taken her bra off. My dick was hard as a rock, and I was fighting the urge to take her home and fuck. There was only one reason for that though… Tasmine.

I really fucked with her and in addition to her having a dope personality, her pussy was bomb. She wasn't my girlfriend or anything yet, but I could definitely see things going in that direction. She was what every nigga in my position wanted, just a regular pretty bitch who couldn't care less about how much fame or money you had, and could take the dick. However, despite the fact that she was basically a nigga's dream girl, it didn't stop me from being attracted to other women. And because she wasn't my girl, I was gonna do what the fuck I wanted to do in the meantime. I just hoped it didn't fuck up what we were building.

"She's bad as fuck," Truman stood up, holding hands with Chiina, and fixing his pants with his free hand.

"Ain't she?" I said, glancing from him back to Amethyst.

"Well, I'm gonna head *home*, so I will see you later." He put an emphasis on home to let me know he was going to the hoe crib. We dapped one another up, and then he left the building.

Amethyst's set was finished, so once she left the stage, I went into my phone to answer and delete a lot of text messages that I was never gonna answer from my burner app. I gave out my burner number to pretty much every female I came in contact with except Tasmine, because as soon as they got to acting up, I could burn that shit out and get a new one. Lately, I'd been too busy though, so this little app had been jumping with nonsense.

"I saw you watching," a sweet voice said.

Looking down, I spotted Amethyst who was now in a different outfit than before. Smiling, I waved her into the VIP, and she quickly walked in.

"I watch every girl that dances," I finally replied.

"No, you glance every now and then, but with me, you watched the whole time." She leaned in and whispered the last part into my ear.

"Aight, you got me," I nodded as she chuckled sweetly.

"I know. So where are you going after you leave here?"

"Home."

"Want some company?" she questioned, raising her eyebrow. This girl was beautiful, and had no business shaking her ass for random niggas in the strip club.

"Yeah, I do."

She stood up right away, and pulled me with her; well, attempted to but I was way too heavy. I led her out to my car, and she was acting like a kid in a candy store when she got in.

"I've never been in one of these before. What is it?" We laughed in unison before I responded.

"Lambo… Lamborghini." I cranked it up.

"Boss," she nodded as her eyes continued to roam my interior and center console.

I sped to my house with the windows slightly cracked, blasting Young Jeezy. I handed her one of the blunts from the tray I had, and lit my own at the red light. Baby girl was sexy but I didn't know where her mouth had been to be sharing blunts with her.

Making it to the hoe crib, I swooped into a park right next to Truman's car and climbed out, jogging around to get the door for her. I helped her exit, and then stood there watching her walk for a moment. Damn, her body was ridiculous.

I prayed that tonight wouldn't get me another fake baby mama.

I didn't need that shit, especially not while I was attempting to have something with Tasmine.

Catching up to Amethyst, I let her into my crib so shit could get nasty.

# CHAPTER TEN

# Shayne

Marisol and I were going on a little double date tonight. I wanted to get some alone time with Lloyd, but Marisol thought it would be a good idea for us to chill together. I felt like she only said that because she wasn't feeling the fact that Lloyd wanted me and not her. On the bright side though, Lloyd already text me on the low saying that we were gonna ditch them two and I could not wait. I wasn't the double date type at all.

Tonight I was wearing a tan bustier dress that hugged every curve on my body perfectly. I had matching nude stilettos, gold jewelry, and nude lips to match. My finger and toenails were even painted cappuccino, so as you can see, the nude family was the theme for tonight. Pierce always told me how good I looked in these colors, and he was right, because as I looked myself over in the mirror, all I could do was shake my head.

I patted some glitter on my light golden complexion, and then spritzed some perfume on before letting my long ass hair down to show my body waves.

"Damn, bitch, we're just going to dinner and the club after," Marisol peeked into my bedroom, lip turned up just like the hater she was. She was wearing a simple red strapless dress, but her big butt and breasts made it look like more than just a piece of fabric.

"Exactly, and on the damn strip. It's the weekend too, so you know them out of town bitches are gonna be showing out. I refuse to have Lloyd looking at anything but me."

"So what about Pierce?" she folded her arms.

"Look, Marisol, we're cool, but not cool enough to be discussing my relationship and shit, okay?" I glanced at her before turning away to check out my backside in the mirror.

I didn't even like the fact that she knew about Pierce, because I was paranoid that she'd run her mouth to him. I didn't wanna be with him, because shit, you know why, but he was all I had right now. I wasn't trying to jump ship until I had another one waiting for me, and I was hoping Lloyd was that other ship. But I knew if Pierce found out about me cheating, he would kick my ass out, and I didn't have the funds to support myself yet since my dance checks wouldn't be coming in yet. And if that happened, where was I gonna live? With Alanna's depressed ass? Or in the dorm with my little sister? Negative.

"My bad, Shayne. I don't get why we can't be friends. I mean, I understand you're a little salty about the Oden situation, but neither of us got him, so…" she shrugged.

"It's not about who got him, it's the fact that you would purposely come at him, knowing that was exactly what I came to the club for. That's shady, and I don't like shady bitches."

"Oh, so you have to be the only shady one, Shayne?" she stepped further into my room. "You and I are just alike, and that's why we've been hanging out more than you and Alanna lately. We click, you just don't want us to. And I didn't know you then so I didn't care about your goal. I saw Oden, he was fine, and I wanted him. But now that we're 'cool' I promise I won't do that shit anymore."

Staring at her for a while, I gave her a fake smile and said, "Fine, we can start again." I wasn't starting shit with this bitch; she was shady and that was it. Yeah, I had some fucked up ways too, but I didn't want friends like me, and Marisol was like a mirror image.

"Good, come on before Pierce gets here," she hugged me lightly.

I gave myself one more look in my full-length mirror, and then hit the lights.

About 15 minutes later, we were pulling into Caesar's Palace hotel, where the guys were staying. I gave my keys to valet, and then the two of us headed inside and up to their suite.

Like last time, you could hear music coming from behind their door as I knocked on it. This time Lloyd answered, looking sexy as hell. I'd never seen a nigga this fine in my life outside of Oden, and had I known that niggas down south looked like this, I would have been relocated.

Lloyd was rocking a long sleeve maroon polo, white jeans, and some suede maroon Adidas. His neck and wrists were iced the fuck out, blinding me every time I looked at them. And his cologne was so masculine yet not overbearing at all. His dark complexion was smooth like silk, and his scruffy beard and curly hair complemented it well.

"What's good?" he bit down on his lip, gold slugs on full display.

"Hey," I replied shyly. My body was hot already, letting me know that I was nervous. Dudes didn't make me nervous, but Lloyd did.

"Hey, Lloyd," Marisol flirted as we both walked in.

"Y'all want some water or something? Roone is still getting ready."

"No thank you," she and I replied almost at the same time.

"Aye, come here," Lloyd waved me over on his way to the back. I pointed to myself to make sure, even though he was looking dead in my eyes. He nodded with a smile before continuing to the back. I followed him, and when I got into his room, he closed the door.

"What?" I tried to sound irritated even though I wasn't.

"Kill all that attitude shit. Sit down," he demanded. I did as he asked, and he plopped down on the huge bed next to me.

"So why are you cheating on your man?" he raised a brow, catching me off guard like a muthafucka.

"What? I don't have a man—" He shook his head at me, letting me know to cut the bullshit out. "I'm not in love with him anymore." He nodded his head as he lit the tip of the blunt in his mouth. "Is that a problem?"

"Nah, ain't no problem for me." He shrugged. "Only nigga it'd be a problem for is yours. As long as you keep him intact so he don't come at me with no bullshit, we good."

"He's not that type, he's calm," I lied.

"Good, because I don't play them games and I would hate to have to body a nigga before I even get my first paycheck out here." He took a pull. Suddenly, his phone beeped, so he looked down at it, and then stood up. "I'm gonna brush my teeth and then we can bounce." He ashed the blunt and did just that.

When he returned, he helped me up, and while holding my hand, he was fully checking me out, shaking his head in admiration.

"Like what you see?" I giggled, walking past him and allowing him to look at my ass. I didn't have a big stripper booty, but it was enough to grab and make niggas look if in the right dress.

"You know I fucking like what I see. Ain't no girls like you down in Birmingham," he replied, letting his southern accent shine through.

"Ain't no niggas like you on the West Coast either, but I'm glad you moved here."

"Me too." He took my hand into his and led me out of the room and through the living room so we could leave the suite. I noticed Marisol wasn't on the couch anymore, just before loud moaning boomed throughout.

"I guess we're on our own."

"I guess so," he smirked.

We headed down to this Chinese food restaurant named Mr. Chow, located inside of the hotel. It was so pretty and clean, and I just knew it cost a lot of money to eat here. See, this was the life meant for me.

On the way in, I slipped my hand into Lloyd's when I saw some bitches checking him out. You could tell he wasn't from here, and I guess I wasn't the only one who thought that down south shit was sexy all of a sudden. Not to mention he looked like money.

I was surprised to see he had a reservation, but then again, he'd been saying we were gonna be alone for the longest, so he had time to plan. We were seated almost immediately, and had our drink orders taken. The room was currently lit up with purple fluorescent lights, which were so beautiful and not too bright. Pierce would never take me here; maybe if he had have stayed in the NFL, he could have though.

"You ever been here?" I furrowed my brows, sipping my cocktail.

"Just 'cause a nigga from Alabama don't mean he hasn't traveled. I've been everywhere, well almost, from jail to overseas."

"You've been to prison?"

"Yeah, I have. I don't plan on going back though, fuck that."

"That's good," I nodded.

"I get the impression that you don't like niggas who have been to prison," he chuckled, taking down some of his water and never taking his eyes off of me.

"I mean, I've never dated a guy who went to prison."

"Oh, only rich niggas with trust funds, huh?"

"I guess," I half smiled. "I like you though, so looks like prison doesn't bother me as much as I thought it would."

The waitress came to take our orders, and we both asked for a refill on our alcoholic drinks, which she brought over fairly promptly.

"So what's your story? What do you do other than be pretty for no reason."

"Pretty for no reason?"

"Yeah, girls like you should be in somebody's movie or music video. You can't look that good and just be a regular girl." I was blushing even though I didn't want to.

"I dance. I just got hired on for a show in the Harrah's hotel. The pay is only $850 a week, but I love to dance so I don't mind."

"Damn, that's dope. I have to come see you sometime, just don't sit me next to your nigga," he chuckled, and so did I.

"How did you know I had a man?"

"Girls that look like you ain't never single, shawty."

"Why'd you come to Vegas, Lloyd?" I pushed my hair back, allowing the waitress to set down my plate and then his.

"Work. My homeboy Oden asked me to come out, me and Roone, and since shit wasn't happening down in Birmingham no more, I thought why not."

"Oden?" my stomach dropped.

"Yeah, you know him?"

"Yeah, he's dating my little sister."

"Like he's smashing her?"

"No, that's her boyfriend, like spend every day together type," I chuckled at his facial expression.

"Oden having a girlfriend? I don't know, shawty, I gotta see it to believe it," he laughed, sipping his water again. "No disrespect to your kinfolk."

"None taken."

We continued to have great conversation once I was able to get over the fact that he and Oden were homies. I just figured I wasn't gonna let that stop me from pursuing something with him… yeah, a bitch liked him that damn much.

Once we finished our dinner, we had dessert, and then he paid the bill so we could go to Omnia, the club inside the hotel. There was a line, but he got us in somehow, and we danced and drank all fucking night. I'd never been that drunk in my life, but I was still aware of my actions enough to help him book another suite on his phone. We got the key from the front desk, and then retired upstairs.

As soon as we got into the room, he dimmed the lights and our lips met. I loved how soft his were, and despite his demeanor and looks, he was gentle. Unzipping my dress, he stepped back a little so I could get out of it, and admired my half naked body since no bra was present. He ripped my thin panties, threw them to the side, and then took his shirt and shoes off. He then removed his gold slugs to show me his pretty ass teeth. Thank God he wasn't hiding some crooked shits.

Lying on the bed, he said, "Sit on my face." I complied, getting on the bed and hovering over his face. "Pretty ass pussy," he slurred with his southern accent, turning my drunk ass on.

I rode his face as he sucked my button while gripping my ass cheeks. I was damn near screaming out, while gripping the headboard. He had my body shaking from releasing. I slowed down, breathing heavily, as he continued to attack my center like a beast. Finally, he let me go and I pulled away, trying to regain my composure.

"Damn," I panted, prompting a sexy smile to cover his face as I unbuckled his jeans.

Reaching down in his boxers, I found his snake, which was much bigger than expected. Damn, did this nigga have any flaws? Taking the tip into my mouth, I slurped on it, getting my mouth nice and wet. Light moans escaped his full lips, as he rubbed the back of my head. Easing the rest of his length into me, I let loose, sucking him up like a pro. Being drunk definitely helped lubricate my mouth, so I was going in, especially when his moans got louder. His dick got even harder at one point, and that's when he lightly yanked me off.

"Shit." He pulled a condom from his jeans and then stood up to completely remove them along with his boxers. Rolling it down, he pulled me to the edge of the bed to slip his tongue into my mouth. I loved kissing him. "You know you're sexy as fuck," he groaned, pecking me once more before turning me around so that my ass was in the air and my face was in the mattress.

"Mmm," we cooed in unison once he got inside of me.

Gripping my waist, he moved slowly at first, hitting my spot every time he entered me. I was biting down on the comforter each time I hit the base of his dick, whimpering in the process. His big hands roamed my body, grasping my ass cheeks and spanking them every now and then. The pain he delivered with each smack, mixed with the pleasure from his stroke game was too much. I spilled my nectar so heavily that my inner thighs were a little wet.

"Lloyd, baby," I cried out, slurping the drool that he'd damn near fucked out of me.

"What, baby?" he asked in a low sexy tone, as he continued to grind into me.

"I love you," I sniveled, and we both chuckled subtly. That's how good he was fucking me, and he wasn't even doing the most.

"I love this *pussy*," he responded, reaching around to toy with my clit.

He pressed his abs into my back and began pounding into me while rubbing my bud. I had to hold tighter onto the comforter, while biting down on another portion of it. Yanking a handful of my hair, he pummeled me as I yelled out until we both exploded. We collapsed together, and as I panted, he sucked on my shoulder.

"We gotta do this shit again," he grunted. All I could do was nod.

I had to get rid of Pierce's ass.

# CHAPTER TEN

Tonight was Truman's Christmas party, and Oden said he had one every year. Everyone had to wear an ugly sweater, and when I bought mine and my friends, I made sure to get Oden one to match mine. This party would have a lot of the guys' outside friends there, and in case these bitches didn't know Oden was taken, I would be happy to let them know. I made sure my necklace was in full view too.

"You got me looking crazy." Oden walked into his bedroom, frowning.

"You look sexy to me," I chuckled, playing with the soft Rudolph nose attached to the front of his sweater.

"I better look sexy to yo' ass. I don't give a fuck if I got a gut and one shrunken ball, that pussy better get wet upon seeing me," he grinned as I laughed heartily.

"It will, baby." I leaned up so he could kiss me.

We left the bedroom and grabbed the two big bowls of spiked eggnog from the fridge before bouncing.

We made it to this big ass mansion, and I had no idea who it belonged to, but that was Truman for you. He was so crazy and funny. If you hung out with him, Oden, and Anton together, you would be laughing the entire time to the point where it was painful.

Oden and I got out of his Maserati and entered the home, which was damn near jumping because of the loud ass music bumping. Truman had some official ass bouncers, but since they knew Oden, they didn't give him too many problems. And knowing Oden, he definitely had a gun on him. That shit used to bother me but now I was used to it. My nigga was a thoroughbred and that was all there was to it.

"What's good!" Truman smiled, arm draped over some girl. I'd met his girlfriend, Pilar, and that wasn't her. This nigga was bold, because I knew she was gonna be here tonight. At least she should be.

The party was dope, with Christmas lights everywhere, fake snow, and two big ass Christmas trees on each ends of the large home. I saw a table with snacks like gingerbread cookies and houses, as well as candy canes. There were two bartenders also, making all kinds of Christmas like alcoholic drinks.

"Hey," I smiled, hugging Truman after he dapped up Oden. "Where should we take these?" I gestured towards the eggnog bowls, which we'd temporarily set down to greet him.

"Left a space right there. When y'all are done, come up to the balcony, that's like the little VIP area." Truman turned to walk up one side of the winding staircase with the girl.

Oden and I set the bowls down, and then headed towards the stairs. As we walked through the crowd, Oden hugged me from behind, and we danced slightly as we walked. I saw a couple of bitches with disapproving looks, and I just reached behind me to caress the side of his face in response.

Finally, we got upstairs and I hugged Bella, Tasmine, and Perry. Bella and Tasmine were cuddled up with Santino and Anton respectively.

*So when y'all niggas hop off the jet, you better tuck what's on ya neck and get the fuck from round here.*

"Don't Come to L.A." by YG came on, so Bella, Tasmine, and I got up to dance and sing along. Even though they weren't from Los Angeles, they loved some YG just like me, so they knew the words. As we moved our bodies with drinks in our hands, I felt Oden come behind me and kiss my neck, before going to the balcony to look over the party with his friends.

Suddenly, I heard people screaming from the first floor of the party, and before I could react, gunshots rang out. When I looked towards the balcony, I saw Oden collapse to the floor, blood pouring out the side of his mouth. Anton was going ape shit, and Truman had his heat pulled.

"No! What the fuck!" was the only thing I could get out before a crowd surfaced around him, knocking my friends and I backward.

## TO BE CONTINUED

Join our mailing list to get a notification when Shvonne Latrice has another release!

Text **SHVONNE** to **66866** to join!

To submit a manuscript for publishing consideration, email us at
fcpublishinggroup@gmail.com